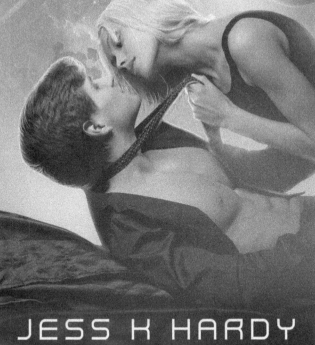

LOVE IN THE TIME OF WORMHOLES

AN IGNISAR NOVEL

JESS K HARDY

MYSTIC OWL

AN IMPRINT OF CITY OWL PRESS

LOVE IN THE TIME OF WORMHOLES
Ignisar, Book 1

MYSTIC OWL
A City Owl Press Imprint
www.cityowlpress.com

Cover Design by MiblArt. All stock photos licensed appropriately.

Edited by Heather McCorkle.

For information on subsidiary rights, please contact the publisher at info@cityowlpress.com.

Print Edition ISBN: 978-1-64898-117-3

Digital Edition ISBN: 978-1-64898-116-6

Printed in the United States of America

PRAISE FOR JESS K. HARDY

"Stars above, *Love in the Time of Wormholes* was an absolute blast. Packed with a diverse crew of characters that felt like dear friends by the end, this interplanetary adventure is full of both humor and fun, at the same time that it tells a sensitive story of grief. Sunny and Freddie's chemistry is fire-hot, and it was impossible not to root for their happily-ever-after from the very beginning. I loved my time aboard the Ignisar!" - *Anita Kelly, author of Sing Anyway and Love & Other Disasters*

"*Love in the Time of Wormholes* is the perfect combination of humor, steam, and heart-felt romance. While set in the far reaches of outer space, the character's struggles are undeniably human, and you will think about them long after you've finished reading." - *Gabrielle Ash, author of The Family Cross*

"*Missing Charlie* is an entertaining, warmhearted yarn about love that persists through extreme transmogrifications." - *Kirkus Reviews*

"*The Bench* was a homerun for me. Both James and Noah have such wonderful personalities. They're both going through a lot and it's nice to have someone to lean on...I liked their growing chemistry as the story played out. Adding in their children and a past complication just added to my enjoyment of this tale. A totally beautiful read I would absolutely recommend!" – *The TBR Pile*

"*Love in the Time of Wormholes* is the perfect blend of clever humor, hotter-than-hot romance, and alien antics! Hardy's animated cast of characters aboard the Ignisar galactic cruise vessel will give you *The Orville* vibes when you join them on one diplomatic adventure after another. As the ship's crew entertains their wild guests, the heat and tension rise to a boiling point between sassy, confident Sunny and sexy, relentless Freddie. Find yourself laughing, crying, and honestly kinda horny through this sci-fi romcom, *Love in the Time of Wormholes*." - Cate Pearce, author of *Traitors of the Black Crown*

This book is for my mom, who raised me on Star Trek and made the mistake of telling me I was too young to read Dune when I was ten. Reverse psychology never worked so well. Love you.

AUTHOR'S NOTE

Content Warning: Prior to the events of this book, the main character lost a child. She continues to process this loss throughout this story.

1

WORTHY

THE ARGOSIAN FARMER TOOK UP MOST OF THE BED, HIS MASSIVE ARM slung over Sunny's waist, pinning her in place like a nova beetle on its back. Surveying his snoring face—and extremely naked body— she wondered, *Did I actually fuck him last night? And if so, how? Physically, how was it even possible?*

Her Viewchip (VC) comm pinged inside her head, alerting her to an incoming message: <Sunny, where are you? You're late.>

Sunny moaned, then froze as the Argosian stirred. <Wrong number,> she told her assistant, Elanie, over the comm in her mind.

<Do not.> Elanie was evidently in no mood. <I've laid an outfit out for you on your empty, unslept-in bed. We have a staff meeting to welcome the new Languages and Customs expert in twenty minutes. Please get your ass to your pod directly.>

<I don't appreciate your tone, Elanie. I am *very* hungover.>

<Really? Because you sound like you're still drunk. And I did say *'please.'*>

Gingerly, Sunny scooted back toward the headboard of the Argosian's bed and sat up. Elanie wasn't wrong. She was still drunk. Argosian ripple didn't take any prisoners.

<What is it that you want?> Sunny asked.

Elanie's sigh gusted between Sunny's ears. <Please, for the love of all the stars in all the skies, bid farewell to whatever disaster you've wrought upon yourself and make your way to your pod. You do not want to miss this meeting.>

<Roger that.> Sunny pinched the purple skin of the arm squishing her belly. "Ahem, darling? Wakey, wakey."

A deep and resonant rumbling erupted from the enormous man whose bed, she presumed, she was currently trying to escape.

"My sentiments precisely," she muttered. "Would you be so kind as to remove your arm from my waist? I'm rather late." She was also rather worried she might break in two when she tried to stand up if what she feared happened last night actually had.

The Argosian rolled onto his back, taking his arm with him.

Air flooded her lungs. "Much better." She slid off the bed. "I'll just find my clothes and—"

"You will not find them," he grumbled, propping his head on an elbow and smirking sleepily at her. Golden tattoos embellished his expansive chest and firm stomach: a scythe, harvest moons glowing over a field of grain, exquisitely detailed seeds—images meant to pay tribute to the agricultural life that drove his planet's economy.

"I can see that. Happen to know where they are?"

"You wore no clothes when I found you." His smirk stretched into a full-fledged grin.

Sunny blinked. "I'm sorry? Can you repeat that?" She enjoyed a wild night here and there, but she had never once in her entire sordid career lost her clothes. Well, unless she counted her shoe, but she'd given that away.

Scratching his chest between his stunning pectorals, he said, "Argos makes a strong drink. Do not feel ashamed."

"Did we...? Did I...?" Sunny gulped.

He shook his head, rueful. "We did not join. We were not *worthy* of each other."

A profound relief buckled her knees. *Worthy*, on Argos—where males tended to outweigh females by one hundred kilos or more—

referred to the way body parts might or might not fit together between two partners. Sunny offered a silent prayer of thanks to the sweet gods of fermentation who had blessed her with complete amnesia of the evaluation of said *worth*.

"Apologies, dear man." She clicked her tongue. "Anatomy strikes again, eh?" Snatching his yellow coveralls—the preferred outfit for all Argosians—from the bed, she wrapped them around her body like a robe.

"No. Those are mine." His deep voice reverberated through her ribcage.

"Yes, well, I can't very well walk back to my pod in the nude, can I? I'm sure you understand. I will have my assistant return your garment to you straight away. You have my word." Her hand reached out awkwardly to pat his big toe, which he wiggled playfully under her palm. She straightened, ran a hand through her hair, and recited her customary closing remarks. "I trust you are enjoying your stay aboard the *Ignisar*, and I sincerely hope you will look no further than LunaCorp for all your future holiday and interplanetary travel needs."

With a curt nod, she scampered from his room while he laughed at her, shaking his gigantic, golden-tattooed head.

Holding up the too-long legs of the Argosian's coveralls, Sunny stumbled as gracefully as she could into the elevator, packed full with two canoodling, sunglasses-wearing Ulaperians, one quad-armed guest from Gorbulon-7—two of those arms busy teasing his hair straight up—and one rather handsome Blurvan. The Blurvan, leaning his humanoid torso against the back wall of the elevator while his gelatinous lower half jiggled above a tapping, seven-toed foot, took one look at her outfit and smirked. "Rough night?"

Sunny pushed the button for deck twelve, mumbled, "No

rougher than usual," and wished for the umpteenth time the crew had their own elevator bank.

After passing a party of hopping, one-legged guests from Vorp on her way to her pod, Sunny winced because there stood Elanie, blocking her door, scowling with her arms crossed tightly under her disgustingly perfect bionic cleavage.

"Staff meeting is in ten minutes, Sunny. I hope it was worth it."

AI with DNA spliced between the wires, all bionics were designed to emulate the pinnacle of their particular species' beauty. Elanie, for example—with her silky brown hair, perfectly straight nose, and big brown doe eyes—always looked as fresh as spring rain. Sunny, on the other hand, felt and likely smelled like the refuse compactor on jettison day.

"Is that a pair of Argosian coveralls?" A look of pure horror overtook Elanie as she realized who Sunny had shacked up with last night.

Always endeavoring to project the appearance of having her shit together, Sunny replied, "It is, and it was completely worth it." Her brow cocked. "Another satisfied customer, if you ask me."

"An Argosian? You could have been killed."

Sunny snorted, waving her off.

Elanie's fist landed on her hip. "You are not a prostitute, Sunny. You are a hospitality specialist. You do not need to sleep with all of these men—"

"And women," Sunny interjected with a finger raised, sliding past Elaine into her room.

"—to be good at your job."

Oh, the naïve little woodsprite. "At the risk of shocking your bionic sensibilities so thoroughly you'll need a hard reboot"—Sunny threw off her coverall robe and donned the outfit Elanie had picked out for her—"I will say only this: life is far too short not to do what you love as often as you can." Her smirk was salacious.

Elanie's groan was lengthy. "You have nine minutes."

Sunny strapped on a pair of kitten heels, tucked a white button-down into a black pencil skirt, and pinched her cheeks. She waved her hand over her body, head to toe. "Yes?"

Elanie frowned. "No. Your hair looks like a trestal's nest."

"Right." Running water from the sink over her hands, she wetted down her jagged blonde hair, then ducked underneath her QuikDri. A dehydrating film made of millions of microscopic sandguppies dropped from the device, clinging to her head and sucking before peeling itself off with a satisfied sigh. "Better?"

One of Elanie's shoulders rose a fraction, the gestural equivalent of *I can't even begin to describe how little I care.*

Sunny's eyes narrowed. "Elanie, darling, are you all right?"

"Fine. Why?" Elanie replied flatly.

"You seem even pricklier than usual, if that's possible. Any chance you finally decided to install your upgrade?" The hormone simulation upgrade had just been released for all bionics generation twenty-six and older.

Elanie shuddered. "No. Absolutely not."

"Why not?" Sunny's brows waggled. "Could be fun, you know."

"I tried the trial version, momentarily. It was not fun. It felt..." Elanie's face pinched in disgust like she'd just sucked the slime off of that elevator Blurvan's seventh toe. "Messy."

"That is a fair assessment. But you should do it anyway. You may find it won't kill you to participate in something other than categorical disdain every once in a while."

"Well, Sunny, as someone once said, 'Life is far too short not to do what you love as often as you can.'"

As Elanie walked into the hallway with a flip of her perfect hair, Sunny burst into laughter.

THE NEW L&C

ACCESSING THE FILES IN HER VC WHILE SHE MADE HER WAY TO THE staffroom, Sunny perused the dossiers of the special guests expected to board this week. A conference of Delphinian magicians arrived earlier in the morning. Delphinian magicians, while mostly harmless, were occasionally disastrous guests. A drunken magician's finger-snap three years ago resulted in the still unfillable pool on deck sixteen. Every time the crew tried to fill it, the water vanished with an infuriating *fizz-pop* sound. Sunny held a bit of lingering contempt for the outer rim planet's enthusiasm for magic ever since. The pool on deck sixteen had been her favorite.

A senator from Tranquis, Sunny's home planet, would arrive tomorrow. Which was...odd. They didn't get many politicos aboard the *Ignisar*—something about the ship's reputation as an orgy-in-orbit tended to keep them from booking. And this senator, Chahna Ramesh, planned to stay with her wife and ten-year-old son until they reached the ocean planet of Portis for the Known Universal Senate meeting. Which would take more than a month. The *Ignisar* was not built for speed, and if the senator wanted to use the ship simply to get to Portis, much more efficient and economical methods of travel were available to her. With much less possibility of destroying her political career after she accidentally ate a piece of warple cake at Sunday brunch and wound up dancing naked in the atrium.

<What do you know of the senator?> Sunny Vcommed Elanie.

<Same as you. Why?> Elanie responded curtly.

<You don't think it's odd? A senator on holiday with her wife and child on the *Ignisar* of all places?>

<I'll admit it is a strange booking. But we have been marketing more to families lately with our Wholesome Deck Initiative, perhaps the WDI is working. Hurry up, you're late. Chan brought cake.>

This information perked Sunny right up. <Ooh, cake! I'll be right there. How's the new *L&C*?>

There was a moment of silence before Elanie replied, <He is...adequate.>

Sunny detected some hesitation in Elanie's response, perhaps even—*gasp*—innuendo. She didn't think Elanie possessed the capability. <Adequate? How very understated.>

<Just get in here.>

When Sunny walked into the staffroom, the crew was huddled at the far end of the big table as someone told a story, the new L&C, she presumed. She saw hands gesturing, heard laughing, and then, in the sexiest, most panty-incinerating Venusian accent she thought she'd never hear again, "And that was the last time I ever went drinking with a Gorbie."

She halted dead in her tracks, the air in her lungs vanishing, her chest constricting like she'd been sucked out an airlock. Her heart kicked so violently against her ribs she was certain everyone on the entire twelfth deck must have heard it. She knew that voice. That warm laughter. Those hands. Months ago those hands had been all over her body, making her moan, cry out, even scream during the most intensely phenomenal sexual encounter of her life.

Noticing her standing wide-eyed in the doorway, Chandler, the *Ignisar*'s cruise director, pivoted his hoverchair Sunny's way and waved her over. "Oh, good! You're finally here. Come meet Freddie. Freddie, this is Sunastara Jeka, our hospitality specialist."

Freddie? When he'd spent the night in her hotel room, fucking her silly into the wee morning hours, when—for the first time in years—she'd considered blowing up her entire life for a man, she hadn't known his real name. She'd only known his high cheekbones, his nose which had been a bit crooked right over the bridge, his soft brown hair falling flawlessly into his blue-gray eyes when he'd been on top of her, nestled snuggly between her legs. They'd met at LunaCorp HQ in the City of All Knowledge—aka (much to LunaCorp's chagrin) the CAK—using her favorite VC dating app, Squee. Nobody ever used their real names on Squee. Her name had been *Phoebe.* His had been *Joshua.* And he had been spectacular.

The wall of her fellow coworkers parted, and when Sunny finally got a look at him, at his long, lithe frame poured into his suit and that wicked sparkle in his eyes, she practically whimpered. And Sunny never whimpered.

When he finally saw her, his eyes grew wide and his mouth stalled open, his fork and the bite of cake perched upon it falling down to clink against his plate. "Phoebe?" he said in pure disbelief.

Sunny's hand clapped over her pounding heart. "Joshua?"

Standing to Sunny's right, knowing full well the alias Sunny used on Squee, Elanie rolled her eyes and groaned.

MOON JELLY

<Stars above, Sunny. Must you sleep with everyone in the entire Known Universe?>

Sunny heard Elanie's snark through her VC, but she sounded like she was a million kilometers away, on a raft, in the middle of an ocean, all the way across the wormhole, maybe on Venus.

"Phoebe?" repeated Joshua—or rather, Freddie, as it happened —while he stood, staring at Sunny with those same earnest, storm-grey eyes she'd been dreaming about for months. "How..."

"You two know each other?" Chan looked curiously between them.

Freddie's expression was blank, and his voice—absent all the sultry swagger Sunny remembered—warbled. But his face; that crooked nose, those full, kissable lips... "Yes, we've met." His voice was a whisper, soft as silk against her cheeks. *This is bad.*

Sunny's poorly hidden lust-filled expression evidently conveyed her indiscretions quite clearly, not that Chan would have had to make much of a deductive leap. As one of Sunny's closest friends, he was fully abreast of her favorite extracurricular activities. As was everyone else on the crew.

"Sunny!" Chan stared at her, his head cocked but his finger flicked out to point at Freddie. "You slept with our new L&C?"

Sunny swallowed what felt like a gwarf—an Aquilinian fruit resembling a golf ball covered in mildly poisonous spikes. She couldn't answer Chan's question. She could barely even speak. Because Freddie was here. The most phenomenal one-night stand of her entire life was now a member of her crew and would work with her every day and live with her on this ship. Permanently. *Holy shit.*

"I'm terribly sorry," she said to no one in particular. "If you'll all excuse me for a moment."

Spinning on her heel, she attempted to walk smoothly from the room but tripped over the threshold and stumbled inelegantly out into the hallway.

"Sunny, wait. Stop." Freddie's honeyed voice had its own gravitational field, slowing her down, pulling her back. Reeling her in.

She took a deep breath and blew it out. *Get a grip, Sunny.* This was her ship. She refused to be stunned into a bewildered silence on her own ship! But when she turned around, Freddie's smile nearly took her out at the knees.

"Sunny, or is it Sunastara? That's quite lovely, isn't it?" he said as an aside once he reached her. "You work on the *Ignisar*? You... I can't believe it." He took her shaking hand in his, pulling her into a quiet alcove next to a moon jelly tank. The watery blue light emanating from the tank danced over his cheekbones in graceful little ripples. "Sunny, say something, anything."

You're beautiful. You smell like the best dream I ever had. I want to eat your face. "Hello, Frederick. Fancy meeting you here," she said stiffly.

"Freddie, please call me Freddie. I haven't been able to stop thinking about you since that night. I thought I'd never see you again. I tried to find you on Squee again, but your profile never reappeared. But, *stars above,* here you are." He released her hand only to reach out and cup her cheek. "Close enough to touch. It's impossible. Isn't this impossible? Put me out of my misery and tell me you've thought of me too. Tell me you feel the same. Please."

Sunny was tempted to tell him that she did feel the same. But fear flooded her, the same cold, paralyzing fear that assaulted her every time anyone tried to get too close since the accident. It was unbearable, this feeling, this panic. Besides, she hadn't even seen this man in months. They probably had nothing in common. He probably liked sardines and hated reality television. Who could say? And they had to work together. Sunny might've mixed work and pleasure on a regular basis, but never with her actual coworkers.

She backed away from him. "Freddie, I—"

His sharp inhale stopped her short. "I didn't even think to ask. Are you taken? Are you already with someone?" He looked completely devastated, like someone just popped a balloon full of puppies.

"No, I'm not with anyone."

"Thank the stars," he wheezed, trying to take another step closer.

Sunny stood taller, clearing her throat. "The thing is, Freddie, I don't ever date my coworkers. It's an absolute nonstarter for me."

He didn't miss a beat, his delicious Venusian accent making her bite her cheek. "Ooch, is that all? Not a problem. I quit." He wheeled around, shouting back toward the break room, "Sorry, Chan, but I qui—"

Sunny couldn't keep the smile from her lips as she threw her hand over his mouth. "Shh! Stop that! You can't quit. We need a good L&C, and I've heard nothing but rave reviews." Once she felt his lips against her palm, she yanked her hand back like it had been electrocuted.

"Pshh. You can find someone else. It's not like it's a difficult job."

"Right, it only takes nine years of higher education, an additional five of fieldwork, and two advanced residencies. Languages and Customs experts practically grow on trees."

"They do, in fact. I can recommend several." His eyes were a storm. "I have to be with you, Sunny. I've never felt anything like the connection I felt...I *feel* when I'm with you. And to meet again, here." He looked around the deck like he couldn't believe his dumb luck. "It's got to mean something."

It was true that when Sunny saw him leaning against that shelf, she wanted nothing more than to run to him, throw herself into his arms, and kiss him until they both nearly died from it. But he had no idea who he was talking to. He knew Phoebe, not Sunny. Phoebe was put together. Phoebe was carefree. Sunny was a disaster. Sunny still spent her days walking over the thinnest layer of ice, knowing that any extra weight at all would shatter the surface beneath her feet and she'd be lost.

Providing a blessed break in the tension, a group of Delphinain Wizards—as this particular group insisted on being called—swept down the hall, their red-and-black robes swishing against their legs. One of them said, "And that's when I realized the incantation, when recited quickly, sounded just like, 'I poured butter on a bear's underbelly,' in the common tongue."

Sunny tried not to grin when another replied, "That's random. Remind me, what is a 'bear'?"

Collecting herself, she finally answered Freddie's question. "What it means is that you and I were meant to *work* together."

He scoffed, shaking his head.

"Listen, we barely even know each other. Trust me, you don't want to throw this job, this very good job with an excellent crew on a beautiful...ish," she clarified, "ship away over one night months ago. You'll love working here. And you and I, well, we can be fr—"

He moved so close that his breath brushed over Sunny's lips. It smelled like cake. "If you say *friends*, I'm going to shout *fire*."

Sunny tried to back away, but she bumped into the moon jelly tank, startling the little blobs into a slightly less slow-motion whirl away from the glass. Freddie's lips hovered a hair's breadth from hers, and she nearly tipped her weight onto her toes so she could kiss him and damn the consequences. Thankfully, some cooler portion of her brain prevailed. "You and I, we had a nice time, that's all. I have lots of 'nice times,' and this was no different." *What a preposterous lie.* "Let's just leave it at that and get on with our lives as fellow crewmembers."

Backing away, some invisible bucket of cold water washing all the heat from his expression, he said, "I see." His hands slid into his pockets.

Sunny felt like shit. "I'm sorry, Freddie. But we should really get back to the party. You're the guest of honor, after all." When she walked past him back to the staffroom, he watched her go without a word.

"Everything all right out there?" asked Chan around a mouthful of cake as Sunny walked back into the staffroom, Freddie filing in behind her.

Freddie's voice was reed thin. "Right as rain, Chan. Thank you." Then, in a lighter tone, "Would you look at that? I leave for five minutes, and you lot try to finish off my cake without me."

Tig, the *Ignisar*'s head of IT, froze, halting the bite of cake currently on the way to her rosebud mouth. She set the fork back onto her plate, shrugging guiltily. "Sorry, Freddie." Pushing her plate away, she flipped the hood of her sweatshirt over her pink hair, her small, round face disappearing until only her pert nose poked out from the hood's shadow.

Freddie slid her plate back in front of her. "I was only joking, Tig. Forgive me."

Sunny pulled out a chair, her heart still pounding, palms still sweating, and pretended she was just perfectly fine. Chan, Elanie, and the twins, Rax and Morgath—identical, hulking, grey-green skinned ex-spec ops from the smaller of the Aquilines' twin planets who ran security aboard the *Ignisar*—and eventually even Tig gorged themselves on yellow sheet cake with chocolate frosting and *Welcome to the Jungle* scrawled across the top in blue-and-white icing.

Chan raised his cup in a toast. "Well," he said with a tight, nervy laugh, "it seems our new L&C has already made quiet the impression on our little group."

Sunny's eyes slid to Freddie across the table. He smiled at her when he met her stare, triggering her head to whip back toward Chan so fast her neck popped. *Well done, Sunny. Very smooth.*

"Chandler, if I may," Sunny recited calmly, psyching herself up by imagining she was both bigger and taller than Rax and Morgath combined. "Before ship gossip reaches critical mass, I will simply say that Freddie and I met on the CAK months ago. We had a—" fire inexcusably seared her cheeks— "nice night. However, that is in the past. We are both professionals and will behave accordingly."

Freddie's eyes ratcheted open in what Sunny guessed was astonishment that this topic was being discussed at a work function, during his first day of his brand-new job, and perhaps this was not her finest decision. "Oh. Um, well. You see," he stammered. "What Sunny says is true. We, er, did..." He trailed off awkwardly. "I am a consummate professional, however—"

Rax snorted. "Y'all got freaky, didn't you?" He grinned, scratching his thick fingers into his unruly mop of green hair.

Morgath elbowed his brother in the ribs. "Shut up, idiot."

"Anyway," Chan said over the chatter. "Welcome to the team, Freddie. Our last L&C was exemplary, so you have some very big shoes to fill. But I'm sure you'll be plenty big enough."

Elanie choked on her VitoWater.

Chan's eyes flew to Sunny, then back to Freddie. "I mean, your feet," he amended, wincing. Poor Chan had a terrible habit of tripping over his tongue. "Your feet are big, not you. Not to imply that you're small..."

Bright-red patches exploded onto Tig's cheeks, Rax and Morgath turned even redder trying to stifle their laughter, and Sunny and Freddie stared industriously at their plates of uneaten cake as if they'd held all the secrets of the universe.

4

HE SEEMS...NICE

PRETENDING HER LIFE WASN'T JUST UPHEAVED BY THE SUDDEN appearance of the only man who had literally made her drool proved immensely difficult. While Sunny bid a farewell to the unbearably demanding celebrity power couple who had monopolized her every waking moment over the last week as they disembarked back across the wormhole to Mars, she should have been ready to celebrate. Instead she barely registered a mild relief. She'd been too busy trying not to remember Freddie's eyes and the way they'd stared up at hers from between her legs.

As she meandered back to the elevator bank from the airlock, a cleaning drone whirred along the carpet beside her, bumping gently against the wall, and she wondered, *Did I recharge my vibrator this morning?*

<Elanie?> Sunny Vcommed, stepping onto the elevator and pushing the button for twelve.

<Yes?> Elanie responded warily.

<What do you think of him?>

<More specific. With you that could mean anyone.>

Sunny groaned. <You really are a twit, you know that, right?>

<More specific, *please*,> Elanie replied with a faux sweetness. <Is that better?>

Sunny exited the elevator on deck twelve, making her way toward the crew pods. <Yes, quite. Thank you. I meant Freddie. What do you think of Freddie?> She placed her hand over her room's security panel and the door slid open.

<He seems...nice.>

<Nice?> Sunny sat on the edge of her bed, staring at her reflection in the mirror. She pressed her fingers into her cheeks, then pinched them.

<Yes, nice. Why do you ask?>

Because he makes my nipples hard, Sunny murmured inwardly. <You and I will be working closely with him. I'm just wanting to make sure you don't have a bad feeling about him or anything.>

<Uh -huh,> Elanie said slowly, not buying the lie.

<So, nice, then?>

<Yes, nice,> Elanie repeated. <And I'm not sure you've noticed, but he's also very, very good looking.>

<Whaaat?> Sunny said, feigning shock. <Hadn't noticed at all. You know Elanie, that is a very unprofessional thing to say about a coworker.>

Elanie actually let her laughter come through the Vcomm. <Please be sure to visit Senator Ramesh and her family first thing tomorrow. They will be expecting you after boarding.>

Ah yes, the senator. And her son. Her young son, Sunny remembered. <Of course, first thing. Thank you, darling.>

Sunny considered taking a nap. Her favorite sleeping shirt, an oversized dark-blue tee with faded glow in the dark constellations as seen from Lathineas, the mountain town on Tranquis' southern hemisphere where she'd grown up, looked more than inviting folded up on her dresser. She'd been running herself ragged this last week, planning the old L&C's retirement party, babysitting the Martians, reuniting with the only lover who'd ever given her seven orgasms in one night. A nap did sound lovely.

<Hello, Sunny. I apologize for the intrusion, but is there any chance you have a moment?>

She jumped. *Speak of the seven-orgasm devil.* It was the first time Freddie had accessed her VC, and the intimacy of it sent a shiver straight down her spine.

<Hello, Freddie. What can I do for you?> she replied, trying to sound professional, feeling anything but.

<I have found myself in a bit of a predicament. I'm currently in the small ballroom on deck five with a very intoxicated Argosian who claims to know you. He refuses to leave unless you come talk to him. He is, um, very large. And he's, well, I think he's *dancing?* With a serving drone. The other guests are alarmed—as am I, I'm not too ashamed to admit.>

<Oh dear.> She kept her laughter off the Vcomm. <I'm on my way.>

5

GARRAN THE VERDANT

<Morgath, are you busy?> Sunny stepped back onto the elevator and pushed the button for deck five.

Morgath's response was swift. <I'm never too busy for my favorite hospitality specialist.>

<It's probably nothing, but there may be a need for some increased security in the deck five ballroom.>

<Mechs or men?> he asked, straight to the point in the way Sunny always appreciated about both Morgath and his brother.

The elevator dinged, and the doors slid open, emptying Sunny out onto deck five. <Mechs will do. Only one or two.> Sunny always kept her estimates low because in Rax and Morgath's world, one meant eight and two meant twenty.

<They're on the way. Let me know if you need more.>

<Will do. Thank you, darling.>

She hightailed it down the hall, and as she neared the ballroom, loud, warbling singing echoed off the walls, interrupted by ground-trembling hiccups. She opened up a Vcomm to Elanie. <Elanie, dear?>

<Yes.>

<Did Freddie by chance contact you regarding the situation on

deck five?> She weaved through a gaggle of gaping-mouthed guests, all staring with rapt attention, and peered inside the ballroom.

Yellow coveralls sleeves slid along the floorboards as the half-naked Argosian, *her* Argosian, spun in circles with...yep, that was indeed a serving drone.

<Negative,> Elanie replied.

<If you're not too busy, I could use your help. Small ballroom please, and do hurry.>

<I'll be right there,> she said, then clicked off.

Four of Morgath's security mechs—titanium balls a meter in diameter that housed all manner of weaponry, crowd dispersal tech, and ultra-intimidating voice programming—floated to Sunny's location, roving red lights encircling their circumferences like ominous Yuletide decorations. Sunny positioned the mechs at either side of the ballroom doors, more to keep any lookie-loos out than to present a show of force within, but she'd learned never to be too careful.

Slinking silently into the ballroom, she spotted Freddie sitting at a table by himself, his chin resting in his hand, his suit jacket folded over his chair back, his tie pulled loose. His face brightened when he noticed her. <Oh, thank goodness you're here. He's tried to pull me onto the dance floor with him twice already.>

Sunny remembered how funny he'd been when he'd been Joshua and she'd been Phoebe, how charming. *Damn.* She continued to slide along the wall until she reached his table where he quietly pulled a chair out for her.

"What happened?" she whispered, taking the offered seat.

Freddie rubbed thoughtfully at his chin. "I couldn't say, to be honest. He's been in here for about an hour, ten minutes of that spent sobbing in the middle of the dance floor, another ten drinking—and this is not an exaggeration—five bottles of rum, and the rest dancing with that drone he's taken to calling 'Kasa.'"

"Kasaaaa!" the Argosian roared, squeezing the serving drone so tightly it *bleep-bleeped* out a warning and flared a bright-yellow light from its central panel.

Sunny winced. "Was that its pressure censor?"

"Third time it's gone off. I'm a little worried he'll crush the poor drone to bits."

"Those aren't cheap," she said.

"Precisely." Freddie leaned in close. "If he breaks it, who will give him the bill?"

"Not me, thank you very much," Sunny replied, wanting to laugh. This was easier than she'd thought it would be, working with Freddie. Perhaps they actually could become friends. Partners, even. Vertical, fully clothed partners.

"He asked for you—and only you. He said you'd know what to do. Do you know him? His name? Whenever I ask he just bellows, 'Not worth night soil!' and starts sobbing again."

Sunny watched the Argosian twirl the drone in circles, the crystal chandeliers above him casting kaleidoscopic shadows around his feet. His face was wet, his shoulders hunched, his steps surprisingly graceful. "I don't know his name. But I do know him. He and I, we, well..."

"You didn't." Freddie's jaw fell to the floor. "And you're still alive?"

Sunny did laugh now. "We did not. We were not *worthy* of each other."

"Thank your lucky stars. Never got his name though?"

"Never came up. Or if it did, I don't remember. I was very drunk. Argosian ripple."

"Oof," Freddie said, sympathizing. She'd expected more judgment from him for some reason. Then again, they had met using Squee. Maybe he craved a little strange just as often as she did.

Sunny gasped as the Argosian wailed something in his native tongue. Her VC translated: "Our rows were to travel together! Our seeds to burrow into the soil as one! Now all is *rot!*" The last word came out as a growling sob, followed by a tremendous burp.

"That sounds like heartbreak," she whispered.

Freddie nodded in agreement. "These are old Argosian mating words often recited at the ceremony for hand-joining. Obviously, something has gone amiss."

"Hmm. I see." Sunny got to her feet, pretending her knees weren't shaking. She didn't imagine the Argosian would hurt her, but she also didn't imagine he'd be dancing with a million-credit robot like it was his Vorp Revel date. Yet there he was.

Steeling her nerve, she made to walk toward the giant, distraught, intoxicated man, but Freddie grasped her hand and held her back. Her skin tingled, turned warm.

"Do you want me to come with?" he asked.

The Argosian swayed and spun, now slumped over, resting the full weight of his head on the serving drone's tray, pushing the weight limit of its thrusters.

"No, darling, walk in the park. And Elanie's just arrived. She's all the backup I'll need."

"I will pretend not to feel unmanned by that statement," Freddie said evenly as he released Sunny's hand.

<Where do you want me?> Elanie Vcommed.

<Why don't you come sit next to Freddie. But be on alert, please. Lockdown may be required.> Like all Bionics, Elanie was strong enough to incapacitate almost anyone, even the inebriated mountain of muscle waltzing over the ballroom floor. And since she was so gorgeous, most didn't mind if she was the one putting them in a rear naked choke.

Sunny exhaled, then said, "Wish me luck."

Freddie's eyes sparkled, crinkling at the corners. "Sunastara Jeka, I've a feeling you are far too good at what you do to demean it with something as fickle as luck."

Her heart stuttered mid-beat. She was not a woman who sought out compliments, but she thoroughly enjoyed them when they were given. The prospects of a non-naked friendship with Freddie grew slimmer by the second. Especially when he winked at her and said, "Now go save our serving drone."

Once Elanie tiptoed to the table, Sunny surrendered her chair, girded her loins, and went in.

The Argosian's voice resonated, echoing off the metallic surface of the serving tray his head was still slung over. He sang a mournful song about a once lush field that had gone fallow because nobody had taken the time to water it. Once she reached a spot a few meters from him, quietly, Sunny cleared her throat.

He stopped singing.

She held her breath.

<Be careful,> said Freddie.

<This is asinine,> Elanie weighed in.

"Hello," Sunny said, her chin ducked, hands raised, palms facing out and fingers splayed wide.

The Argosian's head rose to wobble heavily upon his neck as his deeply set purple eyes found Sunny's. "Finally." His voice rumbled like an avalanche. "You came."

Her shoulders dropped from her ears. This man was distressed —devastated, even—but he was not murderous. That much she could see.

"I'm sorry it's taken me so long. What happened, darling? What's wrong? How can I help?"

He pointed a sausage-thick finger down at a half-empty bottle on the floor. "I saved a bottle for you." Squinting at the bottle, he clarified, "I saved *half* a bottle for you. Drink with me."

Sunny's keen sense of self-preservation told her she should absolutely comply with this demand. Besides, rum was delicious and she was thirsty. Bending down slowly, she wrapped her fingers around the neck of the bottle, then stood and pulled out the cork with a *thwup*. The rum was dark and sweet and tasted exactly like the moment the sun set behind ocean waves.

<Do you really think that's a good idea?>

Sunny's eyes slid to the side. <Yes I do, Elanie. Thank you very

much.> Then she took another swig before meeting the Argosian's blurry gaze again. "It might take me a while to catch up with you." She toed the pile of bottles surrounding them. One rolled free, rumbling across the floorboards until it clinked to a stop against the side of a marble pillar.

He blinked several times, like he was straining to focus his eyes on her but they stubbornly refused to obey.

Sunny's hand extended toward him. "Care to dance with someone less...automated?"

He swallowed, then nodded. "Yes, please."

Carefully, Sunny pried his arms away from the serving drone, and while the traumatized drone careened away wildly like a launched pinball, she stepped into the Argosian's embrace, letting him take the lead. He held her close but gentle, like she was precious, delicate. Wrapped inside his tree-trunk arms, nestled against his warm chest, she couldn't help but feel safe and protected. The entire effect was rather nice. *This Kasa person is really missing out.*

<Elanie, I think we're good here. Would you be a dear and take the serving drone to Tig for analysis?>

<I'd be happy to if I could catch the damn thing.> Running after the drone with her arms outspread, Elanie cut this way and that as the drone whirred and squealed, bobbing and weaving away from her.

"She looks like she is trying to wrangle a bokbok into its den," the Argosian slurred, then gurgled a sound that might have been a laugh. As his chin came down to rest atop Sunny's head, he sniffled.

Sunny took another swig of rum, catching Freddie staring at her intently. <You can leave as well, if you have other things to—>

<Not a chance,> he replied before she'd even finished her thought.

Peeling her eyes from Freddie, from his loose tie and disheveled hair and amused half smile, she returned her attention to her dance partner. "I don't think I ever got your name."

She braced herself for the yelling Freddie had described, but the big man only grumbled, "Garran."

Argosians tended to have lengthy names they earned over their lifetimes that spoke of their greater virtues. So she ventured, "Garran the...?"

"Once," he rumbled, spinning her out in two full circles before reeling her back into his arms, "I was Garran the Brave. Then, Garran the Verdant. Now," his head shook slowly from side to side, "they may as well call me Garran the Desolate. Better yet, Garran the Barren." He snorted miserably at his own joke.

"Well, Garran, would you like to talk about it?"

He pulled away to stare down at Sunny, his violet brows tangling together into the most impressive furrow she had ever seen.

"You thought I was a good choice, did you not? There was no *worth* between us, but you chose me for your bedmate. You had many other options." His throaty Argosian accent was thick with sorrow.

Sunny's eyes traced his golden tattoos, rows of corn that originated at the bridge of his nose, growing taller as they swayed to encircle his bald head. She reached up to stroke his cheek, his prominent cheekbone filling her palm completely. He was magnificent, in a gargantuan sort of way. "I did."

He spun her around again, the rum clouding her head so that she still spun even after he let her go. Then his head dropped to hang between his shoulders. He startled a *yelp* out of both Sunny and Freddie as he collapsed to sit hard onto the floor. Sunny thought she heard a floorboard crack.

Glancing at Freddie as Garran sobbed into his hands, she shrugged, unsure how best to handle this particular turn of events. Freddie's answering shrug in return was no help at all.

After one more lengthy pull from her bottle, Sunny sat down on the floor next to Garran. "Is this about Kasa?" she asked.

"Kasa grows in my heart, but I do not grow in hers," Garran said into his hands. "I wanted to plow her fields."

It took significant effort not to laugh at this innuendo, especially since it was unintended. Although the winters on Argos were frigid and brutal, the remaining six-hundred-and-fifty standard days that made up its calendar year boasted an exceptionally moderate climate, giving Argos the longest growing season of any planet in the Known Universe. As a result, most Argosians made their livings as farmers. Garran, quite literally, wanted to help Kasa plow her fields.

"She doesn't want the same?" Sunny asked carefully. "Do you know why?"

He nodded, then hiccupped, his massive shoulders jerking toward his ears. "She says I am too green."

<Too *green*?> Sunny Vcommed Freddie, not familiar with the saying.

<I believe it means too young or, more likely in this case, inexperienced.>

That's hard to believe, she thought. "Is Kasa on the ship?" Perhaps this situation merely required Sunny's unparalleled matchmaking skills.

"She arrived from Argos this morning. But I have loved her since I was a seedling."

"Is there someone else for her? Someone else she wants?"

His head whipped up so quickly, Sunny fell backward on reflex.

"She says there is not. But if there is," he growled, "I will be very unhappy about it."

That's it? Unhappy? *He really is a gentle farmer, isn't he? Never judge an Argosian by their muscle mass,* she supposed.

"Garran the Brave, Garran the Verdant." She took his thumb in her hand because any more fingers wouldn't fit. "The last word I would ever use to describe you is *green*. Kasa obviously doesn't know what she's talking about."

It was small and short lived, but Sunny swore a smile tugged at his lips.

"You have asked for the perfect person this evening," she told him. "Because I happen to be quite good at this sort of thing—worlds class, in fact. In order for me to help you, however, I need you to tell me everything you know about Kasa. And don't spare a single detail."

Sunny sat with Garran for at least another hour while he told her how he and Kasa had met, what sorts of things she liked, what sorts of things she didn't, how her hair reminded him of billowing fields of grain bathed in the violet glow of twilight. Garran, as it turned out, was quite poetic. About halfway through their conversation, she convinced Garran to let Freddie join them, telling him she would need Freddie's help to pull off this matchmaking endeavor.

Freddie sat cross-legged next to Sunny, heat building at the point where his knee touched hers, and shared her remaining rum. By the time Sunny knew enough about Garran and Kasa to get started, the rum had vanished, the tips of Freddie's ears had turned pink, Sunny was good and tipsy, and Garran could barely hold his eyes open.

Sunny sent the security mechs back to Morgath, shot Elanie a <Thank you> Vcomm, and then she and Freddie—supporting the crushing weight of one of Garran's arms each slung over their shoulders—led the stumbling, love-sick Argosian bard back to his suite to sleep it off.

"You did well with Garran," Freddie told her. "Not that I'm surprised."

They walked side by side back to the deck twelve crew quarters, but at a distance Sunny deemed safe enough to discourage any accidental fornication in a dark hallway or maintenance closet.

"Thank you, darling."

"Saved my hide, for certain. I wouldn't have made as graceful a dance partner." His Venusian accent had thickened after the rum, rolling from his tongue like an Old Earth Scottish burr.

"Sometimes a situation just needs a more feminine touch," Sunny replied.

"We make a good team," Freddie said. Then, before Sunny could summon any sort of response, he tilted his head toward a door. "This is me."

His pod was just a few doors down the hall from hers. But no matter what, she would not spend the rest of the night imagining him sleeping a mere hallway away. "Good night, Freddie." She held her hand out to him. It felt intolerably awkward.

Ever the gentleman, he took her outstretched hand in his and gave it a firm and professional shake. "Good night, Sunny." And then he pressed his palm against his security panel and entered his pod, closing his door before she could even peek inside.

Back in her pod, Sunny brushed her teeth and washed her face, then she reached deep into her unmentionables drawer to pull out her secret treasure. She'd kept Joshua's—Freddie's—necktie ever since their night together on the CAK. She'd never wanted to forget him, not his laughter or the hysterical stories he'd told her over dinner, not his lips on her skin or his fingers grasping her thighs.

After that night, before he'd left the following morning, she'd taken off his tie and asked him if she could keep it. He'd kissed her then. One last time. It was the single kiss she'd compared every other kiss to before and after, finding them lacking. Even Raphael, who was a phenomenal kisser, didn't hold a candle. When Freddie had walked into the hallway to leave her, he'd bent down, picking up the shoe that had slipped off her foot when he'd carried her to her room after dinner. Holding her shoe by its heel, he'd smiled and said, "And this is mine." She'd thought those would be the last words she'd ever hear from him.

To this day, even months later, she still occasionally slept with his tie wrapped around her fingers, wondering if she'd made a mistake not staying with him when he'd asked her to, wondering if she would ever see him again. Tonight, as her fingertips slid down the soft grey fabric, the raised bumps from its embroidered detailing tickling her skin, she wondered what it meant, that he was here, just down the hall. She climbed into bed, wrapped his tie around her fingers once more, and accepted the fact that she was in very big trouble.

6

HOW OLD ARE YOU?

THE SENATOR'S DOOR SWUNG OPEN AFTER ONLY TWO KNOCKS, revealing a gorgeous, brown-skinned woman in a soft white wrap-around sweater and ornately detailed green silk pants that Sunny wanted to tear from her body and run away with so they would belong to her forever.

"Hello there." Lena, the senator's wife, had a rich yet delicate voice, like cream poured over ice.

"Good morning. I'm looking for—"

"Chahna!" she interrupted, shouting over her shoulder. "It's for you, love." Turning back to Sunny, she waved. "Please, come in."

"Just a moment," came a deeper female voice from a back room, firm, confident, brimming with self-possession—a senator's voice, to be sure.

"Hi. Have you come to visit my moms?"

Stopping in the middle of the living room, Sunny looked down to find the source of this question. A black-haired and brown-eyed child sat cross-legged on the floor, staring up at her with a quizzical expression. When he hopped to his feet, Sunny wondered if he'd recently hit a growth spurt because he was long and gangly, stretched out like taffy. His fingers worked absently at a small wooden puzzle while his attention roved over Sunny from head to toe. She couldn't say she'd ever had a child look at her quite like that before, like a riddle to be solved. It unnerved her.

"Hello, little one. Actually, I'm here to visit with all of you. My name is Sunastara Je—"

"Jeka," he completed, blinking long, black eyelashes. "You are the *Ignisar's* hospitality specialist. My moms have been expecting you." He flipped a wooden peg on the puzzle into place and handed it to Sunny. The puzzle now assumed the shape of a perfect sphere. "It's not an easy one, but do you wanna try it?"

He wore wide-legged black pants and a pink, long-sleeved T-shirt with a *hang loose* symbol on it, but Sunny's eyes drifted to his bare feet. For as lanky as he was, he still had the short, pudgy toes of a younger child, and they grasped gently at the looping carpet. She took the puzzle.

"Hmm. I've never seen a puzzle like this before." She spun the sphere in her hand, looking for a place to start and not finding one.

"I know you haven't." His smile was wide and toothy. "I made this one myself."

"You did? That's amazing." Sunny swallowed down a sudden lump. He'd had so much time to learn so many things. After turning the sphere around in her hands several times, she handed him his puzzle back. "How long did it take you to make it?"

He popped two wooden pegs out of the sphere with his nimble fingers, twisting the top half counterclockwise while pulling on the bottom. Another peg sprung free. "This one took me two months. It's the hardest one I've made so far."

"Sai, come eat your breakfast," called Lena from the kitchenette.

The boy wobbled away, eyes on his puzzle, bare feet padding across the carpet. Sunny watched him hop up onto a barstool, spin around one full revolution, then take a huge bite out of some savory pastry so fragrant her stomach grumbled.

Senator Ramesh strode into the kitchenette, tying her raven-black hair up into a tight bun at the nape of her neck. Wearing a simple blue dress and black heels, she was short but striking, poised and exceptionally intimidating. "Sunastara Jeka," she said. "Welcome to our suite."

Sunny extended her hand toward the senator and bowed her head, as was custom on Tranquis when meeting someone of high esteem. "It's a pleasure to meet you and your family, Senator. And please, call me Sunny."

The senator shook Sunny's hand, bowing her head as well. "And you will call me Chahna."

"Tell her about the tart, Mom," said Sai from his stool.

Chahna smiled at her son, and it sucked the breath from Sunny's lungs. She remembered that smile, that joy, that pure love.

"Sai would like to report a burnt tart from the instawave," Chahna said. "Apparently, the oven refused to turn off no matter how many buttons he pushed. The fire-suppression system was employed."

"Oh dear. Was there any damage? We will remunerate you for any losses." The thick, white foam used to snuff out fires on the ship could be next to impossible to clean from clothing.

Chahna leaned in close to whisper, "We believe he asked the oven to cook the tart for thirty seconds instead of three. But he maintains this is not the case. We're not pushing the issue. I think he's embarrassed."

"Of course," Sunny said. "Such an easy mistake to make." Then, louder, "We had another instawave malfunction on this ship just last week. Nearly burned an entire pod down."

Sai's head whipped toward Sunny, his eyes wide and mouth sprung open. "You did?"

While he might've been a clever child, he had no poker face whatsoever. "I'm just glad no one was hurt," Sunny said with the most genuine sincerity she could muster. "Dangerous thing, a malfunctioning oven. How about we only let your mothers operate it from here on out?"

Sai nodded vigorously, looking relieved.

"How does he know who I am?" Sunny asked Chahna, her voice low.

Chahna walked to her son, mussed his hair then smoothed it back out. "I receive dossiers on the staff of every ship I travel on. Sai likes to peruse them over my shoulder, and we encourage his curiosity."

"Is that so?" Fear spiked in Sunny. She wondered what Chahna had found in her dossier. How much did they know about her? About her past?

As if reading Sunny's mind, Chahna said, "There is no personal information in the dossiers—just where you're from, how long you've worked aboard the ship, any military or political background, that sort of thing." She planted a soft kiss onto Sai's head, then moved to stand at the end of the counter. "But I did see that we're both from Tranquis."

"Yes, ma'am."

"Lathineas, correct?"

"That's where I grew up. My parents still live there, but I haven't been back in years."

Chahna sighed. "I haven't been to Lathineas in over a decade. But I love it there. It's so quiet, so green, and the mountains..." She whistled. "Breathtaking. What a wonderful place to grow up."

"It was. Very peaceful. Although not much of a nightlife."

Chahna's laughter was low and breathy, a senatorial chuckle. "I imagine not. At my age, that's much less of a concern."

Sunny frowned at this. The senator was only a few years older than she was. She wondered if she would still crave the escape of dark bars, stiff drinks, and warm bodies if her life had turned out differently, if she were in the senator's shoes, if she were a wife now, a mother still?

"Come sit, Sunny," Lena said, setting a steaming kettle on the counter. "Would you like some tea?"

Sunny hesitated, her gaze landing on the empty stool next to Sai, then floating up to the boy's smiling face.

"Yeah, Sunny. Come sit with me. I'll show you how the puzzle works." Sai held up the puzzle, now resembling an exploding star with twenty or so tiny pegs sticking out from a central core.

"Sai, you wouldn't try to trick me, would you? Is that even the same puzzle?" She was skeptical as she stepped forward to touch one of the pegs.

"Of course it is! I'm no cheat!"

Chahna glanced up from the techpad she'd pulled in front of her on the counter. "Sai, manners."

They didn't often have children aboard the *Ignisar*. As a matter of fact, Sunny couldn't recall a single guest under sixteen standard years since she'd started working on this ship five years ago. Being around Sai now, being around a child, felt like hands wrapping around her arms, her neck, pulling her back. She'd already overstayed her welcome.

"Thank you for the offer, Lena, but I'm afraid I'll have to take a rain check on the tea. I have a matter I must attend to." Sunny accessed Chahna's and Lena's Vmails through her VC. "I've just sent you both my direct Vcomm link. Please don't hesitate to contact me if you need anything at all. Any time, day or night."

Chahna nodded. "Thank you, Sunny."

"And I'll take you up on that rain check," promised Lena.

Sunny turned to leave, but Sai's sweet voice stuck her in place. "Hey, you didn't send your link to me. I might need to contact you sometime. I..." He paused. "I get bored."

Sunny smiled at him. "Apologies, Sai." She sent him the link. "Better?"

"Yes!" he cheered, his fist pumping in the air.

"Now, Sai," started Lena, her tone stern and parental, "Sunny is a very busy woman. You are not to contact her unless it's an absolute emergency. Do you understand?"

"I know. I won't bug her, promise." But at that precise moment, the little stinker sent Sunny the link to his Vcomm with a message attached. <I have a ton more puzzles to show you. You know, if you aren't too busy. And please don't tell my moms I sent this.>

She Vcommed back, <I'm never too busy for you, darling. And mum's the word. How old are you, Sai?>

<I just turned ten!>

A sharp and sudden ache throbbed deep in her chest. *Ten years old. That's exactly how old...*

<How old are you?> Sai's blunt question heaved her from her thoughts.

<Oh no, darling. The first lesson in interspecies communications is: no matter what, it's never a good idea to ask a woman about her age.>

<Oops, sorry about that.>

<You didn't know, and now you do. And I am thirty-eight.>

There was a pause. <I bet I can learn a great deal from you, Sunastara Jeka.>

Her breath caught in her throat as she reached the door, and when she turned back around, she had to push past the constriction to say, "Thank you, again," to Chahna and Lena.

"Of course," said Lena, pouring herself tea that smelled like peppermint. "Anytime."

"I hope you're both planning to attend the Fire Ball," Sunny said before she left. "It's my favorite event on the *Ignisar*, aside from New Year's."

"We've heard all about it and wouldn't miss it." Chahna stood beside Lena, sliding an arm around her waist.

"Oh." Sunny held up a finger. "There is one thing. I've asked for it to be removed from the menu, but if you happen to see anything on the dessert display called 'warple cake,' you might want to avoid it."

"Why's that?" asked Lena while blowing on her tea.

Sunny sucked on a tooth. "Warple cake is a powerful aphrodisiac. It might lead to some un-senatorial behavior, if you catch my meaning."

With a knowing smile, Chahna dipped her chin. "Thank you for the warning, Sunny."

As Sunny stepped into the hall, she heard Lena whisper, "Maybe we could just bring some of the warple cake back to the suite with us after the ball." She closed the door on the senator's laughter.

7

FFKS

CHAN CLINKED HIS GLASS OF CHAMPAGNE REPEATEDLY WITH A FORK. The last couple of weeks had passed by with relative ease, aside from how hard Sunny'd had to work to not stare too long or too hard at Freddie, professional Freddie, all-business Freddie. Seemingly uninterested Freddie... But the fact that Chan had brought booze to another staff meeting had Sunny's *what fresh bullshit will this be* hackles rising.

"Let's all raise a toast to our new L&C. In the short time Freddie has been with us, he's already prevented Aquilinian on Martian violence, resolved a Ulaperian scone crisis, and averted a cataclysmic misunderstanding by rerouting that Delphinian flash mob to deck sixteen where they wouldn't upset the Gorbies staying on fifteen, since we all know how offended our guests from Gorbulon-7 get by sudden dancing." Grinning a little too widely, Chan tilted the rim of his glass toward Freddie and continued, "We're so happy to have you and that you are so brilliantly capable because..." His gaze darted around the table while he chewed on his lower lip.

Sunny squinted at him, thinking something was up.

"Now is probably the perfect time to, ah..." He stalled, then steamrolled through the remainder of his sentence with a single breath and no breaks, "...let you all know that we will be hosting a party of Kravaxians in three weeks' time."

Sunny's mouth fell open. Freddie coughed, spluttering on his sip of champagne. Tig pulled the drawstrings of her hood fully closed. And, in unison, Rax and Morgath burst from their chairs and cried, "Over our dead bodies!"

"I'm sorry," Sunny said, shaking her head. "I must be hallucinating. Did you just say Kravaxians will be boarding? On purpose?"

"No," growled Rax, "they will not."

Chan toggled his hoverchair controls, rocking his chair back and forth nervously. "Isn't it, uh, exciting?" He couldn't hide his wince as the words left his mouth.

Rax and Morgath began shouting, Elanie mumbled her dissent, and Freddie kept opening and closing his mouth like he was close to summoning a response but couldn't quite pull it off. Sunny only blinked.

"Everybody calm down, please!" Chan's voice carried over the din of outrage and general bafflement ricocheting off the staffroom walls. "Let me explain."

"Oh, we need no explanation. You've obviously lost your gods-damned mind!" Morgath's hands splayed flat on the table, and he hovered ominously over Chan like a muscle-bound green gargoyle. "There is a senator aboard, for fuck's sake!"

Sunny met Freddie's stare, then they both turned to look at Morgath, then at Chan, then back at each other, mystified. Next to Sunny, Tig slid gingerly back out of her hood.

The problem with Chan's revelation, Sunny thought, was that Kravaxians were, not to put too fine a point on it, monsters. These space pirates were murderers, arsonists, chaos breeders, and if one believed the rumors, raging cannibals. Clever, vicious, brutal, and with no allegiances aside from the all-mighty credit, they were, in Sunny's opinion, exceptionally bad cruise ship guests.

Freddie cleared his throat and suggested with some hesitation, "Perhaps we should give Chandler a chance to explain."

"Explain what?" snapped Rax, flinging his hands into the air. "That we've decided to invite Godzilla into the city?"

Silence descended as everyone at the table stared blankly at Rax.

"What's that, darling?" Sunny asked, having no worldly notion what a *Godzilla* was.

Rax grunted in frustration as Morgath supplied, "Old Earth movie monster. Giant lizard thing. Destroys buildings, shoots lightning-fire out of its mouth, kills everyone. That sort of deal."

"Ah, well then." Sunny nodded, acknowledging the similarities.

Elanie looked up from her nails momentarily to add, "Bright side, we won't have to worry about feeding them. The guests should suffice."

Chan groaned. "It's not what you think. They won't eat our guests."

Tig trembled. "They'll eat me first, won't they? I'm, like, bite-sized."

"Really, Chan? Why do you want Tig to get eaten, Chan?" Morgath, still on his feet, punctuated Chan's name harshly like he might as well have been saying "asshole" or "fuckhead."

Poor Chan, who could barely get a word in edgewise over the irate twins now spiking various objections at him in rapid fire succession, tried to shout above their verbal assault, "Nobody is going to get eaten!"

"I didn't know they made muzzles big enough to fit a Kravaxian," Elanie slipped in under the uproar.

"And the captains signed off on this?" asked Rax in utter disbelief.

"They have." Chan leveraged this bit of distant camaraderie from the captains to wrangle the conversation in. "And if you give me a second, I will tell you why." He leaned over, fishing some brochures out of the side pocket of his chair and passing them out. Wisely, he charged on without waiting for anyone's permission. "The Kravaxians we will host have been hand selected by Luna-

Corp as a local task force leading the Bring Labor and Industry to Kravax initiative, or BLIX, as they're calling it."

Elanie scoffed. "BLIX? That's the best they could come up with?"

Chan shrugged. "They were going to go with BLIK, which is, objectively, much worse."

"Sounds like a load of trestal shit to me," grumbled Morgath.

Sunny turned over the "BLIX" brochure. On the front, Kravax hovered, marbled brown and green with its single tiny moon glinting in the darkness, and on the back, four pale-skinned and raven-haired Kravaxians stood on the front steps of LunaCorp HQ. The Kravaxians smiled—or at least weren't actively scowling—as they shook hands with the young and irrepressible New Earther entrepreneur-turned-new-CEO-of-LunaCorp Becks Karlovich. Sunny stared at Mr. Karlovich with his smug grin and chiseled jaw and—she looked closer—*was he wearing makeup? Some self-tanner? Maybe even blush?*

Tig, always one for gathering as much information as possible, took a brief break from biting her cuticles to ask, "What sort of industry are they hoping to bring to Kravax?"

"Erm," Chan wavered, "I believe they will start with manufacturing, tourism, and...*banking?*"

Freddie snorted. "Banking? With those thieves?"

"Mr. Karlovich feels Kravax presents an untapped resource. Namely, a species that is..." Chan paused again, seemingly girding his loins to utter this next part, "...very good with money."

Freddie laughed outright at this, followed by Elanie, and then everyone at the table erupted into laughter, even Chan.

"That's one way to put it," said Freddie with this giggle that was too delightful for Sunny to even talk about.

Rax shook his head. "This is completely idiotic."

"I agree it is not ideal," offered Chan. "But the Kravaxians have been training with LunaCorp execs and PeaceKeepers for the last six months. They have evidently earned a holiday aboard the

Ignisar. We are to show them a 'good time.'" Chan mimed the quotation marks.

The crew groaned while Rax and Morgath spat a litany of Aquilinian expletives that would have curled their mother's toes. LunaCorp owned the *Ignisar*, along with most of the ships and asteroids streaking through the KU as well as several moons, including the one orbiting New Earth. When LunaCorp snapped its fingers, you jumped. But last time LunaCorp instructed the crew of the *Ignisar* to show their special guests—some sportsball team from New Earth they'd been trying to recruit to Mars—a "good time," the hooligans stole an oorthorse from the Cosmic Spectacle stables and hid it in their pods, where what it didn't ruin with its copious shitting, it ate. And then shat that out too. Sometimes, Sunny thought, working for one of the colossal conglomerates that ran pretty much everything in the KU felt like being squished under an enormous boot heel, not uncommonly covered in shit.

Apparently recalling those very same events, Chan said, "It won't be like last time. For starters, we've tripled the security mechs around the Cosmic Spectacle. Secondly, I've read all the reports on the Kravaxians, and I will make them available to Freddie directly after this meeting." Chan turned to Freddie. "If you aren't convinced of their civility after reading the reports, we won't allow them on board."

Freddie's brows floated up toward the swoop of his bangs. "*But...*" he started, as if waiting for the inevitable shoe to drop.

Chan sighed. "But we have been strongly encouraged to take them."

"Of course." Freddie's smile was resigned.

"How many are there?" Sunny asked, wondering what sort of strings she'd need to pull to meet the Kravaxian's unique hospitality needs—trying to secure, house, and milk a kurot alone would be a nearly impossible feat. Kurots were a bit like New Earth cows but meaner, and Kravaxians bathed only in their fresh milk, or so Sunny had heard.

"Four. Two men, two women."

Rax hissed, "Four fucking Kravaxians."

"There goes the neighborhood," muttered Elanie.

Rax gave Morgath a meaningful look, and they both stood from the table. Morgath rolled his head, his neck cracking like a grollnut shell. "We'll need time to work out the security logistics of protecting the rest of our guests from the FFKs."

"FFKs?" asked Tig.

"Four Fucking Kravaxians," sneered Rax.

Freddie hid his laughter behind a cough.

"Of course," Chan replied, looking relieved that the meeting might end without a staff resignation—or a fistfight. "Whatever you need, it's yours."

After Rax and Morgath stalked from the room, Freddie blew out a breath and said, "Forgive me for asking, but there's no chance this is all some hysterical initiation prank you're pulling on me, is there?"

Chan frowned. "I'm afraid not." His hoverchair rose. "Drink your champagne—sorry it's so cheap—and then get some sleep. We're all going to need it."

"Hell of a first couple of weeks," Freddie mused. He walked next to Sunny, closer this time because she'd let herself walk a bit closer to him every night on their way back to their pods. He always kept his hands in his pockets though, his eyes facing forward, most of the time anyway. "At this rate, I wouldn't be surprised if we wake up tomorrow with the ship overrun by fungus rats."

Sunny shuddered. "That actually almost happened once."

"No," he gasped. "Really?"

Sunny nodded, allowing a small smile to curl her lips. "They'd snuck into one of our guest's bags after they'd visited Gorbulon-7 and got lost in the mold swamps. Must have picked up some rats along the way. If you think Rax and Morgath were upset tonight, you should have seen them when they saw fungus rats scampering around the decks."

"I can only imagine." He turned to face her once they reached his pod. "Most horrific thing I've ever seen—and that was just a baby fungus rat in a cage at the Foulest Creatures in the KU exhibit on Venus. The teeth, the growths," he grimaced, "the smell." He straightened, closing his eyes for a moment. "I just received the FFKs' file download from Chan, so I suppose I'll be spending the rest of the evening perusing the reports and brushing up on my Kravaxian nonverbals. Wouldn't want to offend a vicious killing machine with an accidental thumbs-up."

Sunny's eyes popped wide as she realized quite suddenly the very real dangers inherent in FFK visitation. "Good idea," she managed. "And note taken: no thumb movements. What would that mean if I did give them a thumbs-up though, just out of curiosity?"

Freddie took a step toward her, his left eyebrow floating up. "It would indicate that you were *interested* in them."

"Interested?" Sunny repeated, heat rising into her cheeks, almost enough to fan them.

He backed away to lean a shoulder against his door. "That is correct."

"Well," Sunny laughed, brushing her bangs back off her forehead, "I won't be doing that then, will I? No, sir. And I thank you for the warning."

"Of course." He winked. "It's kind of my job."

"Ha! Too right." Sunny's voice was all wrong, too loud. She cleared her throat.

"Tell me, Sunny. What should I expect from the upcoming Fire Ball?"

At some point, she'd started staring at his mouth. Tearing her eyes away from his juicy lower lip, she replied, "Anything and everything, darling."

He hummed. "That sounds...intimidating."

"Oh, it is. But it's also wonderful, exhilarating. A night without inhibitions."

The way he stared down at her, like he wanted to say something, like he wanted to *do* something... Sunny retreated, extending the distance between them just a little. Taking the hint, Freddie took a breath and said a very polite, "I can't wait. Well, good night, Sunastara."

"Good night, Freddie."

Sunny tried to deny it, but it was useless. She was swooning, dizzy from the way her full name rolled off his tongue. She turned on her heel so that she didn't inadvertently grab him by the lapels of his suit and shove his face between her breasts.

An alarming portion of her brain, and an even larger portion of her heart, wondered if maybe, just maybe, Freddie was a man she could trust. She knew he was a man who could blow her mind, but maybe he was a man who could understand her mind as well. Or maybe he'd just gotten her hopelessly cock drunk months ago and she desperately needed to sober up.

8

THAT IS LAUGHTER, RIGHT?

<Sunny. Fire Ball prep meeting in the staffroom in ten minutes. Don't be late.>

Sunny nearly jumped out of her skin. She'd spent much of the day stumbling around in an *I love the way Freddie says my name*-induced haze, a haze Elanie's Vcomm had snapped her out of.

<I won't be late,> Sunny grumbled. <When am I ever late for anything?>

<Where should I begin? Morning meetings, Rax's birthday, the Solaris roast. I could go on.>

<I was not late to the Solaris roast,> Sunny protested. <I was an hour early, and then left and was late returning. By twenty minutes. So all in all, I was forty minutes early.>

<That is not math that exists,> Elanie said. <Not on any planet.>

<Whatever. I'm here.> But when Sunny walked through the door, much to her shocked surprise, she found the staffroom empty —aside from Freddie. He sat across the table, staring at her. Silently, she wondered if Elanie had planned for them to meet like this, although it seemed unlikely.

"First ones here, hmm?" A twinkle danced in his eyes. His cheeks were flushed, his hair just slightly out of place, the top button of his shirt undone. He looked deliciously loose. He looked like...

"Sunny, why are you looking at me like that?"

"Like what?" she asked, but she knew exactly how she was looking at him. Like he was a snack, and she was hungry. He'd been a perfect gentleman, honoring Sunny's boundaries, treating her with unending respect, giving her all the space she'd stubbornly asked for. This behavior had only served to make her pink parts even more inappropriately perky in his presence. Freddie was the perfect cocktail, the warmest bath—comfort and heat all at once.

He squinted and said, very slowly, "You are looking at me like you know something I don't."

Sunny licked her lips. "Well, it's just—"

"Just what?"

Heat raced up Sunny's neck, pooling at the base of her throat. "You look... The way you look right now... You're reminding me—"

"Sunastara Jeka." He leaned forward onto his elbows, smirking. "I'm fairly certain this is the first time I have ever seen you flustered."

"Ugh," she groaned and may even have stamped her foot. "Fine, you look like *him* right now, all right?"

His head tilted. "Him?"

"Oh, for fuck's sake! *Joshua.* You look like *Joshua.*"

He frowned, looked down at his shirt. "I do?"

"Yes." Sunny covered her eyes with a hand. "Messy hair, loose shirt, a little flushed." She removed her hand—because he was laughing at her now—and waved it up and down to encompass the whole of him. "This is how you looked when you first walked into the bar on the CAK. That night we..." She stopped herself. "Anyway, it's a whole *Joshua* thing."

"Well," he said, still laughing but also combing his hands through his hair to straighten it back into place. "I didn't mean to." He hiccupped.

Now it was Sunny's turn to smirk. "And I think I might know

why." She clicked her tongue. "Tell me, darling. Is there any chance that you are currently intoxicated?"

He grimaced. "Quite, unfortunately. Garran found me this morning and, to make amends for abusing our serving drone, demanded I join him for a mimosa brunch on deck nine."

"Demanded?"

Freddie nodded, trying very hard to look sober. "He did, indeed. He can be very persuasive. And the mimosas were"—hiccup—"very bottomless."

"That's a job hazard, for certain. And with the Fire Ball still to come..." She shook her head. "You, my friend, are going to have a very rough day tomorrow."

"Your *friend*," he repeated deliberately, looking like he'd nibbled on the word and decided he didn't much care for its taste. "Such a benign word to describe one of the greatest disappointments of my life." He stared directly into Sunny's eyes with a boldness only afforded by a morning spent drinking copious amounts of champagne.

Sunny's mouth was suddenly dry as a Neptune desert, her heart racing.

Freddie blinked, his eyes growing wide, like he'd just now realized how uncomfortable he'd made her. "Oh, Sunny. Shit." His hand reached across the table for hers. "I'm sorry. Please forgive me. I'm just... I'm hopelessly drunk."

She sat as gracefully as she could considering her legs wobbled like flicked springs. Carefully, thinking this was probably not a good idea, she took his hand. It was soft and warm and terrifying. She was drawn to him, there was no denying it. But giving in to that pull, letting herself fall into bed with Freddie, it would be like willingly venting herself into space: exhilarating at first, painful later, and ultimately a terrible idea.

She took a shaky breath and squeezed his hand. "It's fine."

"It is not fine. I was completely out of line."

Sunny opened her mouth, then slammed it shut, releasing Freddie's hand as Tig wandered into the room. Her pink hair poking out from under her hood, Tig barely took any notice of them, her attention wholly on the techpad in her hands.

"Afternoon, Tig." Freddie's voice startled Tig into nearly dropping her pad.

She recovered quickly. "Yes. To you too. Um," she pulled back her hood, "to both of you."

"Thank you, darling," Sunny replied as Tig took the chair to her right. She rubbed a hand briefly across Tig's back. "Are you all ready for tonight?"

Tig nodded. "Yeah. It's really not too bad this year. Just some fancy lighting, mist generators, sound effects, and, of course, the pyro." Tig managed all the special effects aboard the *Ignisar* for the ship's various events.

"Any concerns about the magic show?" Sunny asked. Evidently the Delphinian Wizards planned to wow the ship with their magic tricks.

"Oh yes," Freddie said, perking. "I heard about what that last group did to the pool on sixteen. I wonder what they'll accidentally do this year?"

"I think it'll be okay," Tig replied with some confidence. "This batch seems to know what they're doing. I've seen the show. It's quite good and—so far anyway—nothing on the ship has disappeared, and not one of the guests has been turned into a piece of furniture."

"Wait. That's a thing that happened?" Freddie asked.

"Only once," Sunny replied. "And thankfully, unlike the pool, the Delphinians reversed that whoopsie before we had to redecorate the atrium to match our new Mercurian person-couch."

"No organized dancing during the show though, correct?" Freddie asked. "There is a large contingent on holiday from Gorbulon-7, and I'd prefer not to upset them, if possible."

Now that Sunny knew his current state, she could appreciate how hard Freddie was working to mask his mild, drunken slur. And the harder he tried, the more his Venusian accent snuck out. It was incredibly charming. *Why is everything he does so absurdly charming?*

Tig shook her head. "No dancing. But there will be animals."

"Animals?" Freddie and Sunny repeated with a shared concern.

"Well, just one," Tig clarified. "A goat named Dave. But he's very well trained."

"How in the worlds did they get a goat on board?" Sunny'd had a nightmare of a time trying to get a kurot for the FFKs approved for interplanetary travel, and those prats were in possession of a goat?

Tig's grin was mischievous as she twirled her fingers dramatically in the air and whispered, "Magic."

"No shit?" Sunny said. "Any chance they could *magic* me a kurot?"

Freddie snorted.

Sunny was only half joking, but Tig tilted her head in consideration. "I can ask. And speaking of the pool on sixteen," she added with a raised finger, "one of the Wizards fixed it for us. She said it was a fairly simple spell. Any child could do it."

Sunny huffed her disbelief. "Pah! She's putting us on. We've had no fewer than twenty Delphinians try to reverse that spell. They all said it was impossible."

Tig shrugged again. "Like I said, these Wizards seem to know what they're doing."

This news was music to Sunny's ears. Before that drunken Delphinian's spell made it unfillable, she'd visited the pool on deck sixteen nearly every day. It was the smallest pool on the ship—almost private since very few guests even knew it existed—and it had this domed flexglass ceiling above it. She would swim laps in that pool before bed or just float on her back and watch the stars move across the sky. "This is wonderful news!"

Tig grinned. "I knew you'd be happy to hear it."

Chan's booming laughter upended their conversation as it rolled in from the hallway. Through the flexglass wall, they could see him hovering near the elevator bank, speaking enthusiastically to someone Sunny couldn't quite make out because his chair hid them from view.

Sunny scratched her head, watching Chan make grand, sweeping gestures in the air before him. He was never this animated.

"What's that all about?" asked Tig, her pink brows pinched together.

Chan's hoverchair drifted to the left, sliding away to reveal an absolutely stunning woman.

Tig grinned and said, "Ah. It's about *her*."

The woman chatting with Chan was Delphinian, but instead of a black-and-red robe, she wore a pair of skinny blue jeans, a simple black T-shirt, and strappy red flats. Her face was shaped like a heart, her smile was clever, and she'd gathered her long black dreadlocks into a ponytail that reached past her hips. And somehow, impossibly, she was laughing—because of Chan.

Sunny was astounded. Chan was as warm and genuine a person as anyone could ever care to meet, but he had absolutely no game. "Is Chan actually making a woman laugh? That is laughter, right? Not tears?"

"Is that odd or something?" Freddie asked.

Both Tig and Sunny spun in their chairs so they could answer Freddie, but Tig got to it first.

"Chan is, like, the absolute worst with dating. He's a chemistry black hole."

Sunny nodded in complete agreement. "It's catastrophic, really. One time last year, I informed him that some women liked being complimented on their shoes, and the very next woman he took on a date filed a report against him with the LunaCorp HR for being a creepy foot fetishist."

Freddie tilted his head to peek past them through the glass. "Oh, I don't know. Looks to me like he's holding his own."

Tig and Sunny turned back to the window just as Chan said

something else to the woman that, *stars above,* made her laugh again. She flipped the few dreads that had escaped her ponytail back off her shoulder in a move that was unmistakable *I am into you* body language for nearly every species.

"That is unbelievable," Sunny whispered, an overwhelming sense of pride billowing up into her chest.

Rax and Morgath came stomping down the hall, grumbling past Chan and the Delphinian woman without taking any notice of them whatsoever.

"What's everyone staring at?" grunted Rax while he took one of the chairs next to Freddie. Morgath thudded down into the other so that the twins flanked Freddie on either side.

"We are staring at Chan," Tig said. "Because he's out there, somehow not blowing it with that Delphinian."

"For real?" Morgath asked skeptically, staring out through the flexglass.

"Yes," Sunny whispered while Chan turned around to cruise from the elevators toward the staffroom. "But don't say a word. This is a monumental achievement for Chan, and we don't want to embarrass him."

Everyone nodded in agreement, even as they struggled to hide their grins. Then, not two seconds after Chan entered the room, Elanie came striding in behind him, staring over her shoulder at the Delphinian who'd already made her way back down the hall. "Who's that?" Elanie barked at full volume. "She was laughing, Chan, *laughing.* Did you actually make a woman laugh?"

"Never mind," Sunny muttered as Chan began to stammer a nearly incoherent stream-of-consciousness explanation about the Fire Ball and logistics and magic shows and how everything was *completely* professional. The poor man's entire head had turned as red as a strawberry, but when he started spouting something or other about having to organize living arrangements for Dave the goat, Sunny decided to step in.

"What are our assignments for the evening?" she asked, her

voice raised in an attempt to sail over the muffled snorts around the table.

'Not another word,' she Vcommed everyone at the table on an open link, sending it at double the volume to Elanie, just in case.

Eventually, a still-red-faced Chan reined the meeting in and successfully instructed the crew in their duties for the Fire Ball. Elanie would manage the Delphinians (and Dave the goat), Freddie and Sunny would be stationed on the floor to keep the peace, Rax and Morgath would work security at the doors, and Tig—not a huge fan of parties—would run music, lighting, and special effects from the master control booth above the main deck ballroom.

After the meeting adjourned, Sunny gave herself two side assignments: 1. Learn everything she could about the Delphinian woman Chan had been speaking with. And 2. Not allow the night to end until Garran spun Kasa around the dance floor as flawlessly as he'd spun their serving drone.

9

THE FIRE BALL

"Raphael is on his way. He'll arrive in an hour."

Sunny stumbled over a bit of nothing on the carpet. "What did you just say?"

Elanie made a show of staring at her nails as they walked toward their pods. "Raphael. You know—tall, dark, dreamy. Your annual 'fuck buddy.' He'll be here tonight for the Fire Ball."

Sunny was stunned. "Darling, I have never referred to anyone as a 'fuck buddy' in my entire life. And are you serious? How? How is he coming? I haven't seen him on the itinerary." Sunny felt her blood draining from her face, which was shocking because, under any normal circumstances, this news would cause the exact opposite effect.

"I told him he was being ridiculous. But he said he wanted to surprise you."

"That's...sweet," Sunny managed. She was surprised, all right. Raphael was coming. He would be here tonight. For the Fire Ball. And instead of running back to her pod to decide which dress would make her tits look their best or how she could steal twenty minutes with him before the ball, her mind stubbornly traced over Freddie's crooked nose and played with the soft strands of his hair.

Raphael was gorgeous, easy, uncomplicated—a sure thing. And as a private lawyer to one of the largest and wealthiest of the Aquilines' royal families, he was also extremely busy, never able to stay on the ship for longer than a day or two. Sunny was under no illusions as to how much of his precious time he was spending on her tonight. Normally, this was a massive turn on. Tonight though, his visit felt more like an inconvenience.

Elanie sighed. "Sure. *Sweet.* Whatever you say, Sunny."

Sunny stopped walking and shoved her hands onto her hips. "And just what is that supposed to mean?"

Elanie's eyes rolled. "Honestly, Sunny, I endeavor to stay completely out of your love life. The way you choose partners is too much like throwing darts at a board blindfolded: hazardous for any bystanders and occasionally leaves holes in the wall. No offense."

That stung a bit. "What exactly is the point you're trying to make here, Elanie?"

"I don't know." She shrugged. "All these lovers. All these random encounters. It all seems so...futile."

That stung a lot. "Futile, is it?" Sunny snapped. "Do you know what's really futile? Refusing to install an upgrade. That's futile."

Elanie frowned. "No need to get personal. I'm only stating the facts."

When they reached Sunny's pod, she slapped her hand against the security panel to unlock her door and get away from this conversation. "Thank you, Elanie, for letting me know about Raphael. Gives me plenty of time to think about my life choices while I sharpen my darts." She winked, then entered her pod to the sound of Elanie groaning.

After a scalding shower and a few moments under the QuikDri, Sunny sat on the edge of her bed, twirling the longer bits of her hair around a finger. She accessed the ship's manifest and saw that Raphael had already boarded. His room was on deck twenty-three, toward the bow of the ship—about as far from staff quarters as one could get. He did this for Sunny, for privacy. He was very thoughtful when it came to clandestine liaisons. And *oooh*, he'd chosen the Afterglow suite. It was one of the *Ignisar's* most luxurious accommodations, boasting a fully automated bar, a jetted tub so wide one could swim in it, a nullgrav pod (which could be interesting), and with the port-side wall made entirely of flexglass, the views from the suite were phenomenal.

Sunny knew she should be more excited than she was. She knew she should be throwing something on and racing to the After-glow suite before she had to report for duty. She knew she shouldn't feel this...conflicted. She just had no idea what to do about it.

"All right, enough mulling about." She stood, walked to her closet, and, without even thinking, grabbed a dress, pulled it on, and smoothed it over her hips.

The main deck ballroom was an inferno. Serving drones floated through the air with trays so full of fiery cocktails they looked as though they ferried torches from table to table. The ballroom's eight marble columns rose to the ceiling, engulfed in digital flames that crackled and popped as they climbed the pillars to lick at the rafters. Fire danced across the floor in some marvel of interactive lighting so the entire room appeared submerged in a blazing river. Whenever a guest walked across the floor, the flames parted and reformed or slid up their legs to wrap around their thighs. It was stunning, enthralling, and Sunny was so proud of Tig she could barely stand it.

Suspended from the rafters, sixteen iridescent-skinned, long-limbed Ulaperian acrobats dressed in scandalously revealing, jewel-embellished digital costumes spun from metal rings or dangled from wide swaths of silk. They wore black contacts over their round, pearlescent eyes which—while well suited for the darkness of their outer-rim planet—were far too sensitive for the lights at this party. The effect made them look like writhing, erotic, fire demons.

Sunny gasped as one of the acrobat's costumes burst dramatically into flames during a trick where she released her silks, falling in a death drop nearly all the way to the floor before catching herself with a foot hooked around the slippery fabric. The maneuver drew everything from shocked screams to dog whistles to wild applause from the guests in attendance, Sunny included. The performer bowed, then climbed up her silks once more while the fire flickered out over her costume.

The Fire Ball was a celebration specific to the *Ignisar*. Occurring between several planets' major holidays and festivals—the Tranquis Yuletide, the Solstice of New Earth and Mars, Ulaperia's Great Conjunction, and Blurvos's GooFest—the Fire Ball exploited these sacred observances and customs as an excuse for the guests to eat too much, get completely shit-faced, and participate in nonstop debauchery until sunrise sim. Tonight nothing was off-limits, nothing was taboo, hedonism ruled, and unfortunately, Sunny had to remain more or less a sober voyeur until they kicked everyone out.

She spied Elanie ducking behind the lush, red velvet curtain at the far end of the ballroom, presumably to keep an eye on the Wizards and their goat while they prepared for their magic show. Making her way to join Elanie in case there was anything she needed help with, Sunny halted when Freddie waltzed into view, devastating in a fitted black suit, crisp white shirt, slim black tie, perfect hair.

He didn't notice her, so she let herself watch him. He mesmerized her, moving fluidly through the ballroom, winding around tables and guests like a stream around its banks. He bent down to swipe an errant cocktail napkin from the floor, tucked it into his back pocket, then said, "Oop!" while spinning on his heel to snatch a saltshaker from a server before they accidently placed it on a Blurvan's table. He touched the server's shoulder, said something to them—judging by the distaste clear on the server's face, he likely explained what salt can do to a Blurvan's gelatinous lower half—and handed them back the shaker.

"Sunny! Sunny, come say hello!"

Lena Ramesh's voice snatched Sunny's attention. She waved Sunny over to her table where she, Chahna, and Sai sat sipping steaming bright-red beverages in tall glasses shaped like licking flames.

Sunny was surprised they'd decided to bring the boy, but the Fire Ball didn't typically get wild until well after sunset sim so, live and let live, she supposed. On her way to their table, Tig nearly bowled her over, hunched low, her head down as she beelined it back to the control booth.

"Tig. Eyes up, darling."

"Sorry, Sunny. Just trying to get"—she pulled at the neck of her simple black top, her eyes darting around the room—"the *fuck* out of here."

Sunny took Tig by her shoulders, and it felt like she was trying to hold a bolt of lightning in place. "Tig, love, this party is a triumph! The effects are absolutely stunning, your best work yet. Tomorrow, I'm taking you for a spa day to celebrate." Tig's shoulders tensed further. "And a massage. You're tight as a rubber ball."

Tig's nod was tight and nervy. "That's accurate. But I don't really like spas or massages."

"Hmm, all right. I know, how about tea at the bistro on deck thirty? You, me, views of the cosmos, biscuits?" Sunny waggled her eyebrows, running her hands up and down Tig's arms before releasing them.

Tig's blue eyes lit up. "I love that place. That sounds perfect."

"Then, it's a date," Sunny said, beaming like a proud parent as Tig kissed her cheek before skirting around the crowd, heading back to the safety of her control room.

Continuing on her path through fire toward the Rameshs's table, Sunny scanned the expansive ballroom. She doubted

Raphael would arrive this early—he was probably sitting at the desk in his suite and poring over legal documents, his broad shoulders tensed under his tailored shirt, his brows pressed together in concentration, a pen between his teeth, hot cup of coffee steaming beside him—but he'd surprised her before. Like by arriving today unannounced, for instance.

She did very much want to see him. Being with Raphael was like being with a world leader. He was strong, decisive, highly skilled, and she tended to feel more important than she was simply by being near him. He knew what he wanted, was very easy to please, and he was always quick to compliment. In short, he was a hospitality specialist's wet dream. So, yes, she was excited to see him. He made sense. She and Raphael made sense. *Who the hell needs seven orgasms in one night anyway?*

"Hey, Sunny! This is so cool! Isn't this so cool?" Sai's high-pitched voice rang across the ballroom. He leaned over in his chair, swiping his fingers through the flames that danced around his feet.

"It's amazing, isn't it? One of my very best friends made all of this." Sunny waved her hand to encompass the room.

Sai's eyes went wide. "Awesome! Can I meet them? I need to know how they did this. I have a million questions. Two million!"

Chahna patted the seat next to her. "Take a load off, Sunny. Just for a moment."

"Thank you, Senator. And of course you can meet her, Sai. I'll set it up."

The boy's smile stretched from one ear to the other. "Awesome! Thanks, Sunny!" he said before he returned to playing with the fire.

Sunny leaned in close to Chahna. "This ball gets a bit rowdy as the night goes on. You might consider—"

"We are only staying for dinner and the show," Chahna assured.

"And the...what was it called? *Warple cake?*" Lena slid in, nuzzling her nose into the space behind Chahna's ear.

Sunny pointed toward the back of the room. "I spotted some on the table in the corner over there. Just promise me you'll wait until you're back in your suite before you eat any."

Chahna swiped a finger over her chest in an X pattern. "Cross my heart." Her next words stopped Sunny's heart mid-beat. "I heard a rumor that LunaCorp is bringing Kravaxians onto the ship before we reach Portis."

Trying and failing to school her features, Sunny said, "Where did you hear that?"

"I have my sources. Is this true?"

Sunny knew she should neither confirm nor deny the FFK visitation. If word got out too soon, there could be panic, chaos, a mass exodus off the ship. But something in her doubted the senator would be willing to start a riot on the ship her family was staying on by spreading this news. So with some hesitation she nodded and replied, "Only four. But they'll be here purely on LunaCorp business, and they have been thoroughly vetted."

"*Thoroughly*. I see," she said, leaning back in her chair, her tone suggesting that they might as well have attempted to thoroughly vet a Kuiper worm.

"You don't approve," Sunny surmised.

"Of Kravaxians cohabitating in an enclosed space with civilians. No. No I do not approve."

Sunny couldn't hold in her curiosity anymore. "Senator, why are you here? On this ship? I'm sorry to ask, but we don't typically have politicos—let alone their families—traveling with us. At least not publicly."

Chahna cleared her throat, turning her attention to her drink. "That is a question for another time."

And as quickly as it began, Sunny knew the conversation was over.

"How late does the Fire Ball usually last?" asked Sai after taking a sip from his drink out of a swirling straw.

"Believe it or not, Sai, this room will still be buzzing at sunrise sim."

His mouth popped open. "The entire night?"

"Not for you, young man," said Lena, her brow sharply arched.

Chahna clasped her hands on top of her table. "Well, Sunny. I'm sure you have work to get back to."

Sunny knew when she was being dismissed. She stood from her chair. "Of course. I hope you all have a wonderful evening."

"You as well," said Chahna, not even looking up at her. It chafed a little. Sunny understood the senator's concerns—she even shared them, but it wasn't like the Kravaxians had been her idea.

She was about to walk away from the table when Lena took her hand and pulled her close. "Don't mind Chahna. She gets like this when she's worried about something. But I have to tell you, you look absolutely stunning tonight. That dress is flawless. Where'd you get it?"

"Thank you, darling," Sunny said, smoothing the dress down her thighs. "It's my favorite little black..." Her eyes shot open. She hadn't even noticed, but, *stars save her*, she was wearing *the* dress. Her number-one go-to, never-fail hookup dress. The exact same dress she'd worn when she'd met him. The same dress he'd peeled slowly off her body, covering each bit of her exposed skin with his hands and lips and tongue. The same dress she'd worn when she had been Phoebe and he had been Joshua. How could she have not noticed? Had *he* noticed?

"Sunny, you've gone white as a sheet. Are you all right?"

Not bloody likely. "I'm just perfect, Lena. Couldn't be better." She wondered frantically if she could get out of the ballroom and back to her pod to change before Freddie saw her. Maybe he wouldn't even remember the dress. Men so rarely remembered things like what dress a woman wore. Maybe she was being silly.

Turning around slowly, she tried to spot him without being conspicuous. But it was too late. He had seen her. And judging by his expression, he remembered the dress.

He wasn't ten meters away, sitting at a table of Argosian women, staring openly at her. When their eyes met, he stood, his lips parted, a hand pressed over his chest.

Sunny's heart raced. What had she done? Did he think this dress *meant* something? Did she? *Shit. Shit, shit, shit!*

His head tilted toward a hallway leading off from the main ballroom, and then he started walking.

Sunny took a pathetic and shuddering breath, and then, not knowing what else to do, she followed him.

He waited at the end of the dark, quiet hallway, leaning back against the wall, looking up to the ceiling.

"Freddie. I can explain."

Wheeling around, he strode boldly toward her and didn't stop until he was so close that all she had to do was lean forward and the space between them would vanish. "You're wearing her dress," he said in a harsh, almost pained whispered.

His mouth was centimeters away, his lips wet and ready, and Sunny's heart beat so hard and fast in her chest she felt certain he could see it through her dress. And she didn't even care. She wanted to kiss him, badly. She wanted his lips on hers. She wanted to wake up with the sweet taste of him still on her tongue, the smell of him on her skin.

This close to him, it was impossible to deny. She had never wanted a man the way she wanted Freddie, like she was on fire and he was water. Like if she didn't have him, she would burn up completely. The wanting scared the shit out of her—because she couldn't have him. She couldn't. The job was one thing, but there was so much more. Freddie was not some one-night stand anymore. He was in her life, all day, every day. If she gave in to this wanting, he would eventually want things from her in return that she wouldn't be able to give him. He would have questions. Questions she wouldn't want to answer. He would end up resenting her because she would never let him in. Or worse, he would push her so hard to open up that she would resent him. And it would end, painfully and publicly, probably costing both of them their jobs.

So what if she was being a coward. She'd had enough pain in this life already. She couldn't handle any more. Even though choosing to not be with Freddie felt like a fist closing tight around her heart, taking the chance to be with him while knowing, without a doubt, that she would eventually ruin it was unthinkable.

With herculean effort, she pulled her hands—which had somehow found their way to his hips—back to her sides, then pressed one palm against his chest.

"I'm sorry. I didn't mean to wear this dress. It was a mistake. I...I didn't realize."

"A mistake?" he repeated, breathless.

"I am so sorry, Freddie. I'm going to go back to my pod and change this instant."

"Sunny, please." He slid his hand over hers where it still pressed into his chest. "Please don't push me away."

Don't push me away. But couldn't he see? That was all she would ever be able to do.

He touched his forehead to hers, his breath warm on her lips. He would try to kiss her again, and if he did, she wasn't sure she'd have the strength to stop him a second time. So she said the only thing she knew would make him leave. "A man is coming tonight to see me. We have a history."

There was nothing but an empty, unforgiving cold as he pulled the warmth of his body away from hers. "I see." He let go of her hand, his expression unreadable.

Sunny's hand fell away from his chest, and with a horrible tremor in her voice, she repeated, "I'm so sorry." Then, like the coward she was, she ran.

Back in her pod, she stripped off the traitorous dress with trembling hands, then hung it as far back in her closet as she could. She felt cold, heartless, and, worst of all, she felt like a liar. But there was also some relief knowing she'd finally made her intentions crystal clear with Freddie, knowing she would be in Raphael's uncomplicated arms later tonight. Freddie might be angry with her now, but maybe that was okay. Maybe that was easier. He needed to forget about her and get on with his life. He was a good man, and he deserved a good, less damaged woman.

She slid a red dress she knew Raphael loved over her head, pinched her cheeks, and took one last look in the mirror, more disappointed in herself than she would ever actually admit.

<Sunny, where are you?> Elanie Vcommed.

<In my pod. I had to change.>

<You had to change?>

<Don't ask. I'm on my way back. Did you need something?>

<Yes, two things actually. One, Raphael has just arrived. And two, so has your Argosian.>

<Garran is there?> *This could go tits up in a hurry—well, worse than it already had, if that was possible.* <How is he? How does he look?>

<I don't know, huge? Purple?> Elanie replied.

<Elanie. Be serious.> Sunny stepped into the elevator and smiled professionally at the three rangy Vorpols standing along the back wall like floor lamps. She pushed the button for the main deck after tiptoeing carefully over each of the Vorpol's long, single feet. While not as bad as tripping them, she knew from experience that stepping on a Vorpol's foot was a surefire way to cause an immediate interplanetary incident.

<He looks, well... He's smiling, a lot. He won't stop. It's actually terrifying.>

Sunny grimaced. <Thank you, darling. I'll be there soon.> Sunny bit the inside of her cheek. <How does Raphael look?>

<Handsome, I suppose. Very serious. He's looking for you. Freddie told him you were dealing with a wardrobe malfunction.>

<Freddie talked to Raphael?> *That can't have gone over well.*

<Yes. Why? Was he not allowed?>

Sunny sighed. <As always, Elanie, your irreverence is a bright light shining into the darkness of my weary soul.>

<I aim to please.>

<Don't you have some Wizards to gown?> Sunny perked. <Speaking of which, is the woman Chan was chatting with backstage with you?>

<She is. And if you're planning to ask me to gather intel, I'm already one step ahead of you.>

<Well done! Debrief tomorrow?>

<Don't you ever get tired of playing Cupid?> Elanie asked.

<Not even a little.> Sunny might never have another true love in her own life, but she was more than happy to help someone else find theirs.

When she made her way back into the ballroom, the lights had already dimmed for the magic show. Sai was on his feet, clapping and hooting until Lena pulled him back down onto his bum. And Garran stood awkwardly near the bar with what looked like a gigantic fishbowl full of some flaming liqueur. He was still smiling from ear to ear at nothing at all, looking like a toothy, deranged psychopath. Elanie was right, it was terrifying.

Sunny couldn't find Freddie in the crowd, but she knew he'd want to be here for this conversation with Garran. And they still had to work together so she might as well jump into the fire with both feet. <Freddie?> she Vcommed, awaiting the sting of his voice the way a child might await the sting of a spank.

<Yes, Sunny?>

There was no sting or anger, just Freddie, of course. She shouldn't have doubted him. He was nothing if not a consummate professional.

<I'm with Garran, and I could use backup.>

<Of course. I'm on my way.>

"Hello, Freddie. Hello, Sunastara," said Garran with a nod, his smile still pasted into place, looking almost painful now.

"Garran, darling," Sunny said calmly. "Remember when I said that women like a man who smiles?"

His smile blossomed even bigger as a bartender drone zoomed around the counter behind him. "It is good, right?"

Freddie stepped in, placing a hand up on Garran's shoulder. "Everything in moderation, my good man."

Garran's smile faltered. "Too much?"

Freddie laughed. He seemed fine, Sunny thought. Perfectly fine. And that was good. That was great actually. Why shouldn't he be fine? Why shouldn't everyone be just completely fine? Sunny was fine. The weird pressure in her chest was probably just indigestion.

"Good. My face hurts." Garran rubbed his fingertips into his cheeks, then he took a gulping sip of his bowl-drink, the flames finally having died down enough to not sear his throat.

"So which one is Kasa?" Sunny asked.

Garran pointed out a petite—for an Argosian—woman at the same table of Argosian women Freddie had been visiting with earlier. Kasa was striking, and Garran wasn't wrong, her violet hair did resemble a sunset.

"She's here on holiday with her mother," said Freddie, nodding toward a much larger woman to Kasa's left who sat with her arms crossed and a disagreeable expression stamped onto her face.

"Her mother hates me," grumbled Garran.

Squaring off with him, Sunny said, "All right, Garran, here is what you're going to do tonight. You are going to be polite; you will not get drunk—"

He snapped to attention. "What? Why? Really?"

"Really."

"But," he objected, holding up his bowl, "have you ever even tried one of these? They are delicious."

Freddie laughed under his breath.

"I'm certain they are, and after the ball, you can drink them to your heart's content. I'll even bring some to your suite. But as long as you're in the same room as Kasa, you would do well to remain sober. Eye on the prize, big guy."

"Fine," he agreed glumly.

"You will be kind and polite, but mostly you will ignore Kasa tonight. Instead, you will ask *me* to dance with you after the magic show."

"I will?" He looked uncertain.

"Yes," Sunny confirmed. "Kasa needs to see what she's missing. So you and I will put on our own show for Kasa and her mother. And then, before the night descends into complete hedonistic chaos, you will leave the ball and get as inebriated as you desire in your suite."

Freddie nodded in approval. "Devious plan. I like it."

"That sounds wrong," said Garran. "Would it not be better if I showed them how much fun I can be? I can be very fun."

Freddie and Sunny both shouted, "No!"

"Garran, you want to be with Kasa, right?" Sunny asked. "Not just for a night, but forever?"

His eyes glazed over as he stared at Kasa from across the room. "With all my hearts."

"Then trust me. Trust me tonight. If Kasa doesn't come find you tomorrow, I'll eat my hat."

Garran grumbled, setting his fishbowl back on the bar. "Okay. I trust you." He frowned. "But why would you eat your hat? I did not think your kind ate clothes."

Sunny laughed out loud. "It's only an expression, darling."

The matter sorted for the time being, Garran, Freddie, and Sunny settled in to watch the show. As the curtains drew back, spotlights flaring on the Delphinian Wizards taking the stage, Sunny spotted Raphael sitting by himself, watching the show while sipping a martini, looking handsome as ever.

10

DAVE THE GOAT

"WHAT SHAPES OUR LIVES AND INSPIRES OUR DESTINIES? WHAT FILLS our dreams and fuels our passions?" A lanky, bearded Wizard in flowing robes stood under a glowing blue spotlight, his arms sweeping dramatically over his head as yellow and orange flames erupted from his fingertips. His amplified voice thundered through the sound system as he bellowed, "Magic!" to a wild onrush of applause from the audience.

Deafening techno music surged into the ballroom in driving, oontzing beats that vibrated through Sunny's chest while twenty more Wizards took the stage. Sunny noticed a sharp tension radiating off Freddie's shoulders when the Wizards began chanting incantations in time with the music.

<It's all right, Freddie. Tig promised, no dancing,> she Vcommed him.

His eyes roamed the ballroom, landing on the bank of tables where a large party of frizzy-haired Gorbies sat. He winced when a few of them began to stand from their seats, posturing with two of their four hands on their heads, which on Gorbulon-7 was an indicator of outrage. Something like: "You dare to flatten my hair!" On a planet as humid as theirs, big, frizzy hair was as much of a status symbol as bountiful crops on Argos or the number of bathrooms in a Martian's mansion.

<Tig is wrong. They're going to dance. It feels like they're going to dance. Please don't dance. Please don't dance.>

Unable to help herself, Sunny laughed at him while she Vcommed Tig, <No dancing, right? Freddie's about out of his skin.>

<No dancing,> Tig replied. <Tell Freddie I've got his back.>

<How do they do it, Tig?> Sunny asked as two more Wizards rose above the stage with fire shooting from their bare feet like rocket boosters.

<Do what?>

<Come on, you cheeky little pixie. The magic? Are you helping? Is it tech?>

Tig giggled. <It's not me. Have you ever considered that it might be real?>

<Of course not. Wait, are you serious?>

<Did you think I kept that pool on sixteen cursed all by myself? With effects?>

This pulled Sunny up short. <No. I always figured they'd put sandguppies in the filters or something.>

<We replaced all the filters, the drains, everything. Not a sandguppy in sight. It's magic. Deal with it.> Tig clicked off the comm.

Sunny leaned in to yell over the music so both Freddie and Garran could hear her, "I'm going to go in for a closer look."

"Be careful, Sunny. I do not like magic," boomed Garran, making Sunny's ears whine. "It is not natural." As if on cue, a dragon made of fire leaped from one of the Wizard's hands, growing to the size of an Imperion warship as it roared above the crowd. Garran's eyes slammed shut. He uttered some guttural Argosian oath while touching his forehead, making the sign of the Tilth, his planet's three-pointed constellation thought to be the giver and taker of abundance.

Sunny touched Garran's arm, then she gave Freddie a tight and awkward smile—receiving a small nod in return—before she skimmed along the wall to move closer to the stage, and to Raphael. On her way, she spotted Chan staring up at the performance with wide eyes and an even wider grin. She followed his gaze to find the object of his attention.

Dreads lashing through the air around her like willow branches in a windstorm, Chan's mystery woman summoned a three-meter-tall ring of fire in front of her just as another Wizard conjured an oorthorse made of light to leap through it. Before the oorthorse's hoofs touched the ground, the animal exploded into thousands of tiny embers that flitted away toward the ceiling, winking out one by one.

Sunny leaned in close. "She's lovely."

Chan whipped his head around in surprise, nearly causing a nose-to-nose collision. "Shit, Sunny!" he yelled over the music. "You startled me."

Her chin tilted toward the stage. "Who is she?"

With a wistful glance back to the woman, he said, "Someone I don't stand a chance with."

If Sunny was a genie, these would be the words that would summon her from her lamp. "Is that so?"

He nodded miserably.

Sunny stooped to take his chin in her hand. "We'll just see about that."

There was an unmistakable, if fledgling, gleam of hope in his eyes as she released his chin. "We will?"

"Chan, darling," Sunny said, "if it's what you want, I promise to do everything in my power to get you laid."

He snorted, his cheeks flaring redder than the fire rippling below his hoverchair.

After kissing Chan on the cheek, Sunny walked in long, determined strides toward Raphael's table. What she wanted, what she *needed* in order to forget about what she couldn't have with Freddie was a night of pure indulgence in what she could have with Raphael.

Once she reached his table, she licked her lips as Raphael eyed her under his thick, dark lashes. His deep voice slid into her Vcomms. <Sunastara Jeka, as I live and breathe.> His eyes narrowed. <But...you don't look surprised to see me.>

She settled into the seat beside him and explained into his ear, "Elanie."

"She never could keep a secret."

He smelled wonderful, like citrus and sandalwood. He looked even better; smooth black skin, precious dimples that sat above a neatly trimmed goatee, kissable lips, sharp hazel eyes.

"I love that dress, by the way," he said, his lips brushing against her ear.

The sensation was nice. When by all rights it should have been exhilarating, it was...nice. "I'm glad you came, Raphe. But I have to work."

He leaned away and Vcommed, <Of course. Save me a dance?>

<As soon as I'm done making a lovesick Argosian appear irresistible, I'm all yours.>

His expression was puzzled but amused. <You do have the most fascinating job.>

After a quick brush of her lips against his, Sunny pushed her chair back to stand. Before she could leave, however, a spotlight flooded their table.

Raphael shot Sunny a glance, confused and concerned, as she realized all too late that they were about to be part of the magic show.

<Tig,> Sunny Vcommed while the Wizards gathered at the front of the stage, gesticulating wildly at Raphael's table and uttering some indecipherable incantation that sounded nothing like bears or butter. <What is about to happen to us?>

Tig's giggling laughter bounced around Sunny's brain. <Oh no! I should have told you not to sit there.>

<What is it? Tell me this instant.>

"What is going on?" asked Raphael, tensing beside Sunny like he might burst from his chair. Sunny grabbed his hand, holding him in place.

<It's not that bad,> said Tig. <You're just about to meet—>

Before Tig finished her sentence, Sunny let out a "Whoop!" in surprise as a bleating goat popped into existence atop their table, flicking his tail in a furious frenzy.

Raphael reeled back. "What the hell is that?"

<Raphe,> Sunny Vcommed, trying her hardest not to laugh. <Meet Dave the goat.>

Raphael was nonplussed as Dave stared him down. Then Dave blinked back out of existence only to reappear on another table, then behind the bar, then on some unsuspecting Blurvan's paddle tail. Hilarity ensued as the Wizards continued to deploy poor Dave as their magical finale, whisking him through the crowd until Sunny doubted there would be a single Fire Ball attendee who wouldn't go home with some sort of "I touched Dave the enchanted goat" story to tell their friends. It was so incredibly ridiculous yet brilliant that Sunny was overcome by an entirely new appreciation for the showmanship of Delphinian magicians.

She left Raphael at his table with instructions to a nearby serving drone to re-up his martini. The applause died down as the Wizards exited the stage, Dave the goat still wandering around tables like the most irritable party favor in the cosmos. Patting the goat on his rump, Sunny looked up just in time to catch Sai waving goodbye. She returned the gesture as his mothers led him from the ballroom, Lena with one hand looped around the senator's waist, the other carrying a plate with a rather large piece of warple cake atop it. *Good for them.*

Sunny's next stop was the control booth to congratulate Tig once more on the spectacular effects, but across the ballroom, striding from the bar toward the stage, came Freddie.

"That was outstanding!" he said when he reached her. He

pointed delightedly at Dave who was licking someone's dessert plate clean on a nearby table. "That goat bit was smashing, don't you think?"

Sunny said nothing because words failed her. Freddie shouldn't have been smiling at her, not like this, not so genuinely. Not after what she'd done to him in the hallway.

His brows pressed together. "Sunny, are you all right?"

"Sorry. I'm fine." *Far from it.* "I just... I'm headed up to chat with Tig."

He replied with a jolly, "And I am off to congratulate the Wizards," moving past her toward the stage.

Who was this man? How could anyone be so...unflappable? He should've been upset, judgmental, territorial, bitter, anything! But he wasn't. He was just completely, perfectly, infuriatingly fine. It was incomprehensible.

She grasped his elbow before he could leave and, ignoring the spark of white heat where her fingers touched his taut muscles, asked him, "Freddie. Are *you* all right?"

It was immediately apparent that this was the wrong thing to ask. Whatever wall of detached civility he had built around himself crumbled before her eyes. His expression changed, darkening as he glared down at her hand like it might bite him. She yanked her hand back, feeling wounded, but he only kept staring at her intently, his chest rising and falling with every silent breath. Then, right before she could say *"Sod it"* and run away again, he repeated at length, "Am. I. All. Right?"

The lights came up just as the music died down, the booming bass of the magic show techno replaced by softer, atmospheric Delphinain synthwave. Freddie stepped back, shoved his hands hard into his pockets, and then he let her have it. "Well, let's see, Sunny. I just tried to kiss the woman I am absolutely mad about in a hallway because I thought she was trying to tell me something she wasn't. Now I'm left with no other choice but to stand by and pretend that everything is perfectly normal like a complete numpty as she prepares to spend the night with another man. And I'm on the clock, so I can't even get pissed over it."

He forfeited any distance he'd created between them by stepping so close to Sunny he only needed to whisper, so close she saw the flecks of blue in his grey eyes, peering through each delicate space between his lashes like she peered through a field of summer grass.

His voice was a low and desperate rumble. "I know I have no claim on this woman whatsoever and she is free to be with whoever she chooses. But, despite her scarcely logical reasoning, the fact that she isn't choosing to be with me tonight might actually be killing me." His whisper turned harsh. "So to answer your question, no. No, Sunastara, I am very much not all right."

These last three words were an assault, quick, darting jabs aimed at Sunny's chest. She decided—clasping her hands behind her back to quell the temptation to slap him or possibly grab his face so she could disappear into his mouth—that this was all completely unfair. She was abruptly, refreshingly, enraged. "Now you listen here, Frederick. I never once said—"

With a raised hand and an exasperated "Pffft," he shut her down completely, turned around, and started walking away.

The nerve! She ran after him, grasping his elbow again. "Freddie, stop!"

Wheeling around with fire in his eyes—and not just the flames reflected from the floor—he ground out, "That is *precisely* what I am trying to do. I just," he made a choked, frustrated sound, then his features softened as he reached out to gently straighten a twisted strap of her dress, "I'm just doing a piss-poor job of it."

This time when he turned away, Sunny let him go, watching on in bewildered silence as he paused on his way backstage to lean down and scratch Dave between his horns.

Sunny was furious, hurt, and also unforgivably aroused. But this situation was not her fault. She'd been nothing but clear with Freddie since the first time his perfect, storm-grey eyes had found hers in the staffroom. While her feelings for him were an incoherent, illogical, hormone-laden muddle, her actions had been completely aboveboard.

Yes, she knew the dress had been unfair. But it had also been an honest accident. *Hadn't it?* Now she did actually mutter, "Sod it," and stalked like a petulant teenager from the ballroom.

After congratulating Tig, slightly less enthusiastically than she'd planned considering her current emotional state, Sunny gritted her teeth and made her way back into the ballroom. She still had an Argosian love match to make before she could even think about sorting herself out in Raphael's nullgrav pod.

She found Garran kneeling in front of Dave, feeding him happles—a Ulaperian fruit that tasted just like New Earth apples but were shaped like smiling mouths, hence the name—from the hors d'oeuvres table and whispering in Argosian about how he was "a very fine goat."

She cleared her throat, drawing his attention from his new cloven-hooved friend. "Hello, darling. Are you ready?"

Garran's purple eyes raised to meet hers, and she waved a hand over the open dance floor. He stood and wiped his hands on his coveralls. "Are you certain about this?"

Sunny nodded. "Positive. I'll be on the dance floor, positioned near enough to Kasa's table that she will see us, but not so close as to be obvious. Just as the next slow song starts, you will come find me and ask me to dance."

He raised and lowered his shoulders, like a mountain shrugging. "If you say so."

"Trust me, Garran. I'm a professional."

He nodded, then grinned down at Dave. "I enjoy this goat. I have many goats back on Argos. Their milk makes very fine soap." He gazed at the back of Kasa's head, his tone softening. "I made soap for her—jasmine and honeysuckle."

Sunny bit her cheek. *Must everyone be a hopeless romantic?*

"You've got this, big guy. Just follow my lead, and you'll be lathering her up in no time."

He grinned, his cheeks flushing.

Sunny made one more pass by Raphael's table, leaning in close to whisper in his ear, inhaling him deep into her lungs in an effort to remind her flailing mind that *he* was who she wanted tonight. She informed him of her remaining task before they could be off, before she could finally put everything *Freddie* to bed by indulging in the simple pleasure of a single night with a beautiful man and absolutely no strings attached. *Which was all Freddie was supposed to be in the first place!*

On her way to the dance floor, she spied Captain Declan and Co-Captain Morgan Jones finally making their appearance, strolling arm in arm through the fire. Morgan was breathtaking. Black skin glowing against a stunning red satin gown, her hair down in tight spiral curls that bounced gently off her shoulders. She waved, and Sunny waved back as Declan pivoted Morgan toward the bar. Sunny made a mental note to chat with her before she and Raphael left. She had to see Morgan's dress up close.

Dancing with Garran went as expected, awkward at first, painful second (accidental foot stomp), and—as they found a rhythm, his arms slung low around Sunny's waist, her head falling back into ecstatic laughter at something he hadn't said—ultimately a wild success.

Kasa thoroughly impressed Sunny by actually cutting in, stepping into Garran's arms before Sunny even had the chance to back fully out of them. The big man had positively melted when Kasa pressed her body close to his, sliding a hand over his shoulder.

Sunny held up a single finger and mouthed, "One dance, then you leave," waiting with a raised brow for Garran to nod his agreement before she disappeared back into the crowd.

She went backstage to see if Elanie needed any help with cleanup from the show. Once behind the curtain, she found Elanie sitting alongside Freddie, Chan, and—*would you look at that*—the

Delphinian woman, all of them laughing about something or other. Freddie's laughter died like a fire's last ember when he noticed her.

"Sunny. How is it?" asked Chan.

Been better. "Superb! I think this might be the best Fire Ball we've had since I came aboard."

"I saw Raphael. Nice of him to come, huh?" Chan waggled his oblivious eyebrows, and if Sunny's searing, wide-eyed gaze didn't relay how much he needed to shut it, she hoped this would.

"I don't believe I've met this beauty yet." Sunny smiled brightly at the Delphinian. "My name is Sunny."

Chan gulped, Freddie found something enthralling on his shoes, and the Delphinian said, "I'm Makenna. Nice to meet you, Sunny."

Taking the chair next to Makenna, Sunny crossed her legs, doing everything she could to avoid looking at Freddie's face. "That show was just amazing, Makenna."

Makenna beamed. "Thank you. We've been preparing for ages. Really came together tonight, didn't it?" She'd pulled her dreads back again, revealing a long, graceful neck that Chan could not stop gazing at. Sunny noticed Makenna's eyes flitting over Chan too, over his chin, nose, chest.

She Vcommed, <Well done, Chan. I don't know how you've managed it, but Makenna is feeling you.>

<That's ridiculous,> he commed back, blushing <She's just being pleasant.>

<She's just checking you out.>

<She's what? She is? How can you tell?>

<It's as obvious as the stars. Just keep doing whatever it is you're doing, darling. Because it's working.>

After chatting with Makenna, Sunny peered through the curtain and caught Raphael staring at her. The captains had joined him at his table, and he was chatting them up about something or other, probably downplaying the most recent gossip regarding the

Aquilinian royal family. Morgan was obsessed with the Aquilinian tabloids.

Sunny blew him a kiss which he caught and tucked into his pocket without breaking stride in his conversation. With as little fanfare as possible, she snuck out from behind the curtain, strode across the ballroom, and took the seat Raphael had slid out next to him just for her.

He took her hand, pressing his lips to her knuckles. "Hello, gorgeous. Are you finally mine?"

"Hello to you too," she told Raphael, but she wasn't looking at him. She was looking at Freddie. He still sat behind the curtain, raking a hand through his hair. Her breath stalled in her chest when Freddie's eyes found hers. With his lips pressed flat, his brows sinking low, he waved an apologetic hand. And then he smiled at her, and her heart gained twenty kilos. Even so, she said, "Absolutely, Raphe. I'm all yours."

11

BE BRAVE

THERE HAD ONLY BEEN TWO MOMENTS IN SUNNY'S LIFE IN WHICH she'd been uncertain. Once as a girl when her father had given her the choice between a red or blue Yuletide dress, and again when trying to decide what to name her childhood squirtfish (similar to a goldfish, only blue, with a horn, and it squirted little clouds of multicolored ink from its tail. After much deliberation, she'd finally christened hers a rather regal *King Jeremy of Squirtleheim*).

Tonight though, as the Fire Ball unraveled predictably into a warple-cake-and-ambrosia-cocktail-infused revel, it had come, slinking over her skin like the cold mist off the mountains above her childhood home: uncertainty. And she did not care for it one bit.

Raphael led her from the ballroom after the crew ushered the few remaining partygoers out the door. Looking back for the one person she didn't have the courage to bid good night to before leaving, she found him with the rest of the crew, making use of the dregs from the bar, the music, and the empty dance floor to have their own party.

Chan's hoverchair tilted from side to side with Tig in hysterics riding on his lap. Rax and Morgath stomped around in whatever bizarre movements passed for dancing in the ranks of the Aquilinian military. And Freddie swayed in time with Elanie, his laughter unbridled, his necktie encircling his head, the ends wrapped around Elanie's hand as she led him about the dance floor like a puppy dog.

Elanie, seeming to enjoy herself more than Sunny had ever seen her do before, laughed wildly at something he said. A blaze of scalding jealousy raced from Sunny's toes to burn up her ears.

"Ouch, Sunny." Raphael winced. "You're squeezing the life from my hand."

"Sorry, darling." She hadn't even noticed. The same way Freddie hadn't even noticed her leaving.

She followed behind Raphael, uncertainty hanging heavily over her shoulders, her steps from the ballroom as labored as if she'd been walking through a Gorbulon-7 bog. In the elevator up to the Afterglow suite, Sunny and Raphael stood side by side but far enough apart to fit two Blurvans between them. She was reminded of the elevator ride up from the restaurant to her room with Joshua before their night together, when her hand had been held tightly in his, his thumb brushing over her skin. When she'd thought she would die if she didn't get his lips on hers. When her body had ached for him, for his mouth, his fingers, the warmth of his skin, so much that she could think of nothing else.

"The captains are looking well. Still can't fathom what brought them to the *Ignisar*. Did you know they were both NESA astronauts before they jumped to the private sector?"

Sunny nodded absently, her mind elsewhere, on another night, another man.

"Those two combined have more space-walk time under their belts than any two other New Earthers who ever stepped foot into the big black. That they've settled for life as captain and co-captain of this ship is—"

"A head scratcher," she admitted. Small talk. She was forcing

Raphael, a brilliant, gorgeous, and entirely too-busy-to-make-small-talk man, to make small talk. *Get your head out of your ass and get yourself laid!* she reprimanded inwardly, eating the distance between her and Raphael to slide her hand under the lapel of his suit coat. The muscles of his chest tensed under her probing fingers. "It is good to see you, Raphe."

"It will be very good to do something other than just *see* you," he purred. His lips, soft and full, touched hers just as the elevator doors slid open. He pulled away. "After you."

The walk to the Afterglow suite was lengthy. Raphael remained a few steps back, but Sunny felt his gaze roaming over her body like flames licking at her skin. When she finally reached his door, he came up behind her, the length of his body pressing into hers. The hardness against her ass was a scorching reminder that his was the type of cock sex-toy manufacturers made molds out of.

Reaching his hand around her to place his thumb on the suite's security panel, he touched his lips to her neck and whispered, "I've missed you, Sunastara."

They tumbled into his room, and she flipped around in his arms so that she could kiss him. His fingers wrapped around her neck, his tongue brushing against hers, but she was distracted by the scratch of his goatee, by the citrus scent of him. He let her go and said, "Give me a moment?"

Yes, absolutely, a moment. "Of course," she replied.

While Raphael walked to the bathroom, Sunny flopped onto one of the couches facing the flexglass wall and thought, *Damn you, Freddie! Damn your smooth, hairless chin. Your linen scent. I will get laid tonight! On my life I WILL GET LAID!*

She stood, stalked to the bar, and took a deep draw straight from the bottle of very expensive New Earth Scottish whiskey that rose up to the bar's surface at her command. Swiping the back of her hand over her mouth, she caught the few drops of liquid courage that had dribbled down her chin.

This is ridiculous! Tonight she would prove to herself beyond any reasonable doubt that her relationship with Freddie was completely platonic. She peeled off her dress, dropped her panties to the floor, and reclined on Raphael's bed in a position that brooked little argument as to exactly what it was that she wanted.

Raphael's gasp as he exited the bathroom was all the encouragement she needed.

"*Gods*, Sunny." His hand clutched at his chest. "This sight could kill a man my age."

She laughed at him, while she may have also ground her hips into his bed. "That's doubtful, darling."

Framed by her bent knees, he slowly, deliberately, one button at a time, removed his shirt, all the while keeping his eyes solely on hers. Eventually, she was able to admire his bare chest which glowed in the starlight seeping in through the flexglass.

This was good. This was working. Her pulse pumped in her veins, her core heating as Raphael narrowed his eyes, studying her the way a hunter would his prey. He was gorgeous, strong, and when his gaze finally fell between her legs, a deep surge of desire shot through her like an arrow.

The weight of his body shifted the mattress underneath her, his fingers hooking around her thighs and pulling, sliding her down the bed until her hips hovered just over the edge. Sinking down onto his knees, he raised one of her legs and then the other over his shoulders.

His lips pressed against her inner thigh, teeth gently skimming along her skin. Sunny slid her fingers over his head, but instead of his close-cropped fullness, they yearned stubbornly for length, for a slightly tousled mess held back by the soft band of a necktie.

"Raphe," she whispered. But her mind recited, *Freddie, Freddie, Freddie...*

Raphe was so good, so divine but, as the trimmed hairs of his goatee brushed against her skin, so undeniably not the man she wanted.

As if sensing her duplicitous thoughts, Raphael raised his hazel eyes to hers, but Sunny only saw Freddie's stormy greys staring up at her from between her legs. This image awakened a shame so profound she wanted to curl into a ball and hide under the covers forever.

"Stop. Raphe, please stop. I can't."

He pulled away immediately, and she scampered back onto the pillows, her eyes shut tight, her hands covering her face.

A breathless and resigned "Damn" was all Raphael said. He climbed onto the bed to lie down beside her. "Come on, Sunny." He pulled her hands down from her face. "You don't need to do this, not with me."

Her eyes still shut, she whispered, "I'm sorry, Raphe. I'm so sorry."

His hand slid over her cheek to angle her head toward him. "Talk to me. Tell me what's going on."

She cracked one eye open and then the other but remained silent. She had no idea where to even begin.

"How long have we been doing this, you and I?" he asked.

"Since I started working on this ship." *Since tragedy shook my life to its very core and I ran to this ship to hide from it all.* "Almost five years."

He sighed, his shoulder rising and falling with the effort. "Not a bad run. But I knew, eventually, it would come to an end."

"Nothing is ending, darling. I just—"

He brushed her hair back from her forehead. "But maybe it should, Sunny. Maybe it's time for you to let go of whatever it is that's been holding you back."

Sunny sat up, her heart lurching into her throat. "Raphe, what are you talking about? I'm just tired. That's all."

He shook his head, rueful. "I secretly hoped it would be me you'd choose, but that man—what was his name? Freddie, was it?"

"Freddie? What about him? We aren't—" Sunny kept trying to

interject, and Raphael kept cutting through her bullshit like a surgeon with a laser scalpel.

"Sunny, that man threw so many longing looks at you tonight, I'm surprised they didn't leave marks."

Sunny blinked. "He did?"

He reached up to pull gently on her arm, sliding her back down onto the bed. She rolled onto her side so they were face to face on the pillows.

"And you," he said slowly, begging her to disagree, "couldn't take your eyes off of him either."

She didn't bother refuting this. "Raphe. I am so sorry. What a miserable date."

He clicked his tongue. "Not my finest hour, I'll admit. I wanted to have you at least one more time before you left me."

She stroked his cheek. "You still can."

Air rushed from his nose. "Sleeping with a woman while she's thinking of someone else the entire time isn't really my thing."

Sunny groaned. "I am awful, aren't I? Dreadful."

"I think, as a point of fact, that what you are is in love."

Her head shook vigorously. "No. It's not that. It's just an infatuation. It will pass." Until that moment, she had never realized a person could taste their own lies, like sour fruit.

"In the five years I've known you, I have never, not once, seen you this taken by someone. If I'm right—and I am rarely wrong—he feels the same way about you. I won't pretend to know the circumstances of your relationship with Freddie..."

Mind-blowing one-night stand that has left me in a complete and utterly unraveled heap ever since.

"But love doesn't just come along every day, Sunny. It is fleeting, precious, and should never, ever be ignored. Whether you want to be with him or not, for whatever reason, you should talk to him about how you feel. So, at the very least, he'll know that he isn't losing his mind."

He was right. She'd been so unfair to Freddie—and to Raphael.

But not without reason. "What if I can't, Raphe? What if I'm too..." She summoned every ounce of courage she had in her entire body to utter the word, "scared?"

He cupped her face, brushing his thumb over her cheek. "You do what we all do when it's required of us: be brave."

12

THE PROPOSAL

Sunny left the Afterglow suite hours later after talking with Raphe until he had to disembark back to the Aquilines. She felt a profound mixture of gratitude for Raphael's kindness and wisdom, concern that she might never see the man again, and apprehension about what would happen once she knocked on the door she stood in front of. With a deep breath, which she blew loudly from her lips, she raised her fist and knocked three times.

She had to smother her laughter with a hand over her mouth when Freddie opened his door. He wore flannel pajamas with tiny bow ties all over them and what looked like a sleep mask pushed up onto his forehead, making his bangs stand straight up toward the ceiling.

"Sunny, what are you doing here?" he said, still sounding a bit drunk. "Let me guess. You haven't wounded me enough already tonight, and now you've come to gloat?"

Sunny's mouth sprang open in bright outrage, the warmth of Raphael's words bubbling over as her blood immediately began to boil. "Excuse me? No. No, I did not come to *gloat*." She spat the word. "As a matter of fact, I have absolutely nothing to *gloat* about, no thanks to you." Elbowing past him, she barged into his pod.

"Oh, well. Just come right in, why don't you." He mashed the button to close his door. "I wasn't doing anything important, like sleeping. And what exactly do you mean by having nothing to gloat about?" he asked, the sting slipping from his voice.

Sunny wheeled on him, her arms flinging out wide in exasperation. "What I mean is that, despite all efforts to the contrary, nothing happened with Raphael tonight."

Freddie remained silent.

"That's right, Freddie. I couldn't do it. And regardless of how much I may have wanted to, we didn't do it."

He sat down on the edge of his bed. "That's...interesting."

Sunny stood opposite him, leaning against his armoire with her arms crossed tightly over her chest. "Interesting? You think it's interesting that I was unable to sleep with a man I've been sleeping with—with much enjoyment—for the last five years?"

His shoulders rose, fell. "Yes. I do."

A petulant "Pah" burst from her lips.

"What, um, what happened?"

He looked so completely absurd in his flannel jammies, his bangs still shoved up vertical by the sleep mask. She pointed at it. "I can't even take you seriously right now. Can you please take that ridiculous thing off?"

He reached up, grimacing as though he'd completely forgotten about this hair accessory. He slipped the mask over his head and folded it neatly into his lap.

Sunny girded her loins. "What happened was that every time Raphael touched me, every time he kissed me, every time he breathed, all I could think about, all I could see, all I could feel was you. And, well, he didn't find that very appealing. Neither did I, for that matter."

Freddie's eyes grew wide. "Sunny."

She raised a hand, stopping him. "I don't know what any of this means, Freddie, but I will not be a very enjoyable person to be around if I can no longer have sex."

He laughed, then fell silent under the weight of her scowl. "Sorry."

"Honestly, you are looking far too pleased with all this."

"Can't say that I'm not. Pleased, that is," he murmured.

And as much as it made her feel like she was going off the deep end, she couldn't say she wasn't pleased either. She took a single step toward him. "I don't know what to do here, Freddie. This is all very confusing." She took another step. "But I'm thinking, maybe..." This next step brought her up to his knees, which he spread apart for her. She took another breath and one final step. His hands slid slowly up her thighs as she settled into the space between his legs. "If I can't have sex with anyone else," she said while his eyes found hers, "maybe I can at least have sex with you."

His arms moved to encircle her, and he pulled her close, turning his cheek to rest it against her belly. And then he said a soft and sweet and completely confounding, "No."

What! "No?" Sunny repeated, incensed. "What do you mean, no?" She pushed against his shoulders, trying to break away, but he kept her pinned against him. "Let me go!"

"Hold. Wait, wait, wait," he pleaded, his cheek still flush against her belly. "Just wait. Sunny, please. Let me explain."

"Explain what? That I'm being denied by two men today? Of all the ludicrous horseshit!"

His laughter rumbled against her belly.

She squirmed in his grip. "Stop laughing. This isn't funny."

"Stop fighting, and I'll stop laughing."

With an exasperated grunt, she tried for one last escape, was met with his firm resistance, and then relented, submitting to her confinement. "Fine! Get on with your *explanation*, then," she said, dropping her voice to mock him.

Her treasonous core tightened as he turned his head, his chin resting against her stomach, his eyes blazing up into hers. "Sunny," he said, "I can't have meaningless sex with you. I won't. I refuse."

"And why not? We've done it before. And I believe we both found the experience," she cleared her throat, "adequate."

"I can't have meaningless sex with you because," he swallowed, "as it happens, unfortunately, I am deeply, hopelessly, and madly in love with you."

Her heart thumped against her ribs, once, twice, three times. "Shit."

His arms around her loosened, releasing her at last. "Yes, shit."

Despite her newfound freedom, she didn't move away from him. "Freddie, I can't... I'm not—"

"No, I know. I know, Sunny." He leaned back, his hands settling softly onto her hips. "I know there's something other than this job keeping you from wanting to be in a relationship. I won't ask you what that thing is, but I've been thinking about this—a lot actually. And I have a proposal for you."

"A proposal?"

He nodded once. "Yes."

Sunny considered this for a moment, unintentionally spending a lengthy portion of that moment staring into his eyes, which pulled on her the way a planet pulled on its moons. Yanking herself free, she straightened to her full, unimpressive height and said, "All right. I will hear it."

His voice fell quiet, timid, his gaze sinking from hers to land somewhere above her navel, which produced a distracting sensation there, like the uprush of waves onto the shore. "I know you aren't ready for a relationship. But I don't think I can stay away from you anymore. What if there was a way we could be together, more than just sex but less than a relationship, not as Sunny and Freddie but"—he paused to take a deep breath, as if readying himself, then he charged forward—"as them. As Phoebe and Joshua."

"As Phoebe and Joshua?" Sunny repeated, not following.

He winced, like he knew precisely how mad he sounded. "I know, but bear with me. Freddie and Sunny work aboard the *Ignisar*. They are professional, friendly, and in no way involved with each other. But maybe, after the workday ends, we could assume different identities. We could be Joshua and Phoebe, vacationing singles who made an undeniable connection and now want to feel each other out. See where things might lead."

She tried to speak, but no words came to her. Either he'd gone completely off the rails, or he was perhaps the most genius suitor in the entire KU.

"I don't want to mess this up with you, Sunny. You're it for me. Without question. And I thought I could be patient. I thought I'd be able to stand by and wait until I charmed you so thoroughly you had no other choice but to realize how perfect we are for each other. But if tonight taught me anything, it's that I cannot handle seeing you with someone else. Unless, perhaps, that someone else is me—or a version of me anyway."

A long, profoundly stunned silence followed. In the middle of this silence, Sunny imagined how it might go. A late-night movie at the Rialto, a walk along the twenty-eighth deck promenade, a dip in the pool on deck sixteen, a stolen kiss overlooking the atrium. It could be very romantic. It could be fun, and Sunny loved fun. A hidden romance, hidden lives, hidden pasts. It might not be real, but the real world was a place she'd been hiding from for years. It might be nice to have someone join her in the make-believe.

"Say something, please," he whispered. "Anything."

She slid her fingers under his chin, raising his eyes back up to hers. "Darling, you must know how completely insane this sounds."

His answering breath of a laugh, his unassuming smile, the warmth of his hands closing around her hips, she was undone.

"Sanity is overrated," he said. "Besides, I don't think I could possibly be more insane than I've been since the first moment I saw you on this ship." He tucked his chin again, resting his forehead against her. "I think this could work, Sunny. Please say yes."

Her fingers reached out, trembling until she let them run through his hair. She didn't know if fingers had the capacity to feel relief, but considering how long hers had been aching to touch his soft, thick strands, they positively sighed.

"Sunny still isn't certain. But," she started laughing as her brain, apparently pushed over the edge of some bottomless cliff, plummeted into the void, "Phoebe thinks it's one of the best ideas she's ever heard."

Without a word, his arms wrapped tightly around her and he pulled her into a crushing embrace. She leaned over him, burying her nose into his hair, breathing in his linen scent, and something else, lavender and vanilla maybe. Once again, he was mouth-wateringly edible. And then, with any uncertainty scampering back into whatever dismal den it came from, she climbed into his lap and started unbuttoning the top button of his ridiculous jammies, her fingers desperate to touch his skin.

He reached up, stilling her hands with his. "Wait. Stop."

Her head tilted like a dog hearing a whistle. "Stop? Why?"

"Well, you see," he said, flushed, "Joshua would like... He'd like a chance to—"

"Yes?" Sunny encouraged, feeling suddenly impatient.

He took a deep, steadying breath. "He would like a chance to, um, woo Phoebe."

Her eyelids falling heavy with desire, or possibly exhaustion, she brushed her thumb over his lower lip. "I believe that ship has sailed. No wooing required, I promise."

He kissed the tip of her thumb with an achingly sweet tenderness that turned her bones to mush. "Joshua disagrees. And I'm afraid he's rather committed to the endeavor." Abruptly, he stood from the bed, taking her with him, and set her down on her feet. "Therefore, respectfully, I will need to ask you to leave."

Her disappointment must have been noticeable because Freddie raised his hands and said, "I don't think you'll have any regrets. Not to toot his own horn, but Joshua is pretty good at wooing."

She scoffed. "Did you say 'toot his horn'? Are you eighty?" Her eyes narrowed. "And how good?"

He licked his red lips, and her mushy legs nearly went out from under her. She tucked her lower lip securely between her teeth as he said, his voice wobbling, losing its resolve, "You'll just have to wait to find out."

Standing on her tiptoes, moving her mouth so close to his that they shared the same breath, she asked, "How long?"

"Not long," he squeaked, practically leaping back away from her. His voice assumed a firmer quality as he ushered her to the door, being careful not to touch her too much on the way. "But tonight, Joshua needs his beauty rest. He has sonnets to compose— or limericks at the very least."

She tried to object, but he had her out in the hallway in no time, waving with a tight, "Good night," before shutting the door.

Head spinning, heart pounding, mouth smiling so wide it hurt a little, Sunny stood outside his door for a full minute, two. She couldn't seem to leave. She didn't want to leave. She was not going to leave, not without *something*. She knocked once, and the door slid open.

"Yes?"

Now that she was face to face with him again, she wasn't entirely certain what to say. So she blurted out, "How do you think they did that trick? The one with the goat?"

He stepped forward, just enough to straighten the strap on her dress that seemed to prefer being twisted. She angled her head away from his fingers, just enough to elongate the slope of her neck. *Phoebe knows a thing or two about wooing too, Joshua.*

He swallowed audibly as he retreated back into his pod. "No clue. Let's ask them later. Good night, er, good day actually, I suppose," he stammered, then closed his door again.

Damn. Not even a kiss.

Carrying a mountain of sexual frustration but a light heart, she turned away from his door and walked toward her pod. She wasn't two steps away, however, when his door whooshed open again, and he muttered, "Bugger it," before grabbing her wrist, pulling her back inside, taking her into his arms, and kissing her.

His mouth was hot and greedy, and Sunny moaned into it, grasping at him with frantic fingers, pulling him closer, craving as much of him as he would give her. This kiss was hungry, ravenous as his arms wrapped tightly around her and lifted her off the floor, one of her shoes left behind to tip onto its side on his carpet. His tongue slid into her mouth, and somehow through the demanding, blistering heat of the kiss, his tongue was soft, gentle as spring rain as it caressed her own.

She shuddered in his arms, her heart pounding. She wasn't sure she'd be able to stop if this kept up any longer. But then, mercifully, like the sky right after the sun finally sank below the mountains, the fiery red surge of the kiss cooled to soft streams of violet, blue, pink. His hand rose to cradle her head, his fingers firmly supporting its weight, and everything slowed as he deepened the kiss, pulling her down with him, setting her feet back onto the ground.

Sunny had thought by now she'd experienced every known variety of kiss. Not so. This kiss was a novel species, an unidentified element, an uncharted star she would place her finger over in the night sky and proclaim, *This, this one is mine.*

When they finally parted, breaths coming heavy, foreheads touching, he said, "Sorry about that. I couldn't help myself."

She nestled into the space between his neck and shoulder, resting her cheek upon the soft, adorably bow-tied fabric of his pajamas. He breathed in a slow, hypnotic rhythm that pulled her eyelids lower with every centering inhale and exhale.

"Are you falling asleep?" he asked, his lips brushing against her ear.

She shook her head in firm denial, all the while thinking, *Not asleep, darling. But falling, nonetheless.*

13

SWEETS AND SECRETS

SUNNY WAS CERTAIN SHE WAS EXHAUSTED. SHE HADN'T SLEPT A WINK, and sunrise sim had been hours ago. But as she meandered back to her pod, all she felt was exhilaration. And perhaps a touch of concern that the kiss had broken her because she couldn't stop smiling or thinking about flannel pajamas and soft hair and lavender and vanilla, and, *damn,* why did Raphael always have to be right about everything!

She practically fell into her pod, stumbling to the bed and flopping face first onto her pillows.

<Don't forget you have tea with Tig in three hours.>

Sunny groaned. <I nearly did. Thank you, Elanie.>

<Have fun last night?>

How to even respond? *No, and then a little, then most assuredly not, and then, for a glorious, smoldering, transcendent moment, absolutely?* Sunny settled on, <Of course. And you? I saw you dancing with Freddie.>

A full minute elapsed. <He was...distraught. Over you, by the way. I was only trying to help.>

<Elanie!> Sunny gasped while rolling onto her back. <Are you blushing? I can *hear* you blushing.>

<No. I do not blush,> Elanie replied flatly.

<Still haven't flipped the old switch, I take it.> It felt a bit silly, but Sunny was concerned that she had, what with how enchanted she'd seemed to be last night while spinning Freddie around on the dance floor. Because if Elanie had finally taken the plunge and installed the upgrade, she might need some sisterly guidance while navigating the peaks and valleys of bionic puberty. Not that she would ever ask for it, or allow it, if she knew that's what Sunny was up to. Proud, stubborn woman that she was.

<Never have. Never will. Not now, not ever.>

The lady doth protest! Sunny thought. <Fair enough. And thank you for the reminder about tea. Now, go get some sleep.>

Elanie clicked off, and Sunny remained supine on her bed, her arms spread wide, gazing up at her ceiling, grinning like a fool. Her hand slipped under her pillow, running up against the coil of Joshua's necktie. She slid the tie out, unraveled it, and looped it around her neck, tying a neat knot at the base of her throat. Threading the ends of Joshua's tie through her fingers, her resolve wavered, logic struggling to rise up through the gooey layers of lips and tongues and fearless, earnest professions.

Perhaps she was too hasty to accept Freddie's proposal. Maybe this was the most ridiculously senseless plan anyone had had the audacity to devise since the evolution of the frontal lobe! She floundered, teetering on some flimsy tightrope of her own design strung over a cavern she'd dug herself.

She couldn't sleep. There was the fear, the apprehension surrounding her agreement to date Joshua. But more than that, there was the raw, aching desire. She couldn't get the taste of him or the feel of his lips out of her mind. So, after a lengthy session talking things over with her vibrator, she left her pod to meet Tig on deck thirty with the delirious, wobbling gait of a two-year-old up past their bedtime.

Sunny found Tig easily, her pink hair glowing in the simulated sunlight that poured in through the bistro's open windows. "Sunny! I was worried you might not come."

The bistro on deck thirty was designed to resemble those found along the Old Earth rue de la Paix in Paris. The floor was a simple checkered pattern of black and cream tiles, and clean white tablecloths adorned each of the twenty or so wrought-iron tables. The table at which Tig perched—half-obscured by a mouth-watering tiered tray of sliced baguettes, brioche, and delicate pastries—sat below a window that overlooked a weather-controlled garden, bursting with violets, lilies, magnolias, and ringed by cherry trees in full bloom.

Sunny stooped to kiss Tig on both of her cheeks. "I'm not late, am I?"

Tig shook her head. "No, but I was still worried."

"Tig, darling, I wouldn't miss this for anything in all the worlds. Did you sleep?" Sunny pulled out her chair and flopped more than sat onto its soft cushion. She needed coffee, immediately.

"Thanks, Sunny. And yeah, for a few hours anyway. But I'm wrecked." Tig slathered a flaky croissant in honeyed butter and shoved it all at once into her mouth.

Sunny didn't dally to join her and plucked a pink macaron with cream filling from the tray. She was famished, even though it wasn't only food she craved. She wondered what Freddie was doing right now. Probably sleeping, or maybe taking a shower, all sudsy and glistening as water streamed down his chest.

Moaning in gratitude as a serving drone set a pot of steaming water, several small bowls brimming with a colorful variety of loose-leaf teas, and two cups of espresso with tiny cherry blossoms worked into the foam onto their table, Sunny reached for a cup.

Tig nodded to the espresso. "You can have mine. Caffeine makes me jittery."

This was true, Sunny remembered. Last time Tig accidentally drank something caffeinated, she'd buzzed around like an electrocuted ghostfly and hadn't slept for nearly two whole days.

Sunny pulled both cups of espresso in front of her, downing one in two gulps, then sipping the other like the refined lady that she was. Her macaron was crispy and sweet and iced with some heavenly buttercream concoction that tasted like figs and almonds.

"*Stars*, Tig. This is the most delectable thing I've ever had in my mouth." This was a complete falsehood, but Sunny did her best to keep her lewd side at bay when she was with Tig. Innuendo tended to make Tig break out in hives.

"I know, right?" Tig concurred, dropping a pinch of bright-green tea leaves into a fine mesh satchel. When she poured hot water over the satchel, a sharp and brilliant aroma rose from her cup, ginger and lemongrass.

As they ate and talked and Sunny spent an inordinate amount of time congratulating Tig on the Fire Ball effects, she couldn't help but notice that Tig seemed uncharacteristically distracted, her eyes darting left and right, her hands clenching at the napkin in her lap.

"Is everything all right?" Sunny asked while taking another pastry from the tray, this one a cream puff, soft and warm between her finger and thumb. "Is there something on your mind?" She popped the entire puff into her mouth.

A brief struggle played over Tig's features. "I'm not sure. Maybe. Maybe not."

"That sounds like a yes to me."

Tig glanced around, releasing a breath when she saw that the surrounding tables were empty. "Could be nothing. It's probably nothing."

"Good grief, Tig. You've gone as white as the tablecloth. What's happened?"

"Okay. So, last night I was running an unscheduled security sweep on the ship's network prior to the ball, just a precautionary measure considering the amount of computing power all the effects required. Anyway, I found something—something odd." Her voice dimmed to a whisper. "For the last couple of weeks, someone off-ship has been accessing our manifests and our guests' itineraries."

Sunny frowned. "Is that odd? Could it be corporate?"

"That's just the thing. It isn't necessarily odd for LunaCorp to access our manifests, although it doesn't happen very often. What *is* odd is that while these recent breaches do have LunaCorp credentials, they're all expired, and the origins are all wrong."

"Wrong?"

She shrugged. "Yeah, wrong. They're not from Luna or the CAK or from New Earth or Mars or any location that a legitimate Luna-Corp access would conceivably come from."

Her concern must have been contagious because now Sunny searched the room for anyone who might be listening in. "Where are they coming from?"

Tig scratched her head, ruffling the pink strands of her hair to stand on end. "For the life of me, I can't tell. The origins are untraceable, and in order to do any deeper digging, I'll quickly become *conspicuous*, if you catch my drift."

If a person wanted to keep their job, the last place they ever wanted to be was on LunaCorp's radar. "Have you spoken about this with Chan? Or Rax and Morgath?"

"No. Not yet. And please don't say anything. I need more information first. Honestly it's probably nothing, just an aberration." She took a tiny bite of her pastry, then set it back down on her plate. Neither Sunny nor Tig ate much more after that.

Tig's revelation had Sunny worried, but the crushing fatigue turning her feet into blocks of lead, rendering them nearly impossible to lift with each step back to her pod, made it hard to think of much else besides sleep. After sliding her door open, she made a solemn vow to worry in full after she got a couple hours of shut eye.

Gazing longingly at her bed like it was an oasis in the middle of a Neptune desert, she tripped over a very inconsiderate object that had been placed directly in her path. It was a box. A gift box, to be exact. And the card tucked into the red satin ribbon adorning the box had a single word scrolled across it, a single word that woke her right up: *Phoebe.*

14

THE GIFT

My dearest Phoebe,

Sitting on her bed, the card in her hands, she stared at this opening line, tracing a finger over its slanted cursive letters.

> *My dearest Phoebe,*
>
> *A little bird told me you've likely not slept yet today. I have taken it upon myself to provide you with some items to aid in that endeavor. If these gifts help, and you're feeling up to it, any chance you'd like to meet this evening? Dinner and drinks?*
>
> *Respectfully yours,*
>
> *Joshua*
>
> *P.S. I can still feel your lips on mine. Still taste you on my tongue, sweet like honey. No matter what I try to do with myself today, I will be absolute rubbish until I kiss you again. Please, take pity on me and say yes.*

Setting the card down beside her, she pulled the red ribbon free and raised the lid on the box. Inside, covered in a thin layer of white tissue paper, she found a long pair of the softest, thickest Venusian wool socks she had ever seen and a sleep mask identical to the one he'd been wearing—smelling of the very same lavender and vanilla that had been tempting her senseless since she'd left his room.

She stripped out of her clothes, rolled on the socks, pulled her favorite nightshirt over her head, inhaled the sleep mask deep into her lungs, then crawled onto her bed and opened the Squee app in her VC.

She found Joshua's profile and clicked on Chat.

<This might be the most thoughtful present Phoebe has ever received.>

She awaited his reply, one minute, two, her patience fraying at the edges.

A message from Squee popped over her vision: *Joshua is requesting a video chat. Do you agree?*

Grabbing her techpad from her bedside table, she clicked on the incoming Squee call. "Hello, darling," she said after he appeared on her screen.

"You like them?" His face was dark, barely lit.

"Where are you? I can hardly see you."

A mischievous smirk danced across his lips. "I'm hiding in a utility closet. I'd been reading in the library. I'm just thankful I happened to bring my techpad with me."

"You were in the library? What were you reading?" Nobody read anymore, not actual paper books, not in an actual library. And reading in the library aboard this ship would be a feat in and of itself since it was the size of Sunny's bathroom.

"Oh, nothing much. Poetry, mostly."

"Poetry?" *Of course.* She bit her lip. "Anything notable?"

His gaze fell to her mouth and lingered there. "There was this one verse. It's from a poem by an Old Earth writer named Atwood, about sleep, ironically." He took a breath and recited:

"I would like to be the air

that inhabits you for a moment

only. I would like to be that unnoticed

& *that necessary.*"

"Hmmm," she sighed. "That's lovely."

"You look beautiful but a bit tired."

She appreciated his diplomacy in recognizing her current state of fatigue. "I am exhausted. But now that I have this"—she raised her hand, his sleep mask dangling from her fingers—"I think I might actually sleep."

He cleared his throat. "Did you get the socks too?"

Her laughter was low and seductive. "I did."

"Can I see them?" he asked, his pupils dilating.

Grinning, Sunny propped up the techpad on her table and moved far enough away that her entire body became visible in the frame. She raised her nightshirt a bit to reveal the woolen socks, long enough to reach nearly to her mid-thigh.

"Good lord," he whispered, biting his knuckle. "That is the single sexiest thing I have ever seen."

She chuckled, looking down at her legs. "You are a very strange man." Then, slowly, she raised the hem of her shirt a bit higher. "I have something you might find even sexier."

"Wait. What are you doing? Stop," he blurted out, flustered.

"You want me to stop?" she teased, sliding her shirt up a centimeter higher and then another. "What are you afraid of? It's not like anyone can see you, hiding in a closet as you are."

He groaned. "When they find me dead in this closet with an enormous erection after having suffered a massive coronary, I hope you'll know that you were to blame."

She laughed at him, but she didn't stop. As her shirt reached the tops of her thighs, so close to revealing the soft curls of hair between her legs, Freddie slammed his eyes shut and said, "If I am ever fortunate enough to see you naked again, it will not be on my damned techpad. So you will desist this instant. You will go to sleep. And I will head back to my pod to take another cold shower."

"Another?"

With his eyes still closed, he admitted, "Third one today.

Sleep well." He cracked a lid, looking relieved to find Sunny on her bed again, techpad between her hands. "Dinner later?" he asked.

Sunny schooled her expression into the picture of innocence. "I would love to."

He puffed out a breath, his hand running through his hair. "Good. I'll pick you up."

Before he clicked off the call, she asked, "And, darling, should I wear these socks?"

His sexually frustrated groan was the last sound she heard before she passed out cold.

Sunny woke to a very loud, very insistent knocking on her door. She raised the sleep mask from her eyes and rolled off her bed just as the door erupted into another barrage. "I'm coming," Sunny called. "Please stop trying to break my door."

"Oh, sorry," a voice boomed through the battered mycelon panel.

She knew that voice. Stumbling to the door, she pressed the button to slide it open. "Garran. Hello. How did you—"

"Your pink-haired friend told me where to find you. But then she ran away." He grimaced guiltily. "I think I frightened her."

Sunny looked him over. Garran was so tall he'd have to duck if he wanted to come inside her pod. "Well, darling, you can be a touch intimidating."

Now he looked Sunny over. "You look nice today. I like your shirt. And those socks are very fine. They would get you through a full winter on Argos."

Oh, Garran. "Thank you. They were a gift. What can I do for—"

"A fine gift," he interrupted, grinning. "Very thoughtful."

She did her best to hide her smile. "I suppose it was. Do you want to come in?"

"No. I would not fit," he said, squinting past her into her pod. "Can we talk out here? It will not take long."

"Of course. How can I help?"

For such a large man, Garran did sheepish cowering better than anyone Sunny had ever met in her entire life. "Kasa has asked if I would like to go dancing with her, alone, this weekend."

"Dancing? That's wonderful."

He nodded. "I do enjoy dancing. But I have never been on a date...with a woman...on purpose. I do not know what to do."

Sunny smiled widely, patting his gigantic arm. "Not to worry, big guy. I've got you."

After her brief but insightful chat with Garran, she Vcommed Freddie, <I am awake. It is—> she accessed the time— <seventeen hundred. I just had the most fascinating conversation with our favorite Argosian.>

He responded almost instantaneously. <Good afternoon. About?>

His professional response was a relief. Sunny liked knowing they could keep things separate—work and play, business and white-hot impropriety. Clear lines drawn in molten lava.

<Kasa has asked him on a date this weekend.>

<Good man!> There was laughter in his voice. <He's feeling unsure of himself, I gather. If he came to find you.>

<He is. I could use your help. Care for a late night this weekend?
>

A brief moment elapsed. <A late night *working*, correct?>

This time Sunny took a moment. An evening spent hiding behind the scenes, turning Garran into the Don Juan of Argos, it could be very romantic but also very clearly work. <Yes, that's right. Working.>

<Then I am up to the task.>

<But do let Joshua know that Phoebe is very much looking forward to seeing him in a couple of hours for dinner.>

<I just did, and he replied, "Thank the stars.">

After a scalding shower, Sunny stood in front of her closet, trying to decide what to wear—*not the black dress. Far too on the nose*—when a Vcomm from Chan came through.

<Sorry to bother you on your day off, Sunny, but something has come up.>

<Yes?> She knew his tone, and she could already feel date night with Joshua slipping like sand through her fingers.

<Senator Ramesh has been called in for an emergency meeting of the KU Senate, and her wife has gone off-ship due to a family emergency.>

<Leaving Sai alone,> Sunny surmised, the hairs on her neck prickling as a cold sweat broke out across her forehead. *Please don't ask me to watch him,* she thought hopelessly.

<You are the only staff member available who's even slightly qualified to watch over a child.>

Her cold sweat transformed into an icy shower. What was Chan talking about? How would he know what experience she'd had with children?

<You did such a good job watching over those Martian movie star brats last month, a ten-year-old boy should be a walk in the park by comparison.>

Her breathing slowed, stabilized. Of course Chan didn't know anything—because she never *told* anyone anything. Ever. <I'm not very good with children,> she lied, trying to swallow past the lump in her throat.

<Please, Sunny. I'd ask Elanie, but she watched him once the other day and it didn't go well. Evidently, Sai told his moms that all Elanie did the entire time was sit opposite him on the couch and

scowl. Senator Ramesh asked explicitly that she not watch the boy again. Her meeting shouldn't last the entire night. I'd do it myself, but I have dinner with the captains.>

Sunny wasn't getting out of this. Maybe it would be okay. Maybe she was ready to spend some time with a child again. Maybe...it might even be fun. *Be brave, Sunny, be brave.* <Of course, Chan. What time do I need to be there?>

<Um...> He faltered. <Would right now work?>

So much for date night. <I'll head over to the Ramesh suite presently.>

<Thank you, Sunny. You are a life saver!>

15

SEA LIONS

F<small>REDDIE HAD TAKEN THE NEWS SURPRISINGLY WELL, ALL THINGS</small> considered. Although there'd been a lengthy groan and some choice language—something about a "twally washer," whatever that was. He'd wished Sunny well and asked her to Vcomm him when the senator returned, in case they still had time to grab a nightcap. To which Sunny had replied, "Is that what the kids call making out these days?" She hadn't been able to make out a single word of the string of curses this had pulled from him.

Sai opened the door before Sunny even had a chance to knock. He wore faded jeans and a yellow hoody, his feet bare once again.

"Hi, Sunny! Chan told me you'd be coming, so I've been watching the cams, waiting for you."

"And here I am." She bowed deeply. "At your service."

His smile when Sunny straightened back up was all teeth. "Come in. Have you had dinner?"

"Not yet. You?"

Sai bounced into his kitchenette and pulled a dish out of the fridge. "No, but my mom made me some palak paneer before she left. It's soooo good. Want some?"

The dish he set on the counter smelled incredible. "I've not had palak paneer before."

"You will *not* be sorry. It's my favorite. But," he bit his cheek, his eyes hidden under his thick lashes, "ever since the incident with the tart, my moms won't let me use the instawave anymore."

"Ah, well. That's simple enough."

After Sunny successfully warmed the dish without any fire suppression required, she sat with Sai, and they ate together at the counter. The food was spicy, creamy, and absolutely delicious. It paired surprisingly well with the gigantic glass of lemonade Sai poured for her into a bright-blue tumbler.

"Sweet mercy, Sai. I've never tasted anything like this before. It's amazing."

"Right? I knew you'd love it!"

"Tell me, what are these?" Sunny raised her spoon, which held a small white square of something buttery and delectable.

He studied the object with a deeply furrowed brow. "I think it's cheese. But I'm not sure."

She popped the probably-cheese into her mouth. "And this?" she asked, her next spoonful cradling a bit of wilted green vegetable.

"Hmm," he considered. "That is, uh, lettuce maybe?"

"It is?" She glanced at her spoon again.

"No, wait, not lettuce. Spinach. It's spinach."

"Well it is phenomenal. And this is the best lemonade I have ever had."

He beamed. "I made that! I made the lemonade!"

Pride radiated from him. His expression was one Sunny had seen before, so many times in fact it was stamped onto her mind like a footprint. And yet, somehow, she'd forgotten what it looked like. How could she have forgotten that? What else had she forgotten?

She set down her spoon, her hands suddenly trembling. Her

throat spasmed. She closed her eyes, but no matter how hard she tried, she couldn't catch her breath.

"Are you okay?" Sai asked. "Is it the lemonade? Is it too sweet? My moms always say I make it too sweet. But I can't help it. I just like it better that way. I'm sorry if you don't like it. I can get you something else. NearMilk? VitoWater?"

The poor child doing everything in his power to make her feel better only made her feel worse. She'd made a huge mistake. She shouldn't have agreed to watch him. She'd known it would be too much. Her mouth went dry, her fingers tingling as white light crowded the edges of her vision. And then came the dizziness, the nausea, the buzzing sensation vibrating through her head. The feeling that she was no longer a real person moving through a real world.

"I'm fine, Sai, I just ate too quickly. Please, excuse me. I'll only need a minute."

She stumbled to the bathroom, flipped down the toilet cover, and sat with her head squeezed between her knees. "You're all right. You're all right. You're all right," she whispered, chanting it, trying to make it so. But she was not all right. She would never be all right.

<How's the babysitting going?>

Freddie's voice in her head sent her reeling. She grasped the edges of the toilet, clinging to the sensation of the cool porcelain underneath her fingertips.

<Freddie. Please. I need help.>

<What is it? What's wrong?> he asked, startled. <Is it the child? I'm on my way.>

<Wait, wait. Stop. It's not Sai. It's only me. I'm...I'm having a panic attack. I can't breathe.>

<Ah. All right. Where are you now? Do you want me to come?> His voice sank low, so calm and slow. It settled over Sunny's mind like a heavy blanket.

<I'm hiding in the bathroom. And no, you don't need to come. But don't leave me. Talk to me. Just talk to me, please.>

<Let's see.> There was a brief silence, as if he was trying to think of what to say to her. <Here's something interesting. Have I ever told you about the sea lion population on Venus?>

<No. I don't think so,> Sunny replied, small sips of air making their way into her lungs. A moment passed, and then another. Her panic rose sharply. <Freddie, are you still with me?>

<Sorry. I'm here. I'm with you. I just had to take care of something. Where was I?>

<Sea lions.>

<Right. When we terraformed Venus, the sea lion introduction program went a bit round the bend after their natural predators, namely sharks and whales, didn't fare as well in the harsh early climate on the planet. As a result, the sea lions thrived.>

<That's interesting,> Sunny said, trying her hardest to pay attention to Freddie's centering voice rather than the way her heart was trying to indent itself into her ribs.

<It was very interesting in fact—and rather unexpected. When the first settlers arrived from Old Earth Europe, they had no idea what to do with the millions of sea lions crowding the coastlines. Some they ate and they made furs from others, but they quickly began to notice there was something peculiar about the particular brand of sea lion on Venus.>

Freddie's Venusian burr rolled freely over his words, lending his voice an even more soothing quality. Like vocal valium.

<What was different about them?> Sunny asked while sitting upright, the dizziness and tingling ebbing just a little.

<While the sea lions of Old Earth were not necessarily violent toward humans, the sea lions on Venus were growing fond of the settlers. They'd come up on the shore for pats on their noses, ride the ocean waves for applause and treats, and roll over in the sand for belly scratches. It wasn't long before the settlers could no longer

bring themselves to harm the creatures, often taking them on as household pets.>

The smallest laugh escaped her. <Is any of this true?>

<It is true. I swear it. You see, somehow in the initial cloning and breeding program, something incredible happened.>

<Incredible?> Sunny asked doubtfully.

<Yes. Canine DNA ended up mixing with the sea lion supply!>

She snorted. <This is a load of sea lion shit.>

His laughter caressed her mind. <Aye, you've found me out. But did it work? Do you feel any better?>

Her breaths came more smoothly now, her stomach no longer roiling, her body feeling like it had its own boundaries again. <I do. Thank you. Oh, no!> She bolted to her feet. <Sai! I left him alone out there.>

<No, actually, you didn't. I know you said not to come, but I figured the boy might be frightened, so I came anyway. Forgive me. And what is this amazing food?>

Sunny groaned, burying her face in her hands. <It's called palak paneer. I'm so embarrassed.>

<Don't be. I told Sai that sometimes women just need time alone in the bathroom. To which he scoffed and replied, "I know. I have two moms." We'll be out here whenever you're ready to join us. Take your time.>

<Thank you, Freddie.>

<Anytime, Sunny.>

16

WARMER CLIMATES

Sunny left the bathroom sometime later, when the sound of Freddie's and Sai's laughter drew her out of hiding.

Freddie met her in the hallway. "How are you feeling?"

"I'm fine," she said weakly, then she collapsed into his arms.

His hand came up to stroke her hair. "If I'd have known a little panic would lead to cuddling, I'd have started hiding in hallways to jump out at you weeks ago."

She laughed despite herself. "I'd think twice. I can get violent when startled."

"Even better."

She pulled away so she could smack him on his chest.

"Are you two done making out, or what?" Sai stood at the end of the hallway with his hands on his hips.

Sunny gaped at him. "What do you know of making out?" She ruffled Sai's hair as she walked past him back to the kitchenette.

He nipped at her heels, then slipped around her to hop up onto a stool at the counter. "Blech! They're always doing it in my moms' stories. You know, like this."

Both Freddie and Sunny erupted into laughter while Sai raised his arms as if he held someone and stuck out his tongue, wiggling his head around and making a "muah" sound.

"You're right, Sai," said Freddie, rummaging through a cupboard. "Sunny and I were absolutely embracing the air and sticking our tongues out at each other. And you nearly caught us in the act."

Sai grimaced. "Gross."

Freddie spun around, setting three items onto the counter— flour, NearButter, sugar—and asked, "Tell me, Sai. Where do your mums stand on cookies?"

Turned out—according to Sai—Chahna and Lena were fully in favor of cookies on all fronts. And Freddie, in an entirely unsurprising turn of events, had a secret family recipe all cued up for the occasion.

After stuffing their faces silly with Freddie's warm, gooey sugar cookies, Sai ran himself a bath while Freddie and Sunny cleaned up. Sunny was about to tell Freddie he could leave when Sai, clad in yellow fleece pajamas decorated with round, purple smiley faces, asked specifically for Freddie to read him to sleep. Children, Sunny knew, always had an innate sense of who was the best storyteller in the room.

Freddie retreated to Sai's room while Sunny sat down on the couch and picked up the remote. Even though every show ever created was available in full virtual reality through the VC, the *Ignisar* still supplied all suites with a television. Sometimes, especially when she was tired, Sunny found it nice to disconnect and watch a screen.

With the sound on mute, Sunny listened in as Freddie read Sai a story recounting the outlandish adventures of a deep-space pilot named Captain Zorba and his gorilla second mate named Bartholomew. It was a very funny story, and the voice Freddie used for the gorilla was hysterical. When the story came to an end, a richness entered Freddie's voice while he asked Sai to tell him about his day, if there was anything that happened that he would remember forever. Sai mentioned several options: his visit to the Cosmic Spectacle oorthorse stables, the sugar cookies, Freddie reading to him. Sai's voice was so soft and sweet, his words interrupted more than once by long, sleepy yawns.

"Sunny, you've fallen asleep."

She raised her head from where her cheek had been smushed into the couch pillow. Freddie knelt on the floor in front of her, and as his face swam into view, Sunny smiled at it. "Did Sai do the same?"

"Out like a light." Freddie turned, looking back toward the television. "What are we watching? Looks like, ooh, reality TV. My favorite."

Sunny's brow furrowed. "You can't be serious. You like reality TV?"

He turned back, a gleam in his eye. "I do. Especially this one." His thumb pointed behind him at the screen. "*Kuiper Worm Chasers* is epic. So dangerous, so daring, so stupid."

She reached out to brush her fingers over his cheek, remembering how he'd talked her down from the edge of panic, how he'd baked them cookies, how it had felt to have his arms around her, safe and cared for. "You know, technically, this *is* still our day off."

"Hmm," he purred. "And Phoebe and Joshua *were* supposed to be on a date tonight."

Scooting forward, making room for him, Sunny patted the couch in invitation. He crawled in behind her, his warm body curling softly around hers, his arm resting gently over her waist. They stayed that way for a while, curled into each other, watching grown adults willingly risk their lives to capture three-hundred-meter-long carnivorous invertebrates in the Kuiper belt for not nearly enough credits. And it was lovely. So lovely, in fact, Sunny could have drifted back off to sleep. But she couldn't help but notice

—as a young chap from Uranus gave a harrowing account of his narrow escape from a worm's multi-rowed teeth when his ship's reactor went on the fritz—that long fingers had slipped under the hem of her shirt.

With the softest touch, they brushed over her skin, lightly skimming across her belly. Each slow pass across her body, his fingers rose, just a little, barely enough to be entirely certain he was doing it on purpose. Until they reached the border of her ribs—and kept going.

Her teeth sank into her lower lip as his fingers traveled upward in shallow, dipping switchbacks over her chest, his hand now hidden completely under her shirt. Her heart began to thunder, her breasts swelling, nipples tightening into firm little buds in anticipation of being plucked.

His fingers took a circuitous path over her body, meandering and painfully unhurried as they just barely traced the lacy band of her bra. At first, Sunny thought he must have been teasing her, torturing her with a promise of pleasure that was so close she could taste it but still far enough away that she was a hair's breadth from begging him for it. But then she wondered if this slow, methodical advance wasn't actually his way of asking for permission, giving her plenty of time to stop him if she'd wanted to. *Pah.* She was practically on fire and likely wouldn't have told him to stop to get water if she was.

He didn't make a sound behind her, not a breath, not a sigh, not a single movement of his body aside from his hand, fingertips now sliding slowly under lace, grazing the underside of her breasts. The unanswered craving was agony, and each sweep of his fingers sent flickering pulses of heat straight between her legs. But as much as she wanted to grab his hand and put it where she wanted it, where she *needed* it, she refused to give in. Even if this wasn't teasing. Even if he was seeking her permission, they'd come too far now for her to just give it to him. On this, she would stand firm. She would not break. She would try very hard not to break. His thumb slipped under her bra, his hand so close to cupping her breast she nearly cried. *Fuck,* she was going to break.

As luck would have it, they broke at the same time. Sunny ground her hips against him while he cursed into her ear, pushing her bra up to liberate her swollen, aching breasts and cupping one with his hand.

She rolled toward him as he kneaded one breast and then reached over for the other, gently stroking his thumb over her nipple. Her hand snaked around his neck, and she pulled his mouth down onto hers. He kissed her fiercely, his tongue sweeping in over hers as his fingers continued their exploration of her breasts. When he pinched a nipple and Sunny moaned into his mouth, his hand abandoned her breasts completely, moving south in search of warmer climates.

"Shhh," he whispered when she gasped at first contact. But what did he expect when his hand dove beneath the waist of her pants, slipped under her panties, his finger sinking inside her to the hilt?

"*Stars,* Sunny," he ground out. "You're wet as rain."

She pulled him into another kiss, burrowing her hands into his hair. He withdrew his finger and slid it between her folds to press and hold it firmly over her clit. The sensation was breath-stealing, mind-numbing ecstasy, and then his finger started to move. Brisk, flawless circles. Five, six, seven, eight was all it took until she shuddered under him, burying her harsh, groaning breaths into his neck as release barreled through her, sending light and heat soaring from her toes up into her belly to spread out until a warm, pulsating pleasure wrapped itself around her and squeezed.

Panting against his shoulder, the waves of sensation slowly loosened their grip on her. Lifting her head, she found his eyes just as he brought the finger that had been inside her up to his lips and sucked it into his mouth.

"Freddie," she said, breathless.

He was rock hard now, pressed against her thigh. Grabbing his face with one hand and kissing him again, Sunny reached down between their bodies, desperate to touch him. But he stopped her hand.

"What's wrong?" she asked.

Bringing her hand to his mouth, he pressed a kiss into her palm. "That was just for you. Besides, the senator might be home at any moment."

"Senator? What senator?"

His laughter brushed over her knuckles. "I should go."

"She'll know you were here. Sai will tell her."

He sat up, sliding her legs into his lap and slipping her shoes off to rub her feet. "I know. But it's one thing to bake cookies and quite another to be making out with the babysitter on the couch."

When he put it that way... "Can Phoebe visit your pod later? After the senator gets back."

Releasing her feet, he got to his, trying to smooth his shirt over his obvious, mouth-watering erection. "Joshua would like that very much."

She pulled him back down so she could kiss him one last time, while she might also have palmed him through his pants.

He groaned into her mouth and, when she released him, said, "Yes, Phoebe should definitely visit," adding a "Please?" for effect.

17

THE COUCH OF ILL REPUTE

SUNNY HAD ALMOST FALLEN ASLEEP AGAIN WHEN THE TELLTALE SOUND of a security lock clicking off had her sitting bolt upright.

Chahna released an exhausted sigh as she entered her suite, slipping out of her heels and kicking them off to the side to rest against the wall. She reached back to release the top of her skirt's zipper, then pulled a pin from her hair, running her fingers through her raven-black waves until they settled over her shoulders.

"Welcome home, Senator. How was your meeting?" Sunny's voice sounded wrong, awkward, *guilty.*

With a sharp inhale and a hand clasped over her heart, Chahna exclaimed in a harsh whisper, "*Gods above,* Sunny. You startled me."

"I'm sorry. Long day?"

Her groan was bone-weary. "An understatement. How was Sai?"

"An angel," Sunny replied, trying her best to assume her customary professionalism. "Perfectly behaved."

Chahna snorted, sitting down on the chair across from Sunny. "He is always on his best behavior for anyone who is not one of his mothers."

"Especially once Freddie came over to make him cookies,"

Sunny said, rushed, wanting it all out on the table. Well, not *all* of it, exactly. "Sai said you wouldn't mind."

Chahna's eyes narrowed, almost in accusation. "Freddie came?"

Sunny coughed on nothing as she thought, *Not yet.* She realized in a mortifying flash that Chahna could see straight through her. That she *knew.* There was evidently one thing all beings in the entire KU could not hide, and that thing was having been brought to orgasm on someone else's couch. "I called him in for reinforcements. Sai wanted cookies, and I can't bake."

Chahna's slow nod up and down said: *Bull. Shit.* "That's sounds lovely. I like that Freddie."

It was definitely time for Sunny to leave. This woman was as skilled as a Portisan empath when it came to reading minds. "Well, I should probably go and let you get some sleep."

But before Sunny could stand from the couch of ill repute, Chahna leaned forward and said, "Sunny, please stay. Just for a moment."

Settling back against the cushions, Sunny said, "Yes, of course."

"Thank you. I know your time is precious."

"Not at all," she replied smoothly, even though her time did feel precious right now, seeing as there was somewhere else she would really rather be, something else she'd rather be doing.

A resigned expression moved over Chahna's face. "You'd asked me at the Fire Ball why I was traveling on this ship. As much as possible, I try to keep my professional life separate from my personal life, but I would not be where I am today if I didn't have a keen sense of when to ask for help." She took a deep breath, and as she did, she pulled Sunny down from the heights of brain-scrambling pleasure to land firmly onto the bedrock of this woman's world. A world where the decisions she made daily affected billions. The notion was sobering.

"Do you need my help?" Sunny asked.

Chahna ran two fingers up and down the bridge of her nose. "I fear...no, I'm quite certain that my family is in danger. Tell me, Sunny. Have you heard of Proposition 2126?"

Sunny shook her head, her attention snagged on two words: family and danger.

"What I am about to tell you is highly classified information. Can I trust you to keep this between us?"

Sunny frowned. She wanted to tell her yes, but she knew that she couldn't. If anything the senator was about to tell her would put this ship—or anyone else aboard her—in harm's way, Sunny would have to tell Chan, Rax and Morgath, the captains, Freddie, everyone. "It depends. One of my duties is to keep everyone aboard this ship safe. If what you're about to tell me compromises that in any way—"

Chahna waved her off. "You're right, Sunny. Forgive me."

Sunny's mind rewound to Tig's revelation. "Senator, our IT specialist found something distressing the other day. Someone off-ship has been secretly accessing our guest's itineraries from an untraceable location."

Chahna's eyes flashed wide, for just a moment. "That's troubling."

"These security breaches started around the same time you and your family came aboard. Do you think this has anything to do with your proposition?"

"Perhaps." Her voice was tight.

"If I'm to help you, I need to know what's going on. And I need to be able to share the information with the crew."

Chahna sighed, resigned. "Very well. I have committed myself to introducing a"—she paused briefly, as if searching for the appropriate word—"*controversial* proposition at the upcoming KU Joint Sessions on Portis. Certain information regarding the proposition has been leaked, although I'm not certain how. Nevertheless, my comings and goings have been a source of much interest of late, and my security officers—also guests on this ship, although you won't uncover who they are unless they want you to—devised this plan to travel to Portis on this crowded ship in efforts to dissuade any attacks on me or my family before we reach the meeting."

Sunny's eyes narrowed. "Is my ship in danger, Senator?"

"We do not believe so," Chahna said, sitting back in her chair. "The negative press of anything happening on board the *Ignisar* would make the risks too great."

Sunny found this an odd statement. Who, she wondered, aside from LunaCorp themselves, would care about the negative press of something happening aboard one of LunaCorp's ships? Sunny wanted to ask her what her proposition entailed, when the soft padding of feet down the hall put an end to their conversation.

"Hi, Mom. What are you two talking about? You woke me up."

Chahna rose to her feet and walked to embrace Sai, picking him up off the floor and swaying him from side to side as she kissed his cheek. "Sorry, bubs. I've missed you. Did you have a good time with Sunny and Freddie?"

Sai's arms squeezed tightly around her neck. "We made cookies."

Chahna laughed, then set Sai down and turned to Sunny. "I'm certain you'll need to discuss what I've told you with Chan, and I realize that it was unfair of me to ask you not to. I would request your entire crew's discretion in this matter, however."

"Of course," Sunny said, getting to her feet. She straightened her blouse and said good night, watching Chahna lead Sai back to his room before seeing herself out. Then she headed directly to Freddie's pod.

18

DISCOURTEOUS

FREDDIE OPENED HIS DOOR AFTER ONE KNOCK. HE WORE A WHITE V-neck T-shirt over gray sweatpants, and he must have showered because his hair was damp and that delectably clean linen scent radiated from him. Maybe it was his soap or shampoo or just some pheromone his body produced to snare unsuspecting women into entertaining lurid fantasies of making him all dirty again.

"The senator made it home, I presume?" He backed away from the door to let Sunny inside.

"She did. I told her about the cookies. And she told me that her family might be in danger."

He coughed. "What?"

As succinctly as she could, Sunny told him about Tig's findings and the senator's concerns.

"That's troubling," he stated once she finished up.

She knew they should probably talk more about this, maybe tell other people. But it was very late, and Freddie smelled very amazing, and there was something about a man who typically wore fine suits looking casual and comfy in sweatpants that rendered her mind incapable of thinking of anything other than the feel of soft cotton under her fingers as she pulled those pants down.

Although she'd been in his pod before, this was the first time she'd taken the opportunity to really look around. He'd programmed digpics on his walls, scenes of Venus mostly. One pic between his bed and his table was of Freddie as a child, maybe a few years younger than Sai. He stood between who Sunny assumed were his parents on a black sand beach, waves crashing against rocks behind them. She stepped closer to the pic.

Young Freddie seemed carefree, happy. His parents gazed down at him, warm and loving, as a soft breeze blew through his mother's loose blond curls. She was beautiful. No surprise there, considering how handsome Freddie was.

Sunny stole a glance at his table, covered by a half-completed puzzle of some vivid, multicolored nebula, an empty coffee mug, and a small stack of leather-bound books—more poetry.

When Sunny looked up at him again, she found him staring at her with a patient, almost amused expression.

"What are you doing?" he asked.

"Oh, just checking out your pod. It's quite nice. Although, bring a stranger here and I'm not certain they'd be able to tell if this pod belonged to you or to your grandfather."

He laughed, staring down briefly at his bare feet.

She picked up one of his poetry books, leafing through the delicate pages. "You are very old fashioned."

His hands slid into the pockets of his sweats. "It's not such a bad thing, is it?"

He looked nervous, apprehensive. *Was he concerned she might actually think his classic style and impeccable manners were a flaw?* she wondered. *Ridiculous man. Ridiculous, charming, delightful man.*

She walked to him, stopping a few paces away. "No, it's not a bad thing. Not even a little bit." Staring into his clear, blue-grey eyes, she remembered the brush of his fingers on her skin, his finger inside of her. Her head tilted. "Phoebe still has some unfinished business with Joshua."

He swallowed, his throat bobbing. "She does?"

She nodded, slowly. "Mm-hmm."

With every step she took closer to him, he stepped one away, retreating from her advances until his back ran into his door, until she stood directly in front of him with nowhere for him to go.

Her gaze fell from his eyes to his lips, his throat, to the spot where his pulse leaped above his collar bone, down over his chest, lower. Her fingers followed suit, reaching out to stroke the growing hardness of him over his pants.

His eyelids fluttered, mouth opening in a silent gasp. He whispered, "It's not necessary. Joshua's not expecting any—"

"Shhh." She brushed a kiss over his lips, then slid to her knees, hooked her fingers into his waistband, and pulled. "Phoebe insists."

He sprang free, his pants dropping to the floor, and she nuzzled against him, pressing soft kisses onto his stomach, over the slope of his hip, inhaling him deeply. It *must* have been pheromones because he smelled even more amazing down here, like fresh wash drying in a summer breeze.

He muttered something unintelligible as she took him in her hand and then into her mouth, marveling as her tongue ran over his soft skin, smooth as silk with iron underneath. She kept her pace unhurried, steady, deliberate as she savored him, memorizing the shape of him, learning what made his breath catch, pulling a moan from somewhere deep in his throat.

As he was with everything, he was a gentleman when he got head. He didn't grab her hair or push into her or give her suggestions or orders like some lovers did. Instead, he stood as still as a statue with his arms at his sides, hands clenched into fists. He stayed quiet as a mouse aside from rare, hesitant moans and an occasional breathy, heartfelt praise.

He was perfect, always perfect, *too* perfect. It must wear on him, she thought, the pressure he puts on himself to maintain his impeccable manners, his even temper, his kind and considerate conduct. She wondered, while she was on her knees before him, while she held him quite literally in the palm of her hand, if she could pierce his perfectly polite demeanor here in the safety of his pod and give him permission to be, for a few moments at least...discourteous.

She slowed her pace, lightened her touch. Then, after another whisper-quiet but decidedly frustrated moan, she slowed even more.

"Please," he begged, his voice strained, his fists balled even tighter, knuckles turning white.

But even now, even with her teasing, he'd still asked politely. She pulled off him completely, and as he looked down at her with a pained, confused expression, she let her tongue flick over his tip.

He groaned, his eyes locking onto hers as she gave him a devilish grin. Then, still holding his stare, she slid her fingers up the inside of his thigh. When she reached the apex of his thighs, she stilled her hand, not yet touching him, and hovered her mouth directly over the tip of his cock.

"Please," he pleaded again, not moving, not reaching for her, so restrained, so *well-mannered.*

She slid her hand a bit farther so that she just barely touched him and whispered, "Let go for me. It's okay. I want you to. I can take it."

His eyes closed as her palm finally made full contact, cupping him. She took him into her mouth again, moving faster this time. A tiny thrill pulsed through her as he arched back, his head thudding against his door.

Grasping his hips, she moaned around him. And then, finally, as if unable to bear it one second longer, he let go. His hands unclenched, fingers diving into her hair, and with an exquisitely grunted "Fuck!" and still as politely as anyone ever had, he thrust into her once, twice, and came completely undone.

When she looked up, he was leaning against his door, breathing hard, his fingers releasing their grip on her head to gently cradle her face. "That was... I've never... How did you..."

She placed a sticky kiss right below his navel as she pulled his pants back up and led him to his bed. "I'd say years of practice, but I'm not sure that's what you want to hear right now."

With a breathy laugh, he sat on the edge of his bed and said, "Practice makes perfect, doesn't it?" Then, as if coming to his senses, his brief respite from restraint came to an end. He looked up at her, brows pinched together above wide and guilty eyes. "I'm sorry. I'm so sorry if—"

Leaning forward, she kissed him deeply before he could utter another word. "No apologies. I loved every single second." A corner of her mouth ticked up. "Especially that last little bit."

Sitting down beside him, she let her head rest on his shoulder. The mirror above his dresser reflected a picture back at her of a dazed man and a content woman she didn't quite recognize.

His eyes found hers in their reflection. "We look good together."

It was a simple statement, almost benign compared to other professions he'd already made. And he wasn't wrong. They did look good together. And in another life, maybe they'd live happily ever after. Or maybe, like always, she was just thinking too hard, too much. Maybe she should just let one thing happen without over-thinking it, just one.

She raised her head to face him and cupped his cheek in her palm. Then she told him, "We really do," and kissed him again.

19

DON'T MURDER THE MESSENGERS

"You mean to tell me the senator has her own security detail staying on this ship pretending to be guests? And we knew nothing about this until now?" Rax had somehow skipped over the objectively more important and significant details of the early morning briefing on the senator provided by Sunny and Tig to land on this concern.

"Yes. That is exactly what we mean," Sunny said, holding up her hands. "Don't murder the messengers, darling."

Morgath, evidently sharing Rax's outrage, chimed in with, "That she doesn't trust us to at least *know* who her SOs are is an insult of the highest order." His eyes darted between Sunny and the rest of the staff. "It is an insult to everyone sitting at this table!" He emphasized his point by way of slamming a green fist down on said table.

Chan ran a hand over his head. "I'll admit it is unusual, but given her situation surrounding whatever this proposition is, as well as the fact that someone is hacking into our system to monitor her family's comings and goings, I can't say that I don't understand why she wants to keep her security undercover."

Tig had informed the crew that while several of the guests had their specific itineraries accessed by the hackers, the senator's had been accessed a total of twenty-two times, ten-times more than any other guest.

"Well, I can," snapped Rax. "She should have warned us before coming aboard, given us time to prepare. Or even to decide if we wanted to let her on the ship at all. Now we're caught with our pants down!"

A flush surged up Sunny's throat, her mind flashing back to finely muscled thighs and sweatpants pooled around ankles. When she chanced a glance at Freddie, she found him studying an imperfection in the table, a blush bursting from his cheeks to his hairline, maybe remembering the exact same events.

"So, what do we do?" Tig pulled at the strings of her hoodie. "I could try harder to uncover the source of the breaches, but I might get caught."

"That seems like a bad idea," offered Elanie. "I'm not sure how much we want to implicate ourselves in whatever the senator is wrapped up in."

Chan nodded, Rax and Morgath grunted their agreement, Sunny began to simmer. "If somebody is bypassing our security to obtain protected information on our guests, I believe we have an obligation to do everything within our power to keep those guests safe so long as they are aboard this ship."

Freddie raised his eyes, nodding in a covert show of support. Then, in a very overt one, he said, "I agree with Sunny. Any threat against any one of our guests is a threat against everyone on the ship. Knowing what we know, what can we do to minimize risk?"

Tig cleared her throat. "I think I can trace the breaches without being detected. But it will take time, lots of time. And I'll need some backup."

Chan clicked his tongue. "Funny you should mention that, Tig. Turns out, some relief is on the way."

One by one, everyone turned their heads to stare at Chan.

He avoided their questioning glares to pick at the leather of one of his hoverchair's armrests.

"What 'relief'?" Sunny asked. "Who is coming?" Besides the FFKs, there were no special guests on the docket, and Chan couldn't possibly be implying that some deep-space pirate could assist Tig in high-tech espionage.

"Funny story," Chan blurted. "I mean, it's wild, really. You probably won't even believe it—"

"Chandler, spit it out," instructed Morgath between clenched teeth.

Chan repositioned himself in his chair, shifting his weight from one hip to the other. "Well, conveniently, while they're here, Luna-Corp wants us to train the FFKs—"

The explosion of green intimidation when Rax and Morgath surged to their feet pushed everyone else back from the table and made Tig cry out a "Yip!"

"If the next words out of your mouth have anything to do with giving fucking Kravaxians access to our IT, you can consider our employment aboard this vessel terminated." Fury emanated from Morgath, and Rax grasped the edge of the table with such force, Sunny was worried he might break off a chunk of it and hurl it at somebody.

Although this news was unsettling, the twins seemed more high strung than usual. Sunny wondered if they wouldn't benefit from a day at the spa or an afternoon in the pleasure pods. Maybe she should set something up for them, sooner rather than later so they didn't end up getting themselves fired.

In another uncharacteristic outburst, Tig asserted herself, "Everyone, calm down. If LunaCorp wants me to work with a Kravaxian, I can do that without compromising our intel."

"Our intel has already been compromised though, hasn't it? With these breaches?" asked Elanie in as kind a tone as she was capable.

Tig's shoulders pulled inward. "That's different."

Morgath released a puff of air between his lips, staring at Tig like she was nothing more than a foolish child. She wilted under his glare.

Sunny bristled. "Last I recall," she began, "there is only one person in charge in this room. I know this situation is extreme, but Chan is still our boss. So please, if you would, sit down, be quiet, and let the man speak."

Chan sighed. "Thank you, Sunny. But nobody is going to like what I have to say next, not even me. Just please remember that we are all in this together and," he looked directly at the twins, "if you break anything, it's coming out of your paychecks."

Rax and Morgath grumbled their agreement, but they remained on their feet.

"LunaCorp is using this holiday for the FF—Chan paused, his jaw clenching—for the Kravaxians as an opportunity to provide them some on-the-job training. One will be assigned to IT with Tig. One will spend the week with me. And the remaining two are to shadow"—he swallowed audibly—"security."

Rax and Morgath succumbed simultaneously to the most outrageous fit of laughter Sunny had ever heard from either of them. Doubled over with his hands on his knees, a red-faced Morgath wheezed like a serving drone on its last thruster. Beside him, Rax clapped his hand onto Morgath's shoulder, then leaned back, releasing this lengthy post-laugh "Hoooo!" at the ceiling.

Elanie rolled her eyes at the pair. "Are you two finished? I do have things to do today."

"And the captains are still in agreement with this plan?" asked Freddie, leaning back, his arms crossed thoughtfully over his chest.

Chan nodded. "One hundred percent. They've had briefings on the situation from Becks Karlovich himself, and both feel confident the Kravaxians present no danger to this ship."

In possession of his faculties once more, Rax growled, "I don't give a flying fuck what the CEO of LunaCorp said, we are not training Kravaxians. It's not happening."

Impressively undeterred, Chan fired back, "It is indeed happening, and you and your brother will behave yourselves, do your jobs, and give the Kravaxians a fair shake before you write them off. Or you will find another ship to work on and another director to put up with your tantrums. So, good luck with that."

Like puppies swatted on their noses, Rax and Morgath finally took their seats, muttering profanities under their breaths.

Chan, riding on momentum, ended the meeting in no uncertain terms. "When the Kravaxians arrive, we will be polite, accommodating, and we will not create a Known Universal incident by showing them mistrust and hostile aggression when they have done nothing to earn it. Is that clear?"

After Chan's dressing down, Freddie, Elanie, Tig, and Sunny huddled near the moon jelly tank.

"That was intense," said Freddie.

"That was Chan at his finest," Sunny replied. Her wink at Freddie earned her a knee-buckling smile, all white teeth and crinkled eyes.

"As stimulating as all of this has been, I really do have work to do." Elanie turned unceremoniously on her heel and disappeared down the hall.

Freddie stared after her, shaking his head. "She is a very unique bionic. She's like a breath of fresh air that occasionally, often for reasons unknown, slaps you hard across the face."

Sunny laughed out loud. "That is the best description of Elanie I have ever heard."

Tig stopped chewing on a fingernail long enough to nod her agreement with Freddie's assessment, then said, "I should go too. I've got a hacker to expose."

Sunny squeezed Tig's fingers. "Be careful, darling."

"I'll try," said Tig before walking off toward her office.

Freddie remained behind, the moon jelly tank reflecting blue waves over his face, just as they'd done the first day Sunny had seen him on this ship.

"What are your plans today?" he asked.

"I think I'm on damage control."

"What damage?"

"Aquilinian twin damage. I should probably do whatever it takes today to keep Rax and Morgath from interrogating random guests in order to find out who the senator's SOs are. And then I need to prepare for Garran and Kasa's date later this week."

"Ooch, that's right. Still want my help?"

She nodded enthusiastically. "I could use your charm for my attempts at playing Cyrano. In fact, if you're not too busy, I could probably use your help with the twins today as well."

Freddie grinned. "I'd be happy to, but first things first, did you just imply that you find me charming?"

Sunny batted her eyelashes, her cheeks hot as she admitted, "I think I did."

20

ORDER OVER CHAOS

THE THIRD BAR SUNNY, FREDDIE, AND THE TWINS STUMBLED INTO— after sipping martinis while watching Old Earth early twentieth century flappers dance at the jazz club on deck five, then sampling the creative yet objectively bizarre cocktails at the Blurvan tavern on eighteen—was one of Sunny's favorites on the ship. It was a dimly lit Venusian pub with a long, wooden bar surrounded by rich leather booths, one of which they piled into while a fiddler serenaded them from a small stage in the corner. It had taken far too many drinks, but the twins were finally loose and laughing and no longer eyeing every other guest with suspicious intent. Sunny's sobriety, however, was the first casualty of this mission.

Sitting across from her, Freddie ran two fingers over the deep brown leather of their booth. "I like this place. It reminds me of home."

Sunny nodded, her head swimming, while Morgath, sitting next to her, dropped his forehead onto her shoulder. "I think I'm drunk," he confessed.

Rax's answering laugh at his brother lasted a full ten intoxicated seconds.

Sunny nestled her cheek into Morgath's green hair. "Never

admit to being drunk, darling. We deny it until our faces are deep in the toilet."

"What in the worlds is going on here?" said a terribly sober voice. Chan had caught them out. Sunny wanted to hide under the booth.

"Chandler," Freddie said, jumping to attention and straightening his tie, trying his level best to appear sober. "Sunny and I were just trying to set the twins' minds at ease regarding the FFKs and the business with the senator. We thought that, you know, that whiskey might do the trick."

"Is it working?" Chan asked, his brow sharply arched.

"What are you doing here, darling?" Sunny asked, trying to shift the topic of conversation away from how drunk they all were. Chan rarely frequented any of the drinking establishments on the ship.

He ran a hand over his head. "Well, there was an incident at the bowling alley on deck nine. A Vorpol was 'accidentally'"—he drew air quotes—"tripped by a Gorbie during his hopping approach to the line, and in the ensuing scuffle, a bowling ball found its way first through one of the light fixtures, then halfway through the floor on its way back down."

"Oh dear," Sunny replied. "That's not good."

"Did you say the ball *found its way*?" repeated Freddie, his head tilting, his lips twisting into a grin Sunny wanted to kiss right off his face.

Chan nodded knowingly. "I did. Who threw the ball is a mystery I was unable to solve. And in the name of keeping interspecies peace, any investigation was abandoned in favor of unlimited free bowling for both parties. After that mess, with no help from you lot, I thought I could use a drink."

"Alone?" Sunny asked, suspicion mounting. "You're at a bar by yourself?"

"Well, not exactly," Chan replied, his lips pressed tight, cheeks and ears turning pink.

Scooting to the edge of her seat, Sunny peered around their

booth, trying and failing to be inconspicuous. She spotted Makenna at a two-top table in the corner of the bar. "Chan!" she gasped. "Are you on a date?"

"Chandler! My man!" Rax cheered, extending Chan an unanswered fist bump.

"Keep your voices down, please," begged Chan, turning even redder. "It's nothing. It's a friendly get-together. Because that's what we are. What she is to me. Just friends." He shook his head as if forcing himself to stop talking. "Don't you all have work to do? Doesn't Elanie already pick up enough of your slack?"

"Doesn't look like it's an 'only just friends' situation to me," said Freddie, angling his head to sneak a peek at Makenna. "She's smiling at you."

Sunny beamed with unrestrained pride. "Bravo, darling," she slurred. "But what are you doing here talking to us when you should be over there telling Makenna that her skin is more luminous than the glow of Ulaperia's moons over the Senasar Sea?"

"Sunny," Chan gasped, "that's wonderful. Can I steal that?"

"It is all yours," Sunny said, her words thick and slow and fighting their way out of her mouth. She realized suddenly that she was careening face-first into blackout territory. Keeping up with the drinking abilities of Aquilinians three times her size was a skill she was rapidly aging out of. Even so, when the next round arrived, as Freddie wisely opted for VitoWater, Sunny clinked her glass of bourbon with Rax and Morgath's and guzzled gamely like she was still in her twenties.

While Chan cruised back to his table, Sunny propped her elbow on the edge of hers. Her cheek rested on her hand so her head didn't spin right off of her neck while she spent the next few minutes trying to read Chan's and Makenna's lips. Freddie lured her attention back when he told them all a story about the time his Granda had gotten so drunk he mistook the laundry hamper for the toilet. Everyone at the table cracked up when Freddie impersonated his grandmother screaming down the hall in a shrill and heavily accented, "That's not the privy, ya doaty tadger!"

"What's a doaty tadger?" asked Morgath after he caught his breath.

Sunny's foot inched toward Freddie's, just enough so that her toes touched his under the table. Through her swimming vision, she didn't miss the corner of his mouth tipping upward as her shoe slipped up and down the length of his calf.

"Shit, we've got to go," Rax said, shaking his head so hard that the booth under Sunny's ass trembled.

"So soon?" Sunny managed, swallowing a moan because Freddie had slipped a napkin off the table, diving to obtain it only so he could run his fingers slowly up the back of her leg.

"Your tolerance is staggering, Sunny," Rax told her, sliding out of the booth and gaining his feet. "I'm drunk as shit. I need to sleep."

"But do you feel better?" she asked, desperately wanting a stolen minute so the fingers on her calf could slide a bit higher and make the aching need between her legs feel better.

"A little," grumbled Morgath.

Freddie returned to his seat, and then they all climbed out. When Sunny spotted Chan and Makenna laughing together at their little table, her smile couldn't get any wider. But then Freddie's warm hand settled over the small of her back to lead her from the pub, and, impossibly, it did.

"I think that went well," said Freddie after they'd walked the twins back to their pods.

"So do I," Sunny concurred, and then, because she couldn't wait for one more second, she said, "Hello, *Joshua*," pushed him up against the curved wall of the hallway, and kissed him.

His hand slid up her back to cradle her head as his other arm wrapped around her waist and drew her close. His lips, the way they fit so perfectly over hers, the softness of his tongue, how their bodies moved together, she couldn't tell where she began and he ended. It was as if they had come into the worlds with a precise alignment of mouths and breaths and hands and somehow, despite the trillions of life-forms floating randomly through the void, they found each other. They connected, order rising over chaos in the closed system of their lips.

Her head spinning and her heart pounding, she pulled away from him. "Walk me to my pod?"

He nodded, grabbing her hand, and they practically sprinted to her pod, which, in retrospect, probably wasn't the best idea because by the time they arrived, Sunny's head was spinning, and not in a good way. But she yanked him into her pod anyway.

She kissed his cheeks, his neck, his mouth, and he let her, his hands roving over her body, but something was off. He was holding back.

"What's the matter?" she asked in between kisses. "Don't you want me?"

He grabbed her ass and pulled her close, the hardness of him answering her question. "More than anything, but I think you might be a wee bit drunk."

She snorted, peppering his neck with kisses. "Lies. Dirty, rotten lies. Do you have any idea how much alcohol this liver can process? I am a professional." She hiccupped.

"I have no doubt." He took a step back, assessing her with furrowed brows. "But it's not your liver I'm worried about."

"Darling, what could you possibly mean?" She hiccupped again, swallowing hard.

He brushed her bangs back off her forehead. "It's just that you're not normally this green."

These were evidently magical words because once he'd uttered them, nausea overtook her. Splinting her belly, she stumbled to her bathroom to lose the contents of her stomach into the toilet.

He walked in after her, grimacing sympathetically while taking a knee beside her on the tile.

"I guess I am drunk," Sunny conceded, her face still hidden in the bowl.

His hand ran up and down her back in long, soothing strokes while she vomited again, amazed there was anything left to purge.

Once she was finally finished, he flushed the toilet for her, then handed her a damp washcloth to clean her face.

"I'm sorry. This is so embarrassing."

Helping her to her feet, he tucked a bit of her hair behind her ear. "Don't be silly. You should be proud. I've seen volcanic eruptions that were less productive."

She laughed, then groaned. "I don't feel very good."

He handed her a cup of water. "Drink this."

She did as ordered, but her stomach roiled. "Ugh. That might have made it worse."

"Come with me." He was gentle as he led her to her bed, even more so when he unzipped her dress and slid the sleeves down over her shoulders, kneeling so she could lean on him for support while she stepped out of it. Then he stood, reaching around her to unclasp her bra. He drape her dress and bra on her dresser.

While he opened the top dresser drawer to search for something for her to wear, she took one of his hands and placed it over her breast. He humored her, cupping her breast, rubbing his thumb over her nipple. The deep, centering sensation helped to pull her out of the spinning vortex that had her in its grasp.

"Arms up," he instructed.

She complied, lamenting the loss of his touch while he settled her favorite constellation night shirt over her head.

"Now," he said, turning her around and giving her a swat on her ass, "into bed with you."

When Sunny came to again, it was after midnight. Her head pounded, her throat was dry, but her heart was light.

She Vcommed him. <You are the most chivalrous of gentlemen, although part of me wishes you weren't.>

After a moment, he replied, <Part of me wishes you hadn't consumed the entire bar. How are you?>

<Alive, but barely. Did I wake you?>

<No. I was finishing my puzzle.>

She laughed out loud. <Who are you? Are you a real person?>

<Aye,> he said. <Cross my heart. I've got the parents to prove it and everything.>

<They looked lovely. I'm assuming that's who you were standing with in that picture on your wall.>

<It was. And they are lovely, thank you.>

She rolled onto her belly, immediately regretting the motion as the throbbing behind her temples intensified. <What are their names?>

<Isla is my mum, and Ethan is my da.>

<Your mother is beautiful.>

<She is a vision, and my da is a giant among men. I've been lucky. What are your parents' names?>

Sunny thought she heard hesitation in his voice with this question. He'd been so careful not to ask her anything too personal, so cautious with respecting her barriers. As a result, the strangest thing had happened: all she wanted to do was let them down for him, only for him. Even with the anniversary of Jonathan's accident so close—maybe especially because of that. Five years seemed long enough to hold pain so tightly against her heart when there might be someone willing to share it with her. Someone she could trust enough to take a bit of the hurt and loss and fear and make it theirs so she didn't have to carry it all by herself. She wondered if Freddie could do that for her.

<Charity and Cosmo,> she replied.

< Well, that explains a lot.>

<Hey,> she groused. <What's that supposed to mean?>

His laughter drifted warmly between her ears. <Nothing. Only that Sunastara is a rather unique name.>

<Ah yes. Charity and Cosmo are card-carrying hippies.>

<Where did it come from, your name?>

She reached blindly for the cup of water Freddie had left by her bed, then took a tentative sip, waiting to see how her stomach responded. <My mother wanted to name me Sun, my father Star. They compromised.>

After a lengthy pause, he said, <I love your name. It's beautiful. *You* are beautiful.>

She buried her smile into her pillow. <And you are very charming. And handsome.> Nausea, sudden and unwelcome, churned in her belly. <But I think I need to go back to bed.>

<Should you drink some more water first?>

<Already have. Luckily, someone left me a full glass on my nightstand.>

<Whoever did that must be very thoughtful.>

She bit her lip. <One of the most thoughtful people I have ever met.>

In the ensuing silence, she wondered if he'd clicked off, if she'd said something wrong. But she had only spoken the truth. It was her job to be helpful, thoughtful, to anticipate someone's needs before they were even aware they had them. It was exceedingly rare that someone anticipated hers.

She nearly clicked off the Vcomm and berated herself for being too forward when he finally said, <You take care of everyone aboard this ship. You deserve to be taken care of too. Thank you for letting me. May you have sweet dreams, Sunastara Jeka.>

Her relieved heart swooned. <You too, Freddie... *Wait*, what is your last name?>

After a beat, <It's Carruthers.>

<Frederick Carruthers? Seriously? Even your name is old fashioned!>

<I know. I had little choice in how I turned out. Nobody's asking Freddie Carruthers to the hip hangouts, are they?>

<Certainly not if he'd called them 'hip hangouts.' Well, good night Freddie Carruthers. Is that like the third or fourth? That has to be a family name, right? Handed down from your great-great-great-grandfather, perhaps?>

<All right, missy. I think that's quite enough. But yes, I am Frederick Caruthers the third. And good night.>

<Freddie?> she said before he could click off.

<Yes?>

<Thank you. For helping me. For being kind. For being you. I think,> her eyes slammed shut as she gathered her nerve, <I think I like you very much.>

And then, after another moment: <That is very good news. Even if you are still drunk.>

He clicked off, and she rolled onto her back again, staring at the swirling tile patterns on her pod's ceiling. He was right, she was still drunk. But only drunk enough to have said things she might not have said otherwise, not so drunk she didn't mean them.

21

THE PODS

"WHAT DO YOU HAVE IN STORE FOR GARRAN AND KASA TOMORROW night?" Freddie asked as they made their way from the breakfast buffet on deck seven back to the staffroom for morning meeting.

Sunny felt like a new woman after sleeping straight through the rest of the night. Waking up to a well-dressed Freddie at her door with a cup of coffee and two anti-nox tabs didn't hurt either.

"He's taking Kasa to dinner, then they're going to the masquerave in the small ballroom on deck five, so I'm thinking stealth. We could pretend to be working the party, then listen in through his VC, provide pointers."

"Or," he interjected, "just hear me out. It's a costume party, correct? We *could* dress up, pretend to be attending the masquerave ourselves."

Sunny slowed to a stop. "Darling, have you ever even been to a rave?"

"No. But they've always sounded fun. Flashing lights, loud music, hot." His brow jumped. "Sweaty."

She tried to hide her smile. "I'll consider it." Then she wheeled around again, pointing a finger into his chest. "But it's still work. Only work."

His hands rose in surrender, wide eyes as innocent as a school-boy's. "Of course it's only work." His eyes narrowed. "Why? What did *you* have in mind?"

Morning meeting went as well as could be expected. Rax and Morgath—both looking a bit haggard—reported that they'd tripled the security mechs assigned to Chahna and her family as well as installed an outrageous number of Vcams not only around her suite but all around the ship. How they got the credits approved for the enhanced security was beyond Sunny, and she was not about to ask.

Tig still hadn't found the source of the breaches, but she'd narrowed her suspected targets down to Ulaperia, Vorp, or Gorbu-lon-7. Only two weeks remained before the ship reached Portis and the senator disembarked, one of which would be spent enter-taining Kravaxians. It would be a miracle, Sunny thought, if they made it through without incident.

Rather out of character, Elanie had not attended the meeting. She hadn't answered any of Sunny's comms either, so when Elanie's voice popped into her head just as she and Freddie were about to part ways in the hallway to go about their days, Sunny grabbed his hand and asked him to wait a moment.

<Sunny. Where are you?> Distress rang through Sunny's head. Elanie was never distressed.

<Outside the staffroom. Where the devil are you?> she replied.

<Deck thirty-six. Something's wrong up here. Something is seri-ously, seriously wrong.>

"What is it?" Freddie asked, frowning.

"I'm not sure. Elanie says something's happening up on deck thirty-six."

<I need more information Elanie. What *exactly* is wrong?>

<*Stars above*, Sunny. Everyone is...they're all... Why?> She made a gagging noise. <Just get up here, please.>

Sunny clicked off. "Well, whatever it is, it's enough to make Elanie gag." She straightened. "I guess I'm going up to thirty-six. Care to join me?"

Freddie nodded. "If whatever's going on up there is bad enough to gross out a bionic, you might need some assistance."

Sunny felt it immediately once the elevators opened on deck thirty-six—a thick, raw tension hanging heavily in the air, like someone had pulled back a moon-sized harp string and was seconds away from letting it spring free.

"What is that?" She shook her head, trying to clear the warm, dense fog sinking over her.

Before Freddie could answer, Elanie raced between them to take their place in the elevator. Pale and repulsed, she looked from Sunny to Freddie, then said, "Good luck," as the doors closed on her.

Sunny stared at the elevator doors and then at Freddie, finding a perfect match for her bewildered expression. Music floated through the air toward them, entrancing and atmospheric as they turned and walked warily down the hall toward the central hub of restaurants, stores, and one very popular strip club on this extremely racy deck.

Freddie bent down to pick something up from the floor, pulling Sunny's gaze to his backside. She sucked her lower lip into her mouth.

Freddie turned, his lips red as cherries, his eyes smoldering, lingerie dangling from his finger. "I think someone's lost their bra." Dropping the bra back to the floor, he blinked several times, then rubbed his eyes. "Something's happening to me. I feel"—he tugged on his collar—"strange."

Tearing her eyes from his, she glanced around the hallway. He was right. *Because he was always right and delicious, and she needed to lick his body from head to toe right this instant.* Sunny slapped herself hard across her face, trying to center her spiraling thoughts.

Discarded clothes decorated the hallway—dresses, pants, even Argosian coveralls littered the space, draped over the wall hangings and dangling haphazardly from the light fixtures.

"Follow me," Sunny said, barely hearing her own voice over the blood rushing in her ears. Every step she took felt like fighting the tide as currents of desire surrounded her, spinning her around, pulling her back toward him.

"Sunny. This is... I'm..." His voice came out strained and hoarse. It raised the hairs on her arms, tiny shivers of ecstasy racing through her with each word from his lips.

"I know, darling. Just keep walking."

When they reached the end of the hallway where it opened into the foyer, Sunny couldn't believe her eyes. Writhing on the floor, sprawled over chairs and couches, even half-submerged in the fountain, a naked, moaning, multi-species free-for-all grinded away with reckless abandon.

Freddie's eyes bulged from their sockets. "What the *fuck* is going on here?"

His swearing stunned a barked laugh out of Sunny, providing a respite from the incessant onrush of mindless wanting long enough for a single coherent thought to override her short-circuiting brain: *I know what this is. I have felt this way before, seen people act this way before.*

She scanned the atrium and finally found the perpetrator of this depravity. A bank of pleasure pods along a far wall, all open, bright red light spilling from them like wine from a glass.

"It's the pleasure pods. They're malfunctioning." She fanned her neck as a single bead of sweat made a path down her spine for more to follow. "All of them."

Freddie loosened his tie, then he unbuttoned the top button of his shirt. "That's not good. We should probably tell somebody, right?" He swiped the back of his hand over his brow.

"Yes, definitely. We should tell someone because—" *Because... what?* Because something, she was sure. But she couldn't keep track of her thoughts. She closed her eyes, overwhelmed by the scene before her, by the hormones pumping through her bloodstream as the pleasure pods hacked her hypothalamus and pushed her pleasure center into overdrive.

"Are you okay?" asked Freddie, moving to stand behind her.

Air rushed out of her as his breath skimmed over her skin. "I don't think so," she whispered. The heat radiating from his body warmed her, soothed her, so thoroughly her head fell back to rest against his shoulder.

His fingertips traced softly down the curve of her neck, over her shoulder, down her arm. She reached back, grasping his hip. Lowering his lips to her ear, he whispered the one word that set her on fire, that set her free, *"Phoebe."*

Spinning around, she grabbed him by his tie and pulled his lips to hers. He broke away from the kiss, his eyes blazing as he pointed his chin over her shoulder toward a utility closet. She nodded, licked her lips, and they barreled through the door.

Her hands had minds of their own, and they grabbed at his coat, his shirt, his tie, tearing his clothes from him as quickly as they could. She laughed as he pushed her up against a shelf, then moaned when he bit gently at her neck.

He dropped to his knees before her, raising her shirt with his nose to kiss her belly while his deft fingers undid her belt clasp, unzipped her zipper, and slid her pants down over her hips. Her panties soon joined the rest of their clothes in a heap in the corner.

She let him ease her legs apart, his hands gliding over her hips as his lips skimmed up along her inner thigh. When his mouth reached the apex of her thighs, he only had to breathe on her and she was gone, gasping as waves of pleasure crashed over her again and again in an unrelenting surge.

"I'm sorry," he breathed against her. "I didn't want it to be like this. I wanted to be patient. But, *stars save me*, I need—"

She grabbed a fistful of his hair and pulled until he looked up at her. "If you're not inside me in five seconds—"

It only took him three.

She drowned in phenomenal, scorching, neuro-hacked bliss. The sensations were all encompassing, pulsing through her in time with his hips, every single thrust into her becoming ecstasy incarnate. It was magnificent. *He* was magnificent. It was so much more than she'd ever felt before with a man. She never, ever wanted it to end. And after her third orgasm and his second, she realized in a brief moment of lucidity that it might actually never end. And that would be bad, probably.

"Our guests," she slurred, her head hanging over his shoulder, pleasure so intense she could barely speak coursing through her. "Need help."

"Yes." He pulled back, his eyes heavy lidded, his lips parted. "Who though? Who could help?"

Right. If anyone else came up here, they'd suffer this same fate. Well maybe not this exact same fate—this fate belonged only to them, just them, forever. She kissed him again as he hardened once more inside her. Distantly, she wondered if anyone had ever died from an orgasm overdose.

They moved to the floor, and she sat up in his lap, kissing him and running her fingers through his hair. It felt so soft, each strand unique in the way it slid through her fingers. "Were we talking about something?"

Sweat glistened between their bodies, and they slid slowly over each other, slippery and warm. He drew a single finger down the center of her spine. "Help. We need to get help." He bit her shoulder, and the sharp sensation brought her momentarily to her senses.

"Elanie. She hasn't upgraded yet. She's immune. She was able to walk away."

He nibbled on her earlobe. "Vcomm her. She can help."

It was insurmountably difficult to access her VC, like sifting through wet sand. <Elanie. Help. It's the pleasure pods. You're our only hope.>

Elanie groaned into her mind. <I have to come back up there? Are you kidding me right now? Why can't you fix it?>

<Too...hard,> Sunny replied, laughing at the irony before a thrusting of Freddie's hips pulled her back down to drown in the sea of sensation. <Only you. Hurry.>

She could feel the moment Elanie finally unplugged the pods, like the silent calm after the storm, waves receding back into the ocean, like waking up from the most wonderful dream. She still sat in his lap, his hands cupping her ass, sweat dripping down her back, his forehead resting against hers. Not a bad place to come to, all things considered.

She ran her fingers up his back, over his shoulders, along his neck, burying them into his hair. "*Holy hell.*"

He laughed, his shoulders shaking as he leaned back to look at her. "Are you all right?" His eyes were glossed over, his cheeks flushed, his hair sticking to his forehead in little sweaty strands.

"I'm not sure I'll be able to walk tomorrow, but I'm fine." She smiled. "Better than fine."

Blinking once, twice, as if clearing out the last remnants of wildness, he asked, "How long have we been in here?"

She accessed the time. "An hour and a half."

"Good lord! That long? How?"

She brushed his damp hair back from his forehead. "Have you never been in a pleasure pod before?"

He shook his head. "They've always intimidated me—and for good reason, it seems."

"You don't notice time when you're in one, or if you're hungry or thirsty or if your hair is on fire, for that matter. The only single thing you notice is the pleasure."

And with this word, they realized at the same time that they were still joined, that he was still inside her. He made to pull away, but she squeezed her legs around him, grasping at his shoulders. "Wait, don't go. Not yet."

He settled back down, his arms slung low around her hips, one hand pressed against her lower back. "No?"

After what they'd just done and how many times they'd done it, it seemed ridiculous to be as nervous as she was. What they had just shared was intense, carnal, worlds-shattering ecstasy. It had left her breathless, her body heavy, muscles loose, skin as warm as an afternoon lying under real sunlight. But she still wasn't sated. She still wanted...him, so much it terrified her. But for this, for him, for his unfailing kindness, his enormous heart, his old-fashioned and impossible-to-deny charm, she would be brave. *Congratulations, Joshua, you king among men, you have managed to woo Phoebe into complete and utter submission.*

Boldly, she whispered, "Stay with me. Make love to me," into his ear.

For a moment, he simply stared at her as they shared breaths, softly, in and out like the tide. Then he leaned forward to lay her down, pulling a towel over from one of the shelves for her to use as a pillow.

They were exhausted and sore, but it didn't matter. And even with the frenzied drive of the pods diminished, they still had enough hacked hormonal encouragement racing through their veins that they were both ready and able.

Propped above her on straight arms, he gazed down, his nose still glistening with sweat.

She ran her fingers over the crooked line of it. "How did this happen? Did you break it?"

"Aye," he said, and her toes tingled—she loved it when he said *aye*. "When I was fourteen. It was a misguided attempt at chivalry when an older and much larger boy made unwanted advances on a lass from my class. I told him to stop, he broke my nose, and that was that."

Her hand moved to cup his cheek. "Did he leave her alone?"

He turned to kiss her palm. "He did actually."

"Did she thank you?"

"Aye, Molly McDay. My very first kiss."

Her hand snaking around his neck, she said, "Lucky lass," before pulling him down onto her, bringing his mouth to hers.

This kiss was deep and sweet, and she disappeared into it as they moved together, of their own free will, slowly at first, then faster, pushing each other up one side of the wave to crest, break, and collapse onto the shore, clinging to each other throughout the entire ride.

22

BLISS

THE FALLOUT FROM WHAT WOULD GO DOWN IN HISTORY ON THE SHIP as "Podgate" wasn't as dire as Sunny had feared. The general consensus from early interviews of the beings on deck thirty-six during the pod malfunction was that fun was had by all. Not necessarily surprising, Sunny thought, considering the typical state of affairs on that deck. The final rule on the pod malfunction—"excessive overuse"—didn't surprise Sunny either. All the same, new and more stringent safety measures were being installed on all pleasure pods throughout the ship.

And while fun was certainly had by Sunny as well, she was brutally sore—everywhere. She'd never been so completely worked. When she'd checked in with Freddie this morning, he'd reported finding himself in a similar condition. After making sure she felt okay with everything that had happened between them, which she did, he'd also reported, multiple times, that yesterday had been phenomenal.

Despite the delicious aching in her muscles, her bones, her *loins*, Sunny still had a job to do. And today that job entailed first meeting with the senator, Sai, and Lena for breakfast in their pod where they'd discussed any continued security concerns while

Sunny had tried her hand at one of Sai's new puzzles, this one a complicated series of lock tumblers and hidden switches that she'd been entirely unable to solve.

But now, much to her chagrin, it was her duty to shepherd a gigantic, hairy, stinky Kravaxian bovine through her ship. The smell originating from airlock A-6 was rank enough to put a Gorbie off their lunch, and Gorbies thought fermented bog slugs were a delicacy.

Even though the Delphinian Wizards couldn't magic Sunny a kurot (Dave the goat was evidently a one-trick pony), she still managed to call in some favors and wrangle one of the foul, wooly beasts onto the ship before FFK day.

Burying her nose into the crook of her elbow to keep the stench out, she pressed her thumb onto a techpad to sign the shipping receipt and accepted the kurot's lead rope from the postal droid.

There were times in a person's life, Sunny thought, when the realization that they were in so far over their head felt as tangible as the ground beneath their feet. Walking from the airlock, pretending she could control a two-ton ungulate with a rope half the size of her wrist, was without question one of those times.

"Need help with that?"

Sunny wheeled around halfway to the Cosmic Spectacle stables and nearly fell to her knees as Makenna strode toward her.

"Yes. Yes, I do. Do you know anything about kurots? It keeps trying to chew on my hair. And, *stars above*, it stinks."

Makenna laughed, low and throaty. "Well, no. Not really. But I have been taking care of Dave for the last week, so... Heading to the stables?"

Sunny nodded, and as Makenna took the lead, she placed a hand onto the taller woman's shoulder and said, "Thank you, darling. With all my heart."

Makenna's petite slope of a nose scrunched. "Woof! It does stink, doesn't it? Like rotten cheese left in the sun."

"I'm not sure I'll ever get its scent out of my nose. And don't let it eat your hair."

Makenna pulled her dreads over her shoulder and away from the kurot. "Thanks for the warning."

The temptation to question Makenna about Chan as they continued their journey to the stables was significant. But every single effort Sunny had ever made to interfere in Chan's love life since he'd hired her onto the *Ignisar* had failed miserably. As difficult as it was to hold her tongue, she did. Well, almost.

"How long will you be staying with us, Makenna?"

Pulling free one of her dreadlocks that the kurot had managed to get into its mouth despite her attempts to hide them, Makenna muttered, "Yuck," while shaking a long string of its drool from her hand. "We're here until we dock in Portis."

"That long?" *Interesting.* "You'll be here for New Year's, then."

"I suppose so. Does the *Ignisar* celebrate?"

Sunny scoffed. "We certainly do. If you thought the Fire Ball was something, just you wait. I'm glad you're staying. It was nice seeing you and Chan out together the other day. It's so rare that he does anything other than work." *Oops,* Sunny thought, *that was* definitely *interfering.*

Makenna slowed, her head turning. "Can I ask you something, Sunny?"

Successful interference, perhaps? "Of course, darling."

Her lips pursed thoughtfully. "Why hasn't Chan...? Why does he still...?" She trailed off. But Sunny knew what she was after.

Modern medicine could repair the damage to Chan's spine. But —as he'd confided in Sunny one very early morning a few years back while they'd watched sunrise sim over an empty bottle of Venusian bourbon—his injury was important to him.

"Did Chan ever tell you that he'd been a lieutenant in the Asteroid Belt Wars?

Makenna shook her head while the kurot stamped one of its front hooves impatiently.

"Of his entire unit, only he and a handful of his soldiers survived an ambush on the asteroid he was ordered to secure for LunaCorp. I'd asked him once why he kept his injury. He'd told me that the men and women he'd lost could no longer breathe or laugh or love or have children or grandchildren...and he could no longer walk. He'd said this was a small price to pay so that he never forgot them or their sacrifice."

"*Saints*," whispered Makenna. "I guess I understand why he would feel that way. But still, does he honestly think they'd want that from him?"

Sunny considered this, her brows knitting together, but the kurot diverted them from any further discussion on the matter by blowing a massive snort at a passing cleaning drone the beast was quite certain had been sent to kill her.

"Whoa, big lady," Makenna soothed before leading the kurot into the stables. She handed the animal's rope over to one of the stable hands, a young, rangy human with a beak of a nose who accepted the rope from her the way one might accept a rotten fish.

"What the hell is this?" the man asked, his accent placing him squarely from New Earth, New York. "Looks like a cow on steroids." The kurot sneezed into his face, generating a barked string of profanities from the man. Outrage percolated up his neck, covering his throat with bright-red patches as Sunny took the time to explain what the kurot was, why it was here, and how it would need to be milked twice daily, by hand. Wisely, she chose not to add, *for Kravaxian bathwater.*

Makenna and Sunny left man and beast to each other, but before they went their separate ways, Sunny reached out and squeezed her shoulder. "Thank you, darling. You are a life saver."

"Nothing to it, Sunny," she insisted, but a touch of color had climbed into her cheeks.

Sunny could never resist capitalizing on a blush, so she made her move, staring directly into Makenna's eyes. "Chan was right, you do have the most magnificent eyes. And he described them perfectly, like amber poured into a bright-blue sea."

Sunny left Makenna red faced and stammering, a skill she'd honed over many years and one in which she felt immensely proud.

"How do I look?"

Garran wore his customary yellow coveralls, but his eyes hid behind a silver satin mask with a sun on one side and two intersecting half-moons on the other, both encrusted with sparkling black gems. He'd also applied a healthy smudge of eyeliner to each eye, giving his eyes a depth under the mask and making his purple irises pop.

"Very sexy, darling. The eyeliner is perfection." Sunny blew a chef's kiss into the air. "How do you feel? Are you ready?"

He rubbed a hand over his freshly shaved chin. "I am. We have been speaking over our VCs at night, Kasa and I. After her mother goes to sleep."

"Ooh, do tell," Sunny encouraged.

He dipped his chin, his cheeks turning a deep burgundy. *Two for two with the blushing today.* Sunny gave herself a mental high five.

"She is very funny. And we both love the same flowers. When we get back to Argos, I will plant an entire field of tulips on my farm, in a rainbow pattern, just for her. And she is very proud." His eyes flashed up to Sunny's. "She is like you—proud, competent. I like that in a woman."

It was Sunny's turn to blush. "Darling, I'm not certain you need my help at all tonight. I think you've got this."

His eyes flashed wide beneath his mask. "No. I need you. Please. This is too important. I will mess it up." After a beat. "Is Freddie coming?"

"I'm on my way to pick him up." Sunny held her arms out wide. "How do *I* look?" When she'd opened her closet this evening, what to wear hadn't even been a question. Tonight she wore her favorite little black dress—Phoebe's dress—and she wore it proudly, boldly, and wholeheartedly on purpose.

"Beautiful," he said. "You look beautiful. Freddie will be very pleased."

Sunny coughed. "What's that?"

His booming laughter rattled the digpics on the walls. "Humans are so strange. You and Freddie are drawn to each other, it is as obvious as poppies in the snow. And yet you hide it. Deny it. Why?"

Sunny froze in place, her mouth gaping.

He stepped close, encircling her shoulder with his massive hand. "I have upset you. You look like an infant after dunking day."

She closed her mouth.

"You and Freddie," Garran continued, "there is *worth* between you. You fit." And then he left her, standing in his hallway, speechless.

"Bloody hell!" Freddie's expression was priceless.

Sunny raised her black cat mask from her eyes. "Hello to you too."

His head tilted as he said, very slowly, very carefully, "You're wearing the dress. Do you know that you're wearing the dress?" His hands slid into his pockets. "What I mean to say is did you *intend* to wear the dress?"

Sunny nodded, then held her breath as he took a step toward her, his eyes roving over her body. "You're sure you want to work tonight? We're passing the Spiral star cluster. We could go to the observatory."

Her conviction teetered as he leaned in to trail the tip of his nose along her neck. "Garran would have our heads," she protested weakly, fisting her hands at her sides so they didn't reach out for him. "He's nervous. Besides, after yesterday—"

"Mm-hmm, yesterday." Freddie's voice held a seductive rumble.

Sunny gasped. "Stop that."

"Stop what?" he asked, his breath warm on her neck, his lips just barely touching her skin.

With a hand pressed firmly into his chest, she pushed him back a step. "Stop Joshua-ing me." She shook herself out to the sound of his laughter. "We need to focus. We've got a job to do, and it doesn't involve making out in this hallway or whatever else you're devising behind those depraved eyes."

His mouth popped open, forming a shocked and innocent circle. "I was simply suggesting we go look at some stars. Ahem, those depraved eyes are up here, sweetheart."

Her own eyes snapped up from where they'd been openly gazing at his pants. "*Stars above!* I'm sorry. I don't know what's gotten into me."

"I do," he said without missing a beat.

She snorted, almost a guffaw. *This was atrocious.* "Can we go now? Please?"

"One moment." He disappeared into his pod, returning with his mask in hand. He looked good tonight. Very good. Dark-grey suit, black shoes, black tie, hair expertly coiffed. He was very well put together, and all Sunny wanted to do was take him apart.

He held an arm out, winking. "Ready whenever you are."

With her hand tucked into his elbow, they made their way to the Argosian restaurant on deck fourteen where Garran had planned to take Kasa. They found the pair sitting on opposite sides of a square table, not speaking, barely making eye contact.

"That's not good," Freddie whispered as they slid into a booth at the far end of the restaurant.

Sunny frowned. "Agreed. Let's patch in."

<Garran, darling. Don't look around. Don't panic.>

Too late. Despite Sunny's warning, the big man whipped his head around, knocking over the salt, then his glass of water when he tried to pick up the salt. Kasa scowled at him, unimpressed.

<Sunny, you startled me,> he Vcommed, wiping his coveralls down with a napkin. <But thank the Tilth you are here. I am floundering. We have already talked about the weather. Three times. And the weather is always the same on this ship.>

Freddie covered his laughter with his hand, having joined in on the comm.

<Tell me what to say,> Garran pleaded.

Raising a brow at Freddie, Sunny said, "This sounds like a manly job. He's all yours."

Freddie interlaced his fingers and pushed his palms out in front of him, cracking his knuckles. "I do love a challenge." He winked, grinning at Sunny, the implication clear that *she* was the challenge he referred to.

<Kasa looks lovely, Garran. Have you told her that?>

Through his VC, they heard Garran say, "I do not think I have told you how beautiful you look tonight, Kasa."

<That's good. Very good. You could also add something else, something specific only to her.> Freddie looked directly at Sunny. <Something like, I love what you've done with your hair tonight.>

Sunny reached up, her fingers brushing over the small black clasp holding back her bangs. She rarely did anything with her hair other than run her fingers through it. She smiled. <Yes, say that, Garran. Women love being complimented on their hair, especially if they've done something special to it,> she encouraged.

There wasn't much to Kasa's hairdo, a simple braid pulled tight. But her smile after Garran complimented her was fantastic as she ran a hand down to the tail of her braid.

<Have you asked her about her day?> Freddie inquired.

Sunny could see Garran's shoulders deflate. <No. What is wrong with me? I am terrible at this.>

<Not at all, big man. We all have to start somewhere,> Freddie

said. <But when you do ask her, really listen, don't just think about what you want to say next.>

<That will not be a problem,> grumbled Garran. <I do not *have* anything to say next.>

<Then you let her do the talking for a while,> Freddie instructed. <Don't contradict or interrupt her. Say yes more than no. And don't be afraid of a little silence. Be genuine, be kind, be curious. You've got this, Garran.>

Sunny couldn't stop staring at Freddie. "That was fine advice. Wonderful. *You* are wonderful."

His foot slid forward until his calf rested warmly against hers, and with a wry sparkle in his eye, he said, "Sunny, tell me about your day."

If they'd been alone, if the restaurant had been empty aside from them, Sunny would have joined him on his side of the table, taken his face in between her hands, and kissed him, softly at first, just a press of her lips against his. But then she'd slide into his lap, kiss his upper lip, then his lower lip, then she'd slip her tongue between them—

His head tipped to the side. "Are you still with me?"

Her eyes didn't move from his lips. "Yes. One hundred percent."

Those lips curled upward.

Dinner went off without a hitch. With Freddie's suggestions, the conversation began to flow freely between Kasa and Garran. As an unexpected result, Freddie and Sunny were able to eat as well and talk. He found her kurot wrangling story delightful. And she thought his tale of how he'd rescued a group of Ulaperians by publicly berating the "eejit" teenaged Mercurians who'd been terrorizing them by shining techpad lights directly into their milky, sensitive eyes, was very heroic.

When they left the restaurant and stepped into the masquerave,

Freddie gasped. It was a living, breathing revel. Flashing lights, trance music, phosphorescent glow paint, and guests dancing everywhere. Including, after much prodding, Garran and Kasa. Things appeared to be going smashingly between the pair, if Kasa's hand squeezing Garran's backside was any indication.

Freddie, who'd disappeared briefly, bounced up to Sunny on the dance floor, his black satin mask sitting crooked on his nose.

"Where have you been?" She squinted at him. He looked a mess. "And what have you been doing?"

"I've been over there," he said, waving at some indeterminate corner of the ballroom. "And here's what I've been doing." Grinning widely, he handed her a tiny blue pill.

She took the pill between her fingers. "Oh no. Darling, where did you get this?"

His head flicked over his right shoulder. "Those are them. Those are...they? I don't know the correct way to say it. The Ulaperian terrorizers. They wanted to apologize for being 'total dicks'—" He drew quotation marks into the air, affecting their bored, indolent, Mercurian accents "—so they gave me these pills."

Two teenaged boys stood against the wall, their heads hanging down, hands in their pockets, nodding to the beat of some song that wasn't actually playing.

"Tell me you haven't taken one yet." What they'd given Freddie, and what he'd given her, was a party drug called Bliss. It was a designer euphoria enhancer, fast acting and extremely potent.

"Two actually. They told me to take two. I've always wanted to try them." His smile was practically incandescent as he reached out to brush a finger down her arm. "Everything feels so *good*."

He took two! He'd be face-first in the punchbowl in another hour!

"Dance with me, Sunny. Please." His head fell back, his eyes glued to the ceiling, transfixed by the kaleidoscopic fractal lights swirling into one another above them. He started to move his shoulders. "I can feel the music. It's moving through me. It's part of me."

Sunny was going to murder those hooligans!

His eyes found hers. "Take yours. You need to feel this with me. It is phenomenal."

Not that she was averse to such things, but after swallowing a double dose of a mind-altering drug he had never taken before, he was going to need a babysitter. "Not tonight, darling."

<Garran. How are you fairing?> she Vcommed. She wasn't sure she could spare more time for Garran since she was about to have her hands full with Freddie once he became compelled to lick everyone in the ballroom.

<Good. Very good. Kasa says she wants to leave soon. What do I do?>

<That's wonderful, big guy,> Freddie chimed in brightly. <Do you want to know what I'd do? I'd take her back to your pod, run a steamy shower, and—>

Sunny muted Freddie from the conversation.

<What has gotten into him?> asked Garran

About one-hundred credits' worth of Bliss. <I think he's coming down with a cold. Listen, let her take the lead, do what feels right. Have fun, be safe, and make sure she comes first.>

Sunny clicked off the comm, watching on with pride as Kasa led Garran from the ballroom with her hand around his, Garran's masked eyes locked on her swaying hips.

Freddie's eyes, on the other hand, darted everywhere, his pupils blown, his mouth open in an awed expression. "It's all so beautiful. So...beautiful. I love every single person in this room. I feel like I know them, like I've always known them. Ever since I was a tiny baby, maybe even before then, when I was only stardust, I knew them. And I loved them."

Trying not to laugh, Sunny held her hand up in front of his face so he could touch it. His fingers ran over the lines of her palm, up and down the peaks and valleys of her fingers. She remembered enjoying this sort of thing when she'd been in his condition.

His fingers slid in between hers, grasping and drawing her to him. "Dance with me."

She straightened his mask and placed her hand onto his shoulder.

"You are breathtaking, Sunny," he told her. "And so considerate and funny and brilliant. I think we were meant to meet. There is a gravity between us." He pulled her flush against him. "Can you feel it?"

She knew he was rolling, but she found his sincerity difficult to ignore. She *could* feel it, this force drawing her to him. What was more, she was beginning to realize that she was powerless against it. Because here, in this crowded ballroom, against every single one of her better judgments, she closed her eyes, and she let him kiss her. Not only that, she kissed him back, slipping her fingers into his hair as his arms wrapped tightly around her waist.

This was bliss, right now, enveloped so completely in his arms. No pharmaceutical enhancement was required. This was true bliss. And maybe it was time she stopped fighting it and let it in, let him in. With the anniversary of losing Jonathan only days away, she needed to try. She needed to take a chance on having the kind of life she knew her son would have wanted her to have. But not tonight. Tonight she needed to get Freddie to bed before he started taking off his clothes.

Freddie had the focus of a child in a toy store as she ushered him from the ballroom to his pod. Everything was "fascinating" or "magnificent," that light fixture, this doorway, even the carpet. The carpet on deck twelve was evidently the most amazing thing since the discovery of faster-than-light drives. When they finally reached his pod, she took his hand and pressed it to his security panel, which he spent another thirty seconds marveling at.

"How do these even get made? Who? Who is able to make

these?" His voice dropped to a reverent whisper as he ran a fingertip over the panel again. "Geniuses, that's who."

Sunny couldn't hold back her laughter anymore. He was absolutely absurd.

"All right, you. Water, then bed," she instructed, finding a glass on his dresser and filling it with water from his sink.

"No." He shook his head. "No bed. Shower, let's take a shower. Take a shower with me. Please. Please, please, please."

His pleading would have been much more persuasive if he hadn't already crawled onto his bed, fluffing one of his pillows between his hands in pure wonder. "These are so fluffy. How have I never noticed how *fluffy* these are?"

She placed the back of her hand over his forehead. "You're hot, darling. Drink."

"No, you're the one who's hot, and gorgeous. And why does my mouth feel like I've eaten fifty balls of cotton?" He opened and closed his mouth in demonstration.

"I think this will help," she said, handing him the glass of water.

"Yes. Yes, you're right. You're so smart." After staring at the water, spinning the glass in his hand for a moment, he guzzled it down.

Sunny spun to fill the glass a second time, but when she turned back around, he had already passed out with his face smushed into one of his fluffy pillows, looking like a contented little baby. She slipped off his shoes, then his suit jacket and tie.

He mumbled something into his pillow, so she moved a bit closer. "What's that, darling?"

"So much. I love you so much," he said softly.

Her heart clenched painfully in her chest. Kneeling beside the bed, she traced feather-soft fingers over his eyebrows, down the crooked line of his nose, across his full lips. She'd done this same thing to him when he'd fallen asleep during their night together on the CAK. She'd wanted to commit him to memory then, to make him real for as long as she could before they'd left each other forever. And now, against outrageous odds, he was here. She didn't need to remember him. She didn't need to make him real. He *was* real. He was real and he was here and she could have him. If she wanted to, she could have him.

The words hovered on the tip of her tongue, *I love you too, Freddie*. She only had to say them. Just as she opened her mouth to whisper them into his ear, he spoke again.

"Serena. Serena, I love you."

23

WHO THE FUCK IS SERENA?

IN THE SPACE BETWEEN WHERE SUNNY KNELT PARALYZED AT THE SIDE of his bed to where Freddie slept peacefully, the universe expanded, pushing a cold and infinite emptiness between what was and what Sunny had only believed to be true. He was not hers. He never had been.

She'd never asked him if he had another woman. And she'd done little more than keep him firmly at arm's length, forcing him to pretend to be someone else entirely just to get close to her. It was no wonder he'd found another lover. Or maybe he'd been with one all along. She'd been so naïve to assume they were exclusive. He wasn't perfect. He was just a man. And she was just a fool.

She closed the door to his pod and stumbled numbly back to hers. With each step she took, one single question kept beating itself against her brain, *Who the fuck is Serena?*

Was she on this ship? A woman from back home on Venus? Maybe she was just his auntie. Some long-lost auntie he confessed his love for in his sleep. *Oh, for fuck's sake!*

She would not let this Serena person ruin her. She would not become a jealous woman. This was a blessing, really. A chance to take a step back—several steps, in fact—and reexamine things.

Things like, what kind of grown man enjoyed doing puzzles? And who wore bow-tie jammies? *Honestly?*

Once in her pod, she stripped down, seriously considered throwing her little black dress into the flash incinerator, then she stood under a shower so scalding it turned her skin red and tender when she emerged twenty minutes later, still not feeling clean.

She knew she wouldn't sleep. She knew she was in shock. She knew that her heart would hurt more in the morning than she could possibly fathom tonight. So she sat cross-legged in the middle of her bed, flipped on her TV, and stared at red, green, and blue pixels until her eyes stung.

Turned out, it didn't take until morning for her heart to realize it was broken.

< What happened to me last night?>

She hadn't moved from her spot in the middle of her bed, even though she'd heard lark song—her preferred alarm—through her VC nearly twenty minutes ago. She'd known he would Vcomm her this morning, but she was still not prepared for the way his voice grabbed the jagged pieces of her broken heart and squeezed until they pierced one another.

<*Bliss* is what happened, darling. Never take more than one pill at a time.> Her tone came out harsher than she'd intended. She'd been aiming for nonchalance but had landed on *And you said you loved another woman in your sleep* completely by accident.

He noticed. <Is everything all right? You sound upset. Did I do something awful? Did I embarrass you? I am so sorry if I did. I don't remember a thing.>

Dammit, Freddie. <Everything is fine. You were fine. *You* had fun.>

<Something's wrong,> he stated, his voice deadly serious.

Her heart pounded, her mouth bone dry, her fingers numb,

panic gripping her. She didn't want to say any of what she was about to say. But what choice did she have? She was in no way capable of having any sort of rational discussion with him about another woman he had feelings for. She was in love with him, desperately. As much as she'd tried to deny it, for the first time in five years she'd felt love again, hope. She'd rather not know the truth than risk learning for certain that her feelings were based on a lie. She wasn't that brave. Better to just cut it off before it was too late.

<Listen, Freddie—>

He responded quickly with, <Sunny. Please, don't,> and pain seared her chest.

<Please, Freddie, just listen. Last night I realized that this is all moving a bit too fast for me.> Sunny swallowed back the bile rising up her throat.

Silence responded on his end of the comm.

<I think I need some time. I need things to slow down.>

He uttered one single agonized word, <Why?>

She was not proud of what she was about to say, but it was the best she could come up with while she'd had this conversation with him in her mind two thousand times last night. <I don't understand why you would have taken *Bliss* without asking me first. You made a fool out of both of us. It *was* embarrassing.>

<Sunny, I am so sorry. You're absolutely right. I don't know what came over me. It just seemed like fun, and I thought for certain you'd take it with me. I was an inconsiderate, selfish wanker, and I am so, so sorry. Please forgive me.>

Listening to his apology, his very kind, very rational apology that she knew she could not accept...a single tear slipped down her cheek. She didn't recognize the sensation at first—a prickling behind her eye, wetness down her face. When she wiped the tear away, an icy self-loathing punched her in the gut.

Sunny had not cried, not once in five years. She'd never shed a single tear after Jonathon died. So many nights she'd sat up in her bed, trying to make the tears come, knowing that if they did, maybe she'd feel less guilty, less worthless, less devastated. They'd never come. And now, this was how it happened? This was what she could cry over? Not her son, but a man?

Fury, sudden and formidable, raged through her. She wasn't angry with Freddie but with herself for thinking she could ever have moved on, made a new life, been truly happy. There was no moving on, not from this kind of loss. Not ever.

<I forgive you, Freddie. But I think things have just gotten carried away between us and we—I—need a break.>

His voice trembled. <Please, Sunny. Don't do this. Not like this. I love y—>

She clicked off the comm, eyes dry once again, chest cold and empty.

Avoiding Freddie would be difficult but not impossible. They had a staff meeting this morning, then the entire day would be spent preparing for FFK arrival. She could easily keep herself busy with the work of staging the Kravaxians' rooms, including stocking their refrigerators and minibars with their requested snacks and beverages—gelatinized trestal eggs, dried gwarfs, crater eel jerky, and, surprisingly, fruit punch.

She knew she couldn't avoid Freddie forever but for the next few days, she needed to not see him or talk to him or have anything *explained* to her or be forced to *explain* anything back. She just couldn't do it.

<You're late. Again.>

<Good morning, Elanie. I am on my way. How is it in there?> Sunny asked, trying to sound like she wasn't a walking, talking bruised heart.

<It is aggressively uncomfortable. I don't think Tig has slept in two days, Rax and Morgath won't speak to or make eye contact with

anyone, Chan keeps looking around like he expects the room to explode, and Freddie is an absolute mess. I've never seen him like this. Did something happen to him?>

To him? *Really, Elanie?* <I couldn't say.> Sunny's tone was flat as stone.

Elanie remained silent for a moment, and then she said a simple, understated, and far-too-understanding <I see.>

When Sunny walked into the staffroom, she planned to smile amiably at everyone around the table, take a seat, zone out completely during the meeting, and then be the first one to leave. But when she saw Freddie, she couldn't summon a single grin.

He sat hunched forward, his face pale, his eyes sunken and rimmed in red. Elanie wasn't exaggerating. He *was* a mess. Sunny felt wretched.

<Sunny, can we talk? Please?> His voice was in her head. It wasn't fair. This was not the time. She had things to do, important things. She was a very busy woman.

<Of course,> she replied coolly while taking her seat, the one closest to the door, no longer looking at him—because she couldn't.

<After the meeting?> he asked.

Chan saved her from having to answer. "Good morning, everyone. Today is FFK day! I trust you all know your responsibilities?"

"Keeping trained killers from destroying our ship," interjected Rax.

"Check," supplied Morgath, drawing a checkmark in the air with a finger.

Both men were armed to the teeth with nonlethals: flash grenades, chuck-cuffs, short-range jammers, paresis-darts, sonic cannons. Some sort of massive laser gun thing Sunny had never seen before sat on the table in front of Morgath. She didn't even want to know what that was. The twins would make the warmest of welcoming committees, she thought.

"Good morning." The deep, commanding voice behind Sunny pulled her out of her misery-haze and up to her full attention.

"Captain, Co-Captain," stammered Chan, shocked. "How wonderful to see you both this morning."

When the captains entered the room, silence followed.

"Excuse our intrusion," said Declan. "We won't take more than a moment of your time." He didn't wait for a response. "As you know, LunaCorp is sending Kravaxians to holiday aboard the *Ignisar* today, as well as train with some of you."

Rax grumbled, summoning a scathing *don't you dare* glare from Chan.

Sunny met Morgan's eyes to find them narrowed back at hers. Then, to Sunny's abject horror, Morgan looked over at Freddie, frowned deeply, then looked back at Sunny. Morgan always seemed to know everything about everyone on her ship.

Sunny needed this meeting to be over immediately.

"We want you to know how important this visitation is for this ship as well as for our employer. I have no doubt we will all treat our friends from Kravax with the professionalism and hospitality we are known throughout the KU for." Declan looked directly at Rax and Morgath, who, wisely, remained silent.

Morgan spoke next. "We know there may be some reservations about this visit and that we all have our own preconceived notions about Kravaxians. But we can assure you that there is nothing to worry about. These are not barbaric deep-space raiders. These are bright, dedicated men and women who just want to move their planet into the thirty-first century. Thank you for all your hard work getting ready for this visit." She winked at Sunny. "I heard we were even able to secure a kurot. Prime work."

After Chan thanked the captains for their visit, they left as quickly as they'd arrived, Morgan giving Sunny a concerned glance before following Declan out the door. Even though the mood in the room seemed to lift in their wake—the captain's show of support for the FFK initiative setting nerves at ease—Sunny felt like she wanted to crawl out of her skin.

<Elanie, please do not look at me. But I need your help,> Sunny Vcommed as the meeting wound down.

<What can I do?> Elanie's tone—there was something wrong with it. It was thoughtful and somber and...sympathetic.

<I don't want to talk about it. So please don't ask. But I need you to find me directly after this meeting and tell me there is an emergency situation at the buffet on the main deck that requires my immediate attention.>

<The buffet? And you think he'll believe that?> There was the snark, *thank the stars.* Sunny was worried she and Elanie might have been having a moment, and she couldn't handle that right now.

<I don't particularly care what he believes.>

<Listen, Sunny, I know this isn't my specialty, but if you ever change your mind and want to talk about it, I'm here.>

Sunny swallowed hard because she'd been right and they *were* having a damned moment. <Thank you, darling,> she managed.

When Chan ended the meeting, Sunny stood, turned, and tried very hard not to bolt for the door.

Freddie followed her. He was surprisingly fast. "Sunny, please wait."

She slowed, then stopped, then turned around. Up close, he looked even more miserable.

"Look, I know I messed up. But can we try to work through this."

This filled Sunny with a bright, irrational rage. He wanted to work through the fact that he was in love with another woman?

"There. Right there." He pointed at her face. "That face. You are furious with me. Something else is going on besides me taking drugs at a rave. What is it? Why won't you tell me?"

He looked so innocent, so desperate. It wasn't fair. *She* was supposed to be the one who looked like that right now, not him. Instead, she just looked angry.

"Sunny, there's an emergency situation at the buffet on the main deck that requires your immediate attention," Elanie said after walking up to them, repeating Sunny's request verbatim and without any inflection, just like the half robot she was. Sunny should have asked Tig to help instead.

Freddie's exasperated "Puh!" called out both Sunny and Elanie on this obvious ruse.

Sunny dared to meet his eyes, finding them bloodshot and pained. "I have to go, Freddie. I've got work to do."

His face contorted further, Sunny's heart gripped in the creases that formed between his brows.

"We can talk," she conceded, buckling under the weight of his staggeringly sad, puppy dog stare. "But later. Let's get through the Kravaxians. Then we can talk."

He nodded, relief that she'd thrown him this tiny bone sweeping over his features. "All right. I'm here. I'll be here."

Feeling like the biggest asshole in the entire KU, Sunny spun on her heel and walked to the elevators. After she stepped inside, she turned around in time to see Elanie standing with Freddie, her hand resting on his arm, his head hanging down.

<Sunny, have a minute?>

She was standing in one of the Kravaxian's rooms when this Vcomm came through, programming the walls to display surprisingly beautiful digpics of their planet. Not the barren wasteland she had somehow pictured, Kravax was lush and mountainous. It reminded her a little of Tranquis.

<Of course, Tig. What can I do for you?>

<Well, I've found out some stuff.> Tig sounded knackered.

<Darling, when's the last time you slept?>

She skirted the question. <Remember the senator's Proposition 2126?>

<I do.>

<I did some research to see what about it might make the senator a target.>

<Find anything?> Sunny asked, programming another pic.

<Nothing. By all accounts it's a fairly benign proposition requesting increased Imperion funding for deep-space exploration and practically identical to a bill passed by the senate ten years ago.>

<That's it? Hardly seems like something that would inspire hacking into a LunaCorp database and threatening a woman and her family.>

<I know,> Tig agreed. <It doesn't make any sense at all. But it makes me wonder why the senator brought it up. Think you should talk to her?>

Sunny nodded. <I will. Just as soon as I can. Thank you, Tig. Did you find anything more about who the hackers might be?>

<No. The signal keeps bouncing between Vorp and Gorbulon-*Seven* and occasionally, oddly enough, Portis. Once it even pinged across the wormhole to Neptune of all places. It's maddening.>

After selecting the last digpic, Sunny sighed at the walls. <Take a break, love. Get some sleep before your trainee arrives.>

Tig groaned. <I hope they don't expect me to make conversation. You know how awkward I am with new people. Can you imagine how awkward I'm gonna be with a Kravaxian?>

<If it's any consolation, I think we're all going to be feeling awkward and nervous. But it's only for a week. It'll be over in a blink.>

<The longest blink in the history of the cosmos,> Tig grumbled, then clicked off.

Sunny sat on the edge of the bed, exhausted, mentally and physically. With Freddie, the Kravaxians, the anniversary looming... it was a lot. And for a moment, sitting there, she let herself feel it— the disappointment, the pain, the sorrow. The sheer crushing weight of it and how easily it could pull her down and never her let go if she'd let it astounded her. But she didn't have time for that now.

Instead, she stood and shook herself out. Only one thing would keep her going, the same thing that had kept her afloat for the last five years. She straightened her shirt, pinched her cheeks, and got back to work.

24

FFK DAY

"WELCOME ABOARD. WE TRUST YOUR TRAVEL WAS UNEVENTFUL." Chan had donned his finest suit and looked absolutely smashing. Sunny was half-tempted to go find Makenna just so she could see him looking so polished.

Chan, Freddie, and Sunny waited outside the airlock where the FFKs' shuttle had just docked with the *Ignisar*, unloading their special guests. The Kravaxians were all tall, all with dark-brown eyes, pale skin, and black hair. Sunny wasn't exactly sure what she'd expected, but she was strangely disappointed. There were no necklaces made of noses or finger-bone earrings. She didn't even see a single menacing tattoo. Instead, the men wore fine suits, the women black skirts and white blouses, and one of the two women stunned in fabulous shoes, red heels with thin straps that wrapped twice around her ankles. If Sunny thought in a million years she'd ever be dying to know where a Kravaxian had bought her shoes...

"I am Sunastara, your hospitality specialist." She nodded to them. It wasn't quite a bow but close. According to the sensitivity training Freddie had provided the crew, Kravaxians found hand-shakes disagreeable.

One of the men stepped forward, the tallest and oldest of the quartet, mid to late thirties in standard years, if Sunny had to wager. He had a heavy brow, a jawline that looked chiseled from marble, and the broad chest of someone who spent a great deal of time lifting heavy things.

"My name is Tano." He waved a hand toward the woman standing grimly next to him, her chin jutting out proudly, her arms held stiffly at her sides. "This is my partner, Marisia." Then to the younger man to his right, who had a naturally wry twist to his mouth and big, friendly eyes. "My associate, Axel." Lastly, he introduced the striking woman wearing the phenomenal shoes. She was younger than the rest, maybe Tig's age, with fine, bird-like features and a hesitant smile. "And this is Reya."

Reya stepped forward and, evidently not finding the practice *too* disagreeable, reached out to shake Sunny's hand.

Sunny took it without hesitation. "It is wonderful to meet you all. Welcome to the *Ignisar*."

"Thank you," Reya said, her voice quiet but unwavering. "It's wonderful to meet all of you as well."

Sunny's gaze slid from the delightfully pleasant Reya back to Tano. He cut an intimidating figure with the efficient air of someone used to being in charge, but he also looked strangely familiar. It was something in the cheekbones, Sunny thought.

He squinted back at her, suspicious, so she concealed her assessment of him with a pleasant, benign smile as Freddie took a moment to introduce himself to the Kravaxians, his hands remaining respectfully in his pockets.

Before Sunny led the FFKs to their suites, she leaned over to whisper into Chan's ear that he should cruise around Makenna's pod before he changed out of his suit.

"Good idea," he whispered back.

Sunny sensed Freddie there beside her, that gravity between them pulling her eyes to his. But while irresistible forces might dictate the movements of the cosmos, they did not dictate hers.

Facing forward, she said, "Please, follow me," to the FFKs and walked straight out of the airlock.

After Sunny showed Tano and Marisia to their shared suite, she led Axel and then Reya to their private rooms.

"This is very nice," said Reya, running her fingers over her bed linens. "Thank you, Sunastara."

"Please, call me Sunny. And you are more than welcome. I'm glad you find the room adequate."

"Oh, it's more than adequate," she beamed. She really did have a lovely smile. "I have never seen such a beautiful room, let alone slept in one. I was raised on a ship, although one much smaller than this. It feels nice to be back off-planet." Her straight, sable hair —just brushing her chin on one side and hanging nearly to her collarbone on the other—slid forward as her head dropped to examine the stitch work on her duvet.

"Who are you training with during your stay?" Sunny crossed her fingers behind her back.

"IT, I believe. Someone named Tig?"

Sunny grinned. Of all the FFKs, Reya was by far the best option for Tig. She was young, talkative, not at all intimidating. "That's wonderful. Tig is one of my dearest friends, and she is absolutely brilliant. I'm certain she'll show you everything you want to know."

Reya's cheeks flushed. "We know how much of a risk it is for you all to accept us onto your ship. We know of our people's reputations. And we appreciate you—all of you. We just want to make our planet safer, stronger, with more legitimate opportunities for young people like me. That's all."

Sunny believed this young woman. She wasn't knowledgeable enough in the ways of Known Universal commerce to deduce what LunaCorp's long game was with Kravax, but she believed this was what Reya thought she was doing for her planet. And who could ever fault her for that?

"Get situated, have a rest. Dinner is in two hours with the rest of the crew. You can meet Tig. The refrigerator and minibar are stocked, and there is fresh kurot milk next to your bathtub."

Reya snorted, then began to laugh through her hand pressed over her mouth.

Sunny frowned. "What's so funny?"

"Only my ancestors bathed in the milk of kurots! That tradition is orthodox and has not been practiced in ages. Where on Kravax did you find kurot milk?"

Sunny's mouth could not open any wider if the kurot currently stinking up the Cosmic Spectacle stables had stomped on her foot. "You're kidding me."

Reya dissolved into laughter again. Sunny couldn't help but join her.

"I had the thing shipped all the way from the CAK! And they only had one because there is an interplanetary petting zoo in their Central Park. It was just dumb luck that the one they had happened to be female."

"Orion's eye!" Reya exclaimed. Perhaps some Kravaxian slang. "I'm so sorry to put you through all that trouble. But, if I am being honest, Tano is very old fashioned and still holds to many outdated religious customs and beliefs. He might actually enjoy bathing in kurot's milk."

"Then it has all been worth it."

When Sunny left Reya's room, she felt sufficiently distracted, better by a sight, and far less worried about the FFKs than she'd been before their arrival. They were only beings, just like everyone else, trying to make something of themselves and seizing an opportunity that had been presented to them. But now she had two hours until dinner with little to do—an uncomfortable amount of time. She *should* get some sleep. She *would*, instead, Vcomm Elanie and ask her to meet up at the restaurant bar to pregame before dinner. Thankfully, Elanie had a break in her jam-packed schedule.

Two martinis later, Sunny felt the tightness binding her chest all day finally loosen. She needed to talk to someone about Freddie, and Elanie cared just enough to listen, not enough to offer advice, and would never tell another soul if Sunny asked her not to.

"You love him?" Elanie asked this as a curiosity, like she wanted to know in what possible equation variable A and variable B could ever be combined to produce the solution of one person falling in love with another.

Sunny nodded, taking a bite of olive from her third martini. "Unfortunately."

"What does it feel like? Love?"

"Right now, it's a bit like an icepick through the heart."

Elanie grimaced. "Why in the worlds would anyone want to feel like they were being stabbed in the heart?"

Sunny's inebriated temptation to serve a heaping portion of sarcasm with her reply was powerful, but Elanie's question was genuine. She deserved to know the truth, as much as it might pain Sunny to tell it. "Well, darling, the problem with love is that it doesn't feel this way all the time. It always hurts, at least a little. But only because it's so precious. You don't want anything to ever happen to it. Because when you are in love, you get to experience feelings that are so much bigger than the hurt."

Elanie leaned in, her eyes big and earnest and surprising because she typically hid her emotions so thoroughly. "What kind of feelings?"

"Well, excitement, for one. The way your heart thumps and your breath catches whenever you see one another. It's intoxicating. And then there is the comfort of knowing you've found another soul in the universe who sees you, *really* sees you—that to them, you matter. It is important to matter, Elanie." Sunny took her hand, and, to Elanie's credit, she didn't pull it away. "And the joy. It is a joyous thing being in love, having someone love you back. And when it's true, it should be cherished."

"But it isn't true with Freddie?"

Sunny released Elanie's hand, downed the rest of her martini, and said an entirely fabricated, "No."

Sunny should not have been this tipsy at a work dinner with special guests but it turned out, thankfully, the Kravaxians weren't opposed to alcohol. After the main course, they were all a bit soused, aside from Elanie who, Sunny knew, would rather shave her head and eat her own hair than lose an ounce of control over herself in public.

Rax and Morgath stood stalwart at the door, arms crossed, scowling. Sunny knew it was unrealistic to expect anything more from the twins at this point. Tig and Reya seemed to be getting on beautifully at least. At one point in the evening, Tig had even gotten animated, waving her arms around and smiling brightly. She must have told Reya something absolutely hysterical judging by Reya's open laughter, her raven hair sliding back from her face as her head inclined toward the ceiling.

Tano and Marisia spent the majority of dinner talking among themselves, occasionally joining Chan and Freddie in whatever they were talking about. Sunny couldn't look in Freddie's direction because every time she did, a deep pain tried to bore its way into her alcohol-induced haze. Instead, she'd spent her time chatting with Axel.

"How long have you worked aboard this ship?" asked Axel, a hint of mischief in his dark brown eyes.

"Going on five years." Sunny took a sip of her fifth martini. No sleep in over twenty-four hours and five martinis deep into drunktown... Tomorrow would be an absolute disaster.

"What did you do before?" he asked.

"I worked on another LunaCorp ship. One across the wormhole

that travelled a course between New Earth and Mercury. How about you? What did you do before LunaCorp snatched you up for BLIX?"

His wink was saucy. "Deep-space piracy, of course."

Sunny nearly spat out her drink.

Axel touched her shoulder. She heard Freddie cough. "I'm only joking," Axel explained, laughing a little at her expense. "Customs. I worked in customs."

Sunny swallowed, clearing her throat. "I see. So your job was to allow all the pirated goods to come into your planet legally, then."

His laughter boomed. "That sounds about right."

Flirting with Axel should have felt better than it did, Sunny thought. He was tall, dark, handsome, and this was what she excelled at—meaningless, fun flirting. Tonight, however, even this familiar terrain was unsettling, like coming home to find all of the furniture in her pod had been rearranged.

As she talked with Axel, she couldn't help but notice Freddie watching her. His deep sighs, and the way his knuckles turned white around the glass of whiskey he held in his hand whenever she laughed at something Axel said made her feel annoyingly awful. As angry and messed up as she was, she didn't actually want to hurt Freddie. She didn't want *him* to think she might be interested in other people because that would be truly terrible of her.

After dinner, Sunny walked the FFKs back to their suites. Axel's suite was located farthest down the hallway, so they were alone when they reached his door. "Thank you." He turned to face her. "You've all been very kind to us."

"My pleasure. If you need anything at all, don't hesitate to call." She sent him the link to her Vcomms. "And that wasn't a line," she clarified. "I give this link to all our special guests."

He stared at her long enough that she began to wonder if he would make a pass, but he only nodded once and said, "Of course. Good night, Sunny."

And that was that. He entered his suite, and Sunny walked

away. Strangely anticlimactic. *This,* she thought, *must be what restraint feels like.*

The next few days flew by in a blur. Security on the senator and her family remained a top priority, but everyone had relaxed considerably knowing the Kravaxians hadn't come on board to scuttle the ship and vent its inhabitants into space. Even Rax and Morgath had behaved as professionally as was within their capability while training Axel and Tano in LunaCorp security protocols. Chan and his mentee Marisia got on as well as could be expected considering the woman never spoke and considering Chan kept running off to have lunch or afternoon tea with Makenna. And Tig and Reya—well, Sunny had never seen Tig so excited about spending time with another person. Which, in turn, made Sunny start scheming possible *whoops, this innocent picnic under the willows in the atrium is actually a date* scenarios she could devise for them.

Freddie had given Sunny all the space she'd asked for. He hadn't Vcommed or Squeed or even tried to speak to her unless it was something work related, and then he'd been all business and, of course, a perfect gentleman. Hurt still hung behind his eyes though, and Sunny could tell he'd wanted to talk to her, but he'd respected her request. Just like he always had and probably always would. And every day that passed, a voice—quiet at first but growing louder—spoke up inside her, *Maybe, just maybe, you've got everything all wrong.*

She knew she needed to talk to him eventually. But not today. Because today she woke up with the weight of a planet sitting on her chest, pushing her back down into her bed. Smothering her.

Today was the anniversary.

25

THE ANNIVERSARY

IT HAD SNUCK UP ON HER SOMEHOW. EVERY YEAR SHE KNEW IT WAS coming, and every year she thought she'd be able to move through it with more ease and grace than the year before. She was always wrong. It never got easier—the grief, the devastation. It was always right there, strong as ever.

She'd struggled through morning meeting like a ghostfly through honey. Freddie's concerned stare across the staffroom table alone had made her dig her fingernails into her palms. After the meeting, she'd asked Chan for the rest of the day off, and he hadn't hesitated to give it to her, looking at her like she might break into pieces right in front of him.

She should have been able to manage this better. She should have been moving forward in her life. But the list of things she should have done stretched out further than she could see. *I should have been there. I should have made sure he was safe. I should have been a better mother. If I was, maybe he'd still be here.*

But he wasn't here. He was gone. So just like every year on this day, she hid in one of the ship's sensory rooms, alone. Sitting on the floor she'd instructed the room to make feel cold and hard, she turned up the wind, the thunder, the crashing waves all around her until these sounds and sensations drowned out everything else—everything, even the opening and closing of the sensory room's door.

When a hand slid over her shoulder, it startled a scream from her.

"Shh," Freddie whispered against her ear. "It's only me. I'm sorry, I didn't mean to scare you." His other hand settled heavily onto her other shoulder as he sat down behind her.

Sunny accessed the room's controls again, dimming the audio.

"What are you doing here?" Her voice rasped. "How did you know I was here?"

His hands slid softly down her arms, then he took them away. Maybe to rest them in his lap. "Elanie."

Sunny turned around so they faced each other, both sitting cross-legged on the floor. "How? How did she... Nobody knows I come in here."

His raised brow and tight smile said all that needed to be said.

Sunny's shoulders sagged. "She knows, doesn't she? That woman knows everything."

"She only told me that today would be hard for you. That every year on this day, it's hard. But you look..." He scanned her face, his brows pressing tightly together in this pained expression, like it was agony for him to just look at her. "Sunny, you're hurting. And this morning at meeting you looked so..." He trailed off again.

"Did Elanie tell you why? Did she say why today would be hard for me?" *How would she have known?*

He shook his head. "When I asked, she said she didn't know." His hand reached out slowly, his fingers gently wrapping around her clenched fist. "You don't have to tell me, Sunny. You don't have to tell me anything you don't want to tell me. And I know there's something going on between us. But do you think that could wait, just for a bit? Can I sit with you? Just so you're not alone."

Whatever anger she'd felt toward him had been dwarfed by her heartache, reduced to a single particle of dust in the vast universe of her grief. She wanted to tell him. She wanted to let him in. She was so tired of being alone. And he looked so genuine, so sincere, so she tried. But her mouth only opened and closed, nothing coming out but little wisps of air. She didn't know what to say, where to start.

He could see how hard this was for her. "*Stars*, Sunny. I'm so sorry. Do you want me to leave? I can go?"

It surprised her, but she didn't want him to go. "No. Don't leave," she told him, then an idea came to her. Something that might be easier than trying to speak. "Can I send you something?"

"Of course," he said, and then he remained still and silent as she sent him the pictures and vids of Jonathan she'd been watching.

After a long moment, he whispered, "Is this... Is he—"

"This is my son. His name was Jonathan. He was five years old, and he was the love of my life." Suddenly, like a river rising over its banks, the words burst from her. "I'd been set to have a busy week planning for New Year's, and my parents had offered to watch him. So I'd put him on a shuttle to Tranquis. It was a Class-Two Euphonia."

Freddie cursed under his breath, taking her other hand in his.

"As you probably know, the Class-Twos had a faulty reactor. They promised me it happened quickly, that he didn't feel any pain. But he was alone. All alone. I should have been with him, but I wasn't. I was on my ship. That was five years ago today. And soon, he will have been gone longer than he was ever here."

Freddie took a deep, trembling breath. "He was beautiful."

Sunny smiled. "He was—and funny. He was really, really funny."

His thumbs ran over her knuckles, then he gently worked her fisted hands open. "I am so, so sorry."

Her shrug felt like she was lifting an asteroid. "Me too."

They sat for a while, holding hands, not speaking, until Sunny finally admitted, "This is why I can't be with you. Why you shouldn't want to be with me. I am a broken woman, Freddie, beyond repair. And I don't think I'll ever get over this."

He was silent. And then, so softly she barely heard him, he said, "I had a wife."

This yanked Sunny's head up. "You... What?"

"I was married," he said, his gaze pinned on their clasped hands.

Sunny's chest caved inward. He'd been married. She knew his wife's name before he said it, but hearing it from him was like hearing glass shatter.

"Her name was Serena. We were high school sweethearts. I loved her. So much."

Sunny's mouth went dry, and her throat kept trying to swallow empty air. "Freddie."

"Bilateral pulmonary embolisms," he continued. "The worst three words I know, in any language. One minute she was fine, and the next she was gone, just like that, in my arms." He blinked, sending a single tear slipping down his cheek. "That was over ten years ago. Feels like it was yesterday. And on the anniversary of that day, I don't get out of bed, still." He looked up again. "Grief is unique for everyone, but you are not alone. And you are not the only broken person here."

She squeezed his hands. She hadn't thought she could possibly feel any more heartbroken that she already had today. But that was the thing about grief: there was no bottom.

"You said her name. After the masquerave, you said her name in your sleep. You said you loved her. I thought," Sunny's jaw clenched, "I thought you were in love with someone else."

He rocked back, reeling like she'd struck him. "Sunny, why didn't you just ask me?"

"Seriously? Don't you remember not one minute ago when I told you that I was broken? I wasn't joking."

A jolt of laughter erupted from him, shaking his entire body. It was relief. He was relieved. Relieved tears streamed down his cheeks. "Sweetheart, I am in love with no one but you. And I'm not telling you about Serena for sympathy or to diminish your loss. I just want you to know, that's all. I want you to know that you are not alone."

But she was. She was so alone. And he deserved to know how fucked up she really was. So she wiped a tear from his cheek and rubbed the wetness between her finger and thumb. "I have never cried for him, for Jonathan. Not when my parents called to tell me he was gone, not during the funeral, not even after, when I told my parents I couldn't see them again, that it was too hard to be around family of any kind. Never. What kind of mother doesn't cry for her dead child?"

He said nothing. *What was there to say*, she supposed. They sat together for a long while, his eyes wet, hers dry.

"Have you ever been to Neptune?" His voice scarcely carried over the muffled roar of crashing waves still rolling through the room.

Sunny shook her head.

"Have you heard about its terraforming? Its people?"

"Only a little." Neptune's inhabitants rarely left their planet. There were rumors about the type of people who lived there— nomadic, fierce, dangerous, wild.

"The terraforming didn't take as it should have. Now Neptune is mostly desert, sand as far as the eye can see. Water is the most precious commodity, and not a drop is wasted." Freddie leveled his eyes at hers, taking her hands more firmly in his. "As a result, for the people of Neptune, crying is strictly forbidden."

Another dry swallow burned in Sunny's throat. "I didn't know that."

"In such harsh climates, the mortality rate is astronomical. Especially infants, children. An entire planet of parents and grand-parents burdened not only with surviving on one of the most inhos-pitable planets in my solar system but forbidden to fully mourn their losses."

Nausea gripped her stomach, her pulse pounding relentlessly against her temples. An entire planet of people locked in grief, just like she was.

But then Freddie said, "Unless it rains."

"It doesn't rain on Neptune though, does it?" Sunny asked.

"It does actually. Only once or twice a year. But when it rains—and only when it rains—the people of Neptune are free to go outside, sit underneath the downpour, and weep over those they've lost."

Her voice shuddered, breath rushing out of her. "I can't do that though. It never rains on the *Ignisar*."

"It never rains on the *Ignisar*," he agreed. "But it can."

Only then did the first droplet of water fall onto her wrist. She stared at the wet spot on her skin when another drop fell and then another. Freddie must have accessed the room's weather controls.

"What are you doing?"

A raindrop landed on his nose. "Let it rain, Sunny."

Scant drops became a sprinkling, a pattering on the floor, in her hair. And then the skies opened up. The rain fell, warm but insistent. It seeped into her eyes, her mouth. It drenched her until she felt suffocated by it.

His hands closed even more tightly around hers. "Just let it rain."

She gasped and water flooded her mouth. She spat it out. But her mouth filled again, the rain a merciless deluge. She shook. She gnashed her teeth. She wanted to scream. She wanted to run. She wanted to hit something, anything. She wanted to fight. She *needed* to fight, but Freddie held her hands pinned in his.

She didn't know when she'd started to cry. But with rain streaming over her face, as if in solidarity, giving her permission, hiding her tears behind its downpour, she collapsed forward, her head resting on the wet ground as sobs racked her body.

Freddie's hands were on her, pulling her into his lap, holding her together as she dissolved, as the rain mixed with her tears, washing them from her face before they dropped from her eyes. His fingers brushed over her hair. He rocked her back and forth, and she clung to him while everything poured out of her. Five years of hidden tears, of fiercely guarded pain.

"I've got you," he whispered. "I've got you, sweetheart."

She'd missed him, his lips, his touch, the warmth of his body and how safe he made her feel. Raising her lips to his, she kissed him while the rain slowly faded away.

"I'm so sorry," she said between his lips. "I should have asked you. I should have been better."

He pulled away to kiss the tears from her eyes, her cheeks. "You couldn't be better if you tried."

Five years without more than a single tear, and now she couldn't stop. When she kissed him again, her tears slipped between their lips, salty and cool.

He broke their kiss, taking her face between his hands. A spark of hope lit his otherwise pained expression. "Who are we right now? Who am I kissing? I need to know." His chin fell to his chest. "Please, I have to know."

More tears fell. She knew what he was asking. *Am I kissing Phoebe or Sunny? Is this real or only more make-believe?*

She brushed a hand down his cheek, her tears intensifying, her voice broken and gasping as she finally confessed, "Frederick Caruthers, I love you—you and only you. I love you like I never thought I could love anyone again. And I have for a very long time."

They were still wet, but they were in Freddie's pod, on his bed, soaked clothes in a heap on the floor. He was on top of her, settled between her legs, kissing her, telling her he loved her, that he was sorry, that she was beautiful.

Sunny told him she had loved him since the first moment she'd set eyes on him. She told him he was the kindest, sexiest, most patient and generous man she had ever known.

He pushed into her slowly, their eyes locked, their breaths soft and even. Sunny had never made love, she realized, not like this, not when her heart was wide open, when it wasn't for pleasure or power or fun but only to let another person inside her completely, holding nothing back, leaving no single dark corner of herself hidden from him.

Her eyes fixed on his as he moved over her, her legs wrapped around his waist, her hands clinging to his shoulders. Propping onto his elbows, he slid his arms underneath her, his hands cradling her head, and she felt held, safe, loved. On this, the anniversary of the single worst day of her life, she felt loved. It was enough to make her start crying all over again.

Freddie kissed her tears away, one by one, and made love to her until there was no sadness left.

26

MOTHERS

THE SOFT RUMBLE OF FREDDIE SNORING WOKE HER. SHE WAS ON HER side, the small spoon, where she'd slept the entire night through nestled against him, safe in his arms. She rolled over so she could place a kiss onto his bare chest and then another and another until he finally began to stir. "Good morning, Freddie."

She felt his lips pressing onto the crown of her head, then he pulled her over on top of him. "Good morning, Sunny," he said sleepily, his eyes still closed.

Smiling, she sat up to straddle him, hauling him up so they sat up together. She ran her fingers over one of his eyebrows, then down along the line of his jaw. "Did you sleep well?"

He kissed her neck, his body still warm and soft from sleep. "Yes. You?"

"I did. Thank you. I love you."

His laughter tickled the skin of her neck where his lips had been. "I love you too, Sunny."

She wondered what it was about saying those words when she truly meant them. And hearing them when they were truly meant? It was addictive. She nearly said them again, when his techpad alarm went off. The sound came from his nightstand, so she leaned over to open his drawer. When she sat back up, it was not his techpad she held in her hands. It was a shoe. *Her* shoe. Her black pump that she'd lost in the hallway during their first night together on the CAK, the one he'd taken when she'd taken his tie.

"My shoe?" she said, awed. "You keep my shoe in your nightstand?"

He shrugged and resumed kissing her neck, her shoulder. "I do. But not all the time. Occasionally I sleep with it propped up on the pillow beside me. It is my prized possession."

She laughed at him, and at herself. "I sleep with your tie under my pillow, sometimes wrapped around my hand or my neck."

His head rose so that his full, pink lips aligned with hers. "I'd pay all the credits in my account to see that." Then he kissed her, deep and slow, his hands grasping her hips. When he pulled away, he was suddenly bashful, blushing and stammering. "There's... There's something else in that drawer for you. I've been saving it."

"Is that so? Like a present?"

"Kind of," he admitted. "It's under the techpad."

She pushed him back down onto the bed, then leaned over again to reach into his drawer. Sliding the now silent techpad out of the way, she uncovered a digcard. It was from the CAK. She sat back up, bringing the card with her. "Is it this?"

His hands slid up her thighs. "That's it. I went to the gift shop directly after I left your hotel room that night to purchase this card. I just never thought I'd get the chance to deliver it to you."

"You've been saving this for all these months?"

"I have."

"Is this something you do after all of your Squee hookups?" she said, trying to play off how much this sweet gesture had shaken her.

It didn't work because his honesty laid her bare. "Believe it or not, you were my first, only, and hopefully last one-night stand."

"What?" she blurted, utterly shocked. *Who only had a single one-night stand?* she thought. *And he was so good at it.*

He laughed. "It's true. I've opened Squee before, scrolled

through suggested matches, but it wasn't until I saw your profile that I changed my status to 'available.' And even then," he said, gazing boldly into her eyes, "I knew right away that one night with you would never be enough."

Sunny stared at him, stunned, until he encouraged, "Read it."

Her gaze sank to the card, and when she swiped her finger up the moving photo of the CAK's Central Park—the massive hedge maze in the shape of Becks Karlovich's face front and center—a stinging sensation pricked behind her eyes.

My dearest Phoebe,

Have you ever had a chance encounter that changed you, that upturned your every notion of why we exist on these spinning rocks so irrevocably that you knew, after meeting this other person, you would never again be the same?

I have.

Here is a secret. I stood outside the restaurant the night we met, watching you before I went inside. You were smiling, talking to the bartender, laughing, and it was like the sun had slipped a ray into that dark bar. For the first time in years, I was nervous. You were the most beautiful woman I had ever laid eyes upon, and I didn't want to do anything wrong, anything that might keep me from at least being able to kiss you. Just once.

I don't know if I will ever see you again, if our paths will ever cross, but wherever you are, I want you to know that for at least this one hopelessly love-struck fool, you shine brighter than every star in all the skies.

Affectionately yours,
Joshua

Tears, fat and hot, fell in broad rivers down her cheeks. "You wrote this? For me?"

He sat up and took the digcard from her hands, placing it back onto his nightstand. "And it's true—every single word."

"I do not deserve you."

He cupped her face in his hands, wiping away her tears with a gentle swipes of his thumbs. "Yes, you do."

Sunny's hips rocked over him, just a little, just enough. Soundlessly, he flipped her over, slid his hand behind her knee to hook her leg around his hip, and took her for all she was worth.

"Sunny, you look..." Senator Ramesh scanned her from head to toe. "You look so different. So—"

"Well served, I believe, is the descriptor you're searching for," added Lena, grinning at Sunny from her spot on their couch. Yes, *that* couch.

Sunny coughed, clutching at her throat.

Lena raised a brow. "Are you all right?"

"Fine." Sunny coughed again. "Just choking on your words."

Chahna laughed as she waved Sunny into their suite. "What brings you to see us this morning?"

After several seconds spent composing herself, Sunny said, "I have a question for you actually. If you aren't too busy."

"Is that Sunny?" Sai burst from his room and thundered down the hall to throw his arms around Sunny's waist.

Although the instinct to pull away still tugged at her, she didn't, not this time. Instead, she leaned forward, picked him up, and squeezed him tight as his feet dangled below her knees. "Good morning, Sai. Did you just wake up?"

He nodded after she set him back down, then his head tilted to the side as he narrowed his big brown eyes. "You look different today. You're all...moist."

Sunny wasn't the only one in the suite coughing now as all three women lost it completely.

"Moist?" Sunny repeated after catching her breath.

Lena buried her face in her hands, her shoulders shaking with muffled laughter.

Sai shook his head, a blush blooming high on his cheeks. "Not moist, shiny, maybe? No, that's not it either. It's...glowing!" he crowed at last. "That's it. You are glowing!" Then he leaned in close to whisper, "Were you and Freddie making out again?"

"That is quite enough, young man." Chahna crooked a finger at Sai, summoning him to the counter for breakfast. After she served him a plate of crispy crepes folded into triangles and served with a chutney that smelled like coconut, she kissed him on the head, then followed Sunny out of their suite and into the hallway.

"What is it you wanted to ask me, Sunny?"

A whirring sound accompanied one of the security mechs standing guard outside her door as it floated closer. Eyeing the heavily armored orb—Sunny didn't particularly care for the mechs —she said, "As you know, Tig has been working tirelessly to track whoever is hacking our system. Although she's had little luck on that front, she has done some research on your Proposition 2126."

Chahna's jaw set, like it was cast in stone. "And what information did she find?"

"Not much actually. That's why I'm here. You'd mentioned the proposition briefly the night I'd watched Sai, but we were interrupted." Sunny lowered her voice, concerned they might be overheard as several Delphinian Wizards wandered by, their customary flowing robes replaced by striped velour tracksuits of all things. "Is the proposition why you're being targeted?"

"I am sure Tig has informed you of the mundane nature of the proposition," Chahna said, her arms crossed tightly over her jewel-blue sweater.

"She said its aim is to increase funding for deep-space exploration, similar to a bill that passed without issue a decade ago."

"That is correct." Chahna squared her shoulders, her expression settling into firm, resigned lines. "So, to answer your question, no. I don't think the proposition is why we're being targeted."

Sunny could spot a lie almost as well as a Vorpol could spot a mismatched-shoe sale. The senator was lying, very clearly lying. Sunny opened her mouth to press her on this, when Chahna derailed her completely by stepping close, placing a hand over Sunny's shoulder, and whispering, "Now, tell me what is going on between you and Freddie."

Sunny stumbled back a step. "Nothing. Nothing is going on. He's a friend. What?"

Chahna laughed at her. "You can tell me. I really don't speak to very many people on this ship. And I know how to keep a secret." She winked. "I'm a senator, it's pretty much all we do."

Sunny's mouth opened, closed, then her head fell forward in defeat. "Is it that obvious?"

"Yes, dear, it is."

Sunny snorted, meeting Chahna's eyes once again.

"You are in love," she stated, as if this fact was as certain as all the stars in the KU eventually burning out. "And thank the Gods for it. We were so worried about you yesterday."

Sunny had stopped by Chahna's suite before heading to the sensory room, and she knew she must have looked terrible. A sudden and acute awareness of how many people aboard this ship have probably been worried about her for years, never asking her about it, never demanding she tell them what was wrong, crashed into her. She took a deep breath and blew it out. "Yesterday was a difficult day for me. My son died five years ago, and yesterday was the anniversary."

Chahna gasped, her hand rising reflexively as if to shield her heart. "Sunny, I'm so sorry."

"Thank you. He would be Sai's age now...if he were still here, that is." *I will not cry. I will not cry. I will not cry.* But when Chahna grabbed her and crushed her tight, hooking her chin over Sunny's shoulder, they wound up crying together.

The way Sunny felt, wrapped inside the senator's embrace, sharing tears with another mother, it wasn't fear or pity or despair.

It was love, just love. It made her wonder why she'd been keeping this pain to herself for so long. And then, like the anchor that had been weighing down her heart gave the rope one final tug before it snapped free, Sunny realized she needed to take care of something long past due.

"Thank you, Chahna," she said, wiping the tears from her eyes. "But if you'll excuse me, I need to go make a call."

"Sunastara?" Her mother's voice was a whispered breath, her eyes already filling with tears on Sunny's techpad screen.

"Hi, Mom. I've missed you. I'm so sorry it's been so long. How's Dad?"

27

ORION'S TEETH

TANO, AXEL, AND MARISIA SAT STIFFLY ALONG ONE SIDE OF THE staffroom table. Since their arrival, they'd all been pleasant and professional, and Tano had even come to the Cosmic Spectacle stables yesterday while Sunny met with that New Earth stable hand to arrange the kurot's shuttle back to the CAK. He'd wanted to thank her personally for the kurot milk. "Finest cleaning I've ever had," he'd said.

She'd made a show of her delight that he'd enjoyed the antiquated custom she'd unknowingly revived, but deep down she couldn't shake that same feeling she'd had on FFK day that she had met this person before. She also couldn't shake the feeling that, with his slippery smile and arched brow, he'd absolutely been checking her out.

She tried not to stare at Tano across the table from her now or at Marisia, whose expression since she'd arrived on the *Ignisar* could only be described as aggressively displeased. Instead, Sunny leaned over to where Reya and Tig sat beside her, chatting intently about the tech effects Tig had planned for the ship's New Year's celebration.

"How are you getting along, Reya? Is Tig telling you all her secrets?" She winked at the pair.

Tig laughed. "Pretty much. Not that I have that many."

When Tig smiled, Reya blushed. Of the two, Sunny would have figured Tig for the more easily embarrassed. But Tig seemed somehow more confident having Reya around. Perhaps it was good for her not to be so isolated in her office all day. Or, fingers and toes crossed, maybe they were making more of a connection than just teacher and pupil, not that the dynamic couldn't be fun as well.

"Have you two exchanged contact information?" Sunny asked innocently. "You know, Reya may have questions once this holiday is over."

Reya's blush deepened as Tig said, "No. We haven't." She turned to look at Reya. "But we probably should. If you want to, that is."

Reya smiled at Tig, and fireworks exploded in Sunny's mind.

<What exactly is it that you're doing?> Vcommed Freddie.

She shot him a sheepish glance across the table. <Nothing. Why?>

<You look like you're scheming. Are you scheming?>

<No. I do not scheme.>

<You do too. You're making poor Reya blush like a rose.>

<I am doing no such thing,> Sunny said, fighting a grin.

<You know, Sunny, you look absolutely amazing today. My productivity's been abysmal. I can't seem to do a single thing other than think about how soft the skin between your legs is. And how when I lick you there, you taste like—>

Her knees crashed together. <Stop. Fine, I see your point. Nobody likes to get all flushed during a work meeting. I will keep my scheming to more private environments. And when this meeting is over, please present yourself to my pod as soon as humanly possible.> It had been nearly twelve hours since they'd been horizontal. An inexcusable length of time.

He gave her a subtle wink. <Roger that.>

"Finally," snapped Elanie as Chan cruised into the room.

"Where have you been? Off doing tricks with your Wizard woman?"

Sunny was apparently not the only person at the table skilled in creating moments of flustered public embarrassment in her peers.

Glowering at Elanie, Chan muttered a simple, if not annoyed, "No," as he cruised to his spot at the head of the table. Chan hadn't quite been himself recently, Sunny noticed. He'd been intensely stressed, staunchly professional, and hadn't made a single wrong move since the FFKs boarded. He was either angling for a promotion, getting ready to quit and looking for a glowing recommendation, or—and what Sunny considered most likely—he was worried. But over what? The Kravaxians had not only been behaving but they would disembark in a few days' time. If something was to go wrong, surely it would have done so already. Perhaps it wasn't the Kravaxians he was worried about leaving the ship. Perhaps it was a Delphinian Wizard with gorgeous eyes and a clever smile.

Sunny had been so wrapped up in her own affairs that she hadn't even considered Chan might've been developing real feelings for Makenna. And when they reached Portis next week, Makenna would leave with the other Wizards and Chan would be alone, again. That didn't seem right or fair, and now Sunny felt profoundly sad.

"Welcome, everyone." Chan nodded to the room. "I've called this meeting to present our special guests with their certificates of completion for this week of training with us. I realize we still have a couple of days left, but with New Year's on the horizon, this may be the only time we aren't all too busy to meet. So without further ado..." He leaned over to the side to pull something from one of his hoverchair pockets.

As this happened, Sunny noticed Marisia grasping Tano's arm as the large man's muscles tensed, some vibrating coil of potential energy within him getting ready to spring free.

Rax and Morgath noticed too from their spots near the door,

their green hands moving to hover over the flash grenades and chuck-cuffs at their hips.

<At ease, gentleman,> Sunny Vcommed the twins. <They are only here for a few more days. We can do this without incident.>

They both looked at her, scowling, eventually lowering their hands when Chan pulled out four digital plaques and placed them on the table without Tano and Marisia going berserk.

<This room is a powder keg,> Freddie Vcommed.

<And far too small for this many large men,> Sunny replied in complete agreement.

After Chan distributed the plaques to the Kravaxians, Tano stood carefully from the table. "We wanted to thank you all as well, for your kindness and hospitality." Tano motioned to Axel, who reached into his bag—triggering the twins to flex once more—and placed what looked like seven slim clear needles made of glass onto the table, each about ten centimeters long, slightly curved, with tips sharpened to a fine point.

Tano held up one of the shards. "These are known on Kravax as Orion's Teeth. They are the first teeth of the sikka and only found by swimming to the bottom of the Rustiun sea and digging them from the sand."

"What is a sikka?" Sunny asked, taking one of the teeth and turning it around in her fingers. It was light as air but felt strong as steel.

Axel answered, "Sikka are carnivorous fish that rule the seas on Kravax. They are cunning, merciless, and resilient—all traits highly prized by our people."

"When you possess Orion's Tooth," Tano said, "it is believed the spirits of our planet will pass these traits onto you."

Sunny's finger hovered over the tooth, then pressed gently onto its sharp point. "Thank you, Tano," she said, placing the tooth gingerly back onto the table. "And thank you, Reya and Marisia and Axel. This is a very thoughtful gift."

"You're very welcome," Tano replied, his brown eyes hooded,

his gaze lingering on Sunny a second longer than strictly necessary. Marisia, noticing the look, scowled at him. "While we are looking forward to your New Year's celebration," Tano said, "we are not looking forward to leaving this ship."

Turning away from Tano's questionable gaze in time to catch Reya sharing a brief, secret look with Tig, Sunny's mind immediately laid out an entire future for them. Reya would be offered a position on the ship, she and Tig would spend every afternoon sharing tea and pastries at the bistro. What started as an innocent friendship would grow—

<If you are going to sit there with that dreamy, devious look in your eyes, I will not be held responsible for the aftermath when I take you right here on this table.>

Sunny coughed so hard and for so long, she had to excuse herself to get a drink of water in the hallway.

<That was highly inappropriate,> she scolded Freddie when she returned to her seat.

<I'll show you inappropriate.>

<Frederick!>

He pushed back from the table.

<What are you doing?> she hissed. <Freddie! Don't you dare!>

"My apologies, Chan, everyone, I have a meeting with the Gorbulon-7 contingent on deck twenty." He held his Orion's Tooth between his fingers and said, "Thank you again for this wonderful gift," to the FFKs.

Then to Sunny, privately, <I'll be in your pod. Please hurry.>

After Freddie left, Chan started talking about something, New Year's maybe or maybe Vorp's position in orbit around their sun. Who could say? Sunny only heard Freddie's voice in her mind, only saw his stormy eyes blazing across the table, only felt the echo of his mouth on her skin. When the meeting finally adjourned, an absolute eternity later, she tried to beeline it to her pod, but hard fingers wrapped tightly around her wrist, stopping her in her tracks.

She spun around. "Axel." *What wretched timing.* "What can I do for you?"

He was tall enough that she had to crane her neck a bit to see his face. He smiled down at her, all charm. "Will you be at the New Year's party?"

Perhaps, she thought, she should not have flirted with him so much. "I will, of course. I'll be working the floor."

His thumb ran over the inside of her wrist, his voice deep. "That's good. I enjoy spending time with you."

Between Tano's ogling and Axel's advances, Sunny was quickly forming an opinion of Kravaxian men. They were opportunists, to be sure. "Axel, I enjoy spending time with you as well. But I must tell you that I am with someone."

"You're *what*?" blurted Elanie, appearing beside them as if the Wizards had conjured her out of thin air.

"What's Sunny doing?" asked Chan, cruising up next to Elanie.

Tig and Reya joined their growing group, and all Sunny needed now was Rax and Morgath shouldering in beside her to make this whole situation turn into her absolute worst nightmare.

Axel raised a brow. "Sunny was just telling me that she's with someone."

Sunny blew a puff of air from her cheeks and muttered, "Thank you, Axel."

"Is it Freddie? Are you and Freddie together? Really? Finally?" asked Tig, her voice rising higher with every word.

Reya weighed in with, "I like that Freddie very much. He's very kind. And funny."

Sunny's eyes rolled like marbles across the ballroom floor. "Well, now that the trestal egg is out of the nest, yes, all right. Freddie and I are a thing. Can we please not make a big deal out of this?"

Chan, apparently afflicted by a temporary bout of deafness, fist-bumped the air and made a hooting noise like a deranged mountain owl.

<Where are you?> Freddie Vcommed.

<Telling everyone on deck twelve, and two Kravaxians, that you and I are involved. Because this is how my day is going.>

<Oh no. Are you all right? Do you need me to come down there?>

Sunny stared at her friends—and the Kravaxians—finding nothing but happy faces. Well, perhaps amused was a better way to describe the tilt of Axel's lips.

<I'm fine. And no, you stay put. I'll be right there.>

Eventually everyone went their separate ways, but Sunny reached out for Elanie's elbow before she could leave. "Elanie, darling. Can I say something to you?"

"Is it brief?" she snipped, true to form.

"It is," Sunny replied, unmoved by her snark. "I don't want to make you uncomfortable, but I know Freddie and I both have one person to thank for bringing us together."

Elanie's brows creased. "Good for you."

Sunny squeezed her elbow tighter, ignoring her attempts at deflection. "You've been there for me for years—a steady, supportive presence. You've also been there for Freddie while I've been dealing with...things. And I know you told him to come find me in the sensory room."

"I'm sure I have no idea what you're talking about." Her voice was stern, but her brown eyes misted.

"Elanie, do you know? Do you know why that day is always so hard for me?" Sunny didn't know how she would, but, somehow, she felt like she did.

Elanie nodded, just once.

"How? How do you know? I've never told anyone."

The expression on Elanie's face was one Sunny had never seen on her before, not her customary annoyance or exasperation or even pity, it was compassion. "*You* did actually, years ago. You were very drunk, and I knew you wouldn't remember, but you told me."

Sunny's chin fell to her chest. "You're right, I don't remember that. I'm so sorry. I shouldn't have burdened you like that."

Elanie's fingers wrapped around Sunny's hand and squeezed. "You have nothing to apologize for. And yes, you should have."

Tears filled Sunny's eyes. "Thank you, Elanie. You are a wonderful person, a true friend, and I love you."

Elanie inhaled sharply. Then, as if coming to her senses, she pulled her hand from Sunny's, flipped her dark hair off her shoulder, then swatted at the tear rolling down her cheek the way someone might swat at a nova beetle crawling across their pillow. "I have to go. I have a lot of work to do. But..." she paused, then whispered, "I love you too," before turning and disappearing down the hall.

Thirty minutes later, after Freddie's head emerged from between Sunny's legs and she remembered how to speak, she told him about Elanie while she rolled him over and climbed on top of him.

His hands cupped her ass. "Elanie told you she loves you?"

Sunny raised her hips enough to guide him into her, then she settled back down with a satisfied sigh. "She did. It was a big moment for both of us."

"So, no more secrets?" he asked, staring up at her, hopeful.

She leaned forward, and just before her lips met his, she said, "No more secrets."

28

NEW YEAR'S

Long swaths of white and silver digital gossamer adorned the main deck ballroom, floating down from the rafters to just brush the floor. Tiny bubbles of golden light shimmered over the soft fabric and rose toward the ceiling so that when Sunny stepped into the room, she felt as though she'd been dropped into the bottom of a champagne glass. It was pure elegance—which, for this ship, was a near miraculous feat.

"You look stunning," Freddie said, coming up behind her, his breath tickling her ear.

She turned to face him. "Thank you, darling." She'd dressed in a sleeveless silk crimson jumpsuit, fitted at the waist and ankles by wide cuffs of matching velvet, and intricately jeweled heels that sparkled in the golden light of the digital effects. "You don't look half bad yourself."

He waved a hand over his immaculate three-piece suit. "What, this old thing?"

Sunny pinched the folded corner of his pocket square between her fingers. She had no idea how he'd managed it, but it matched her dress precisely. Perhaps he had a collection of pocket squares in his "Perfect Venusian Gentleman" kit, nestled directly between his guidebook to flawlessly mussed hair and whatever magical concoction always makes his breath smell minty.

"I like what you've done here," he said, lifting the spindle of Sunny's Orion's Tooth from where it dangled between her breasts.

"I thought it would make a nice necklace," she said, gazing up at him.

He pressed the Tooth back to her chest, his finger following the line of it all the way down to its tip, coming dangerously close to disappearing between Sunny's breasts.

"See you after the party?" she asked, staring down at his finger now, wishing they were alone so he could trace that finger all the way down her body. They would both work the floor tonight, but she'd been assigned specifically to the Kravaxians, which meant, regrettably, she wouldn't see much of Freddie until after the ball dropped.

"Absolutely," he whispered, returning his hand to his side. He kissed her cheek, then she turned her head to stare at his butt as he made his way toward the bar where Garran and Kasa were ordering drinks.

Sunny scanned the room but didn't see Chahna or Lena anywhere. Although they celebrated New Year's aboard the *Ignisar* on this date, it was only because LunaCorp followed the standard year calendar. The actual date of the New Year varied wildly from planet to planet, and on Tranquis it wasn't for another several months. As a result, it wouldn't necessarily be surprising for the Ramesh family to sit this one out.

<Did you know they were leaving tonight?> Freddie Vcommed.

<Who, darling?>

<Garran and Kasa. Their shuttle departs just after midnight.>

Sunny stopped walking. <That's...terrible.> Her heart clenched. <Why? I don't want them to leave.>

<I know. I'm remarkably devastated by the news,> he commiserated. <But Kasa's mother has developed a cough, and Kasa wants to get her back home. Garran will join them.>

<Please don't let them leave without giving me a chance to say goodbye.>

<Of course. I just wanted to let you know.>

<Thank you, Freddie.>

<Have fun with the FFKs—and I've got my eye on Axel. He's going to make a move on you. I can feel it.>

She started walking toward the Kravaxian's table again. <Frederick Caruthers, are you jealous?>

<Yes,> he said, laughing. <Intensely.>

<Well, there's no need for that. The only moves I'm interested in are yours.>

<If I had any moves at all, I'd be flattered. Stay safe.>

Aside from Reya, who spent the evening in the control booth with Tig, the Kravaxians all sat at their table, watching the party unfold with a dour, disinterested silence while nursing their drinks. Sunny was unbearably bored.

Elanie Vcommed, <Having fun?>

<Decidedly not. What are you doing?>

<Helping Freddie manage a table of inebriated Blurvans and watching you stare off into space.>

Sunny glanced around the room until she spotted Freddie sitting at the Blurvans' table with his arm around a young male as they swayed side to side, the Blurvan's gelatinous belly wobbling with his laughter.

<*Stars!* What are they doing? Are they singing?>

Elanie stood next to the table, her arms crossed over her chest. <Yes, if you could call it that. Some Blurvan drinking song. They won't let Freddie leave.>

Just off to Elanie's side, Sunny noticed a gorgeous bionic with bright-blue eyes sitting at a table of other young males and staring brazenly at her ass.

<Don't look now, darling. But you are being checked out.>

<What? Who? Why?> she asked, her shoulders rising toward her ears.

<A scrumptious morsel behind you, and because you are exceptional.>

Across the room, Elanie nonchalantly angled her head, pretending to scratch her chin on her shoulder.

<Nicely done. Very subtle,> Sunny commended.

<He's cute. I guess,> Elanie admitted.

Sunny stifled her smile. <Crew party after the room clears out?>

<Obviously,> Elanie replied, scratching her chin so she could look at the handsome blue-eyed bionic one more time.

When the ball finally dropped at midnight and Marisia, Tano, and Axel retreated unceremoniously to their suites, Sunny practically groaned with relief. She raced to meet up with Freddie so she could say a reluctant farewell to her favorite Argosian. Garran was very happy to see them, maybe a little too happy.

Sunny couldn't speak. She could barely breathe. Freddie's quickly reddening face indicated the same fate had befallen him. She tapped her fingers on the enormous purple pectoral her face was smushed against and grunted, "Darling, release. Please."

Garran held Sunny tightly in his right arm, Freddie in his left, both of them lifted a solid meter off the floor in a crushing embrace. "I am very happy," he cried, squeezing them one last time for good measure. Sunny's back popped.

"Thank you," she managed after Garran set them down. She wheezed, rubbing at her chest as sweet, blessed air made its way back into her lungs.

The big man was all smiles as he looked from Sunny to Freddie and back again. "You two are *worthy* of each other. You fit." The words were simple, but from him they meant the worlds.

Tears burned Sunny's eyes, and she wondered if all she would do for the rest of her life now was sob at the slightest provocation.

"Are you certain you have to leave?" asked Freddie, rolling his shoulders and stretching his neck from side to side. "We have excellent medics aboard this ship for Kasa's mother."

Garran nodded, his tattooed head gleaming in the glow from the overhead lights. "Kasa and I have plans"—he stole a glance at the airlock where Kasa carried her mother's bags into their shuttle —"for making things *official*."

"That is wonderful, Garran." Sunny sniffled. The amount she was going to miss this giant, purple, insightful softie crushed her chest even more than if he'd picked her up and squeezed her a second time.

Freddie wrapped an arm around Sunny's shoulders, pulling her in close. "Garran, this ship simply won't be the same without you."

"You two should come visit Argos." He looked down at his feet and toed the carpet. "Maybe when Kasa and I are joined."

Sunny's hand rested upon his arm. "We wouldn't miss it for all the worlds."

"Is it always this hard?" asked Freddie as they watched Garran's shuttle pull away from the ship through the flexglass. "Saying goodbye to the guests?"

"No. Garran was special, one in a million, like a single piece of hay in a haystack."

Freddie's head swiveled toward her. He frowned. "Where did you hear that expression?"

She shrugged. "Some New Earth American guest, I think. Why?"

"If I may, I'm not sure you're using it correctly. That particular saying is actually 'like a needle in a haystack.'"

Her brow furrowed. "Well, that doesn't make one lick of sense. Why would there be a needle in a stack of hay?"

"Hmm," he considered. "I've never thought about it that way. Why *would* there be a needle in a haystack?"

"Don't look at me." She slid her arm around his waist.

"Baffling nature of the expression aside, it's typically employed to point out how difficult it would be to find a certain thing or person. As hard as finding a single needle hidden in a haystack. For your purpose, to borrow another New Earth colloquialism, you could say something along the lines of 'they broke the mold when they made him.'"

Sunny looked up at him, a smile breaking across her face. She didn't often get to see him playing his role of L&C, let alone benefit from it. His kind, patient competence was, unsurprisingly, a major turn-on.

"Yes, that's exactly what I meant," she replied, then she grabbed his tie and pulled his lips to hers.

After an excessive amount of time spent kissing, Freddie made his way back into the ballroom while Sunny walked to the Ramesh suite, wanting to make sure everything was on the up and up since they'd never showed to the party.

On her way, Tig's frantic voice invaded her head.

<It's not what we thought. I read it more closely, and I'd missed it. I can't believe I'd missed it.>

<Tig, what's wrong? Slow down.>

<The proposition. In the fine print. The funding requested is for deep-space exploration, but only for companies with fewer than twenty-thousand employees. And there's an attached provision to close loopholes and more tightly regulate corporate monopolies. If this passes, it's an extremely expensive slap in LunaCorp's face.>

<Why would the senator want this to pass?> Sunny asked. <Nobody in their right mind would go up against LunaCorp.>

<It's not just her,> Tig said. <Five other senators have helped draft this proposition. Their hope is to support smaller businesses,

increase competition, and provide more diverse opportunities for their planets, especially when it comes to asteroid mining.>

LunaCorp had cornered the market on asteroid mining ever since the Asteroid Belt Wars. It was the key to their wealth and continued chokehold on nearly every industry in existence. This proposition, while noble and courageous, was outrageously dangerous for anyone behind it.

Sunny's heart lurched in her chest. The senator had just made herself, her family, and now Sunny's ship targets for the largest and most ruthless corporate monopoly in the KU.

<And the security breaches,> continued Tig, speaking at a breakneck pace, <they didn't come from Vorp or Gorbulon-Seven. They came from Kravax, Sunny. Kravax!>

Sunny started running. <Where is she? Where is Chahna?>

<She wasn't at the party?>

Sunny sprinted to the Ramesh suite, sliding to a stop at the sight of the twin's security mechs, now disabled heaps of motionless metal on the floor. She banged frantically on the door to no response.

<Rax! Morgath!> she barked. <Override the security locks on the senator's suite!>

<What's happening?> demanded Rax as the lock disengaged.

A bomb had gone off in the senator's suite, tables overturned, broken glass on the floor. Sunny walked past Sai's bedroom—empty. But in the back bedroom, Chahna and Lena were sprawled across their beds, not moving.

<Code white! Code white! Disable all air locks, lock all docking ports. The senator and her wife are down. And the boy is missing. It's the FFKs. It's got to be.>

<The FFKs,> grumbled Morgath. <I knew it!>

<Not the time, Morgath!> Sunny snapped while crossing the room to kneel at the bedside.

<Is the senator alive?> asked Rax.

Sunny placed her fingers against Chahna's throat, feeling a

steady pulse thrum underneath them. <Yes.> She did the same to Lena. <And her wife. But they're out. Drugged?>

<I'm on my way,> Morgath said.

<Opening up comms among all staff,> said Tig on a separate line.

<Sitrep?> came Captain Jones' deep voice over the comm.

Sunny left the senator's suite, listening to Tig and Rax bring the captain and co-captain and the rest of the crew up to speed while she raced down the hall back toward the ballroom.

<Where are the Kravaxians?> asked Freddie, his smooth, calm voice in her head nearly bringing her to her knees.

Tig responded, <They all left their suites about fifteen minutes ago, all but...Reya.>

<Is she with you?> Sunny blurted. <Tig, get out of there!>

<No, she just left. She said she had to use the bathroom. Sunny, you don't think she's with them, do you?>

<I'm so sorry, Tig> Sunny commed, her throat tight as a knot. <Maybe not, but we can't take any chances. You need to lock the door to the control booth. Rax, head to the ballroom control booth to get Tig. Don't send mechs. They're disabling them. Hurry!>

<On it,> he growled.

Captain Jones took control, barking out orders over the open comm, but on a private line, Sunny saw Tig's ID blinking.

Tig's voice warbled with tears. <Sunny, I can see them on the monitors. Airlock B-4. They have the boy. And Reya is with them.>

Sunny had never run so fast in her entire life, thundering down hallways and sliding around corners. <Rax is on the way, darling. Don't worry,> she told Tig.

<Don't let the twins kill her, please.>

Sunny clicked off the comm before she wound up telling Tig that if Reya had a hand in harming Sai in any way, she would kill the woman herself.

Sunny rejoined the shared comm to shout, <Disable airlock B-4. They have the senator's son!>

<Do not engage,> boomed Captain Jones. <Sunny, do you copy? Do not engage. Help is on the way.>

But when she heard a boy's cries echo down the hallway to the B-gate airlocks, Garran himself couldn't have kept her away.

<I can't disable airlock B-4,> said Tig. <It's been disconnected from our system and password protected with a suicide sequence. If I try to disable it manually, it'll blow. All other airlocks and docking ports are on lockdown.>

<Enable exterior mechs,> ordered Captain Jones.

<No!> Sunny cried. <They have the boy! Do not fire on them!>

Freddie found her on a private comm. <What are you doing, Sunny? Where are you going?>

<I'm sorry. I can't let them take him.>

<Sweetheart, stop. Please. You're unarmed.> His next sentence was uttered with such profound sadness that Sunny clutched at her aching heart when she heard it, <Please don't leave me, too.>

She didn't want to leave him. She was caught in the space between her past and her future—they both were, but she knew the choice she had to make.

<I love you. I love you so much, Freddie. And I'm sorry, but I can't lose another boy.> She clicked off the comm, wiped away her tears, and ran for airlock B-4.

29

KRAVAX

<Sᴀɪ. Sᴀɪ, ᴄᴀɴ ʏᴏᴜ ʜᴇᴀʀ ᴍᴇ?> Sᴜɴɴʏ ᴡʜɪᴘᴘᴇᴅ ᴀʀᴏᴜɴᴅ ᴛʜᴇ ʟᴀsᴛ turn toward the airlock and slid to a halt, ducking into a vestibule when the shrill whine of blaster fire erupted down the hallway.

<Sunny?> Sai's voice came through strong in her mind. <Sunny, where are you?>

<I'm close. What's happening?>

<That Kravaxian woman came into our suite—the older one. She shot darts that put my moms to sleep. She took me from my bed. Mom's SOs are here now, but it's too late. They're putting me into a shuttle. I'm scared.>

A man's thickly accented voice shouted down the hall. "Give us the kid, and we'll let you leave." Sunny knew this accent, this voice. It was the New Earther stable hand from the Cosmic Spectacle.

"Put down your weapons. There is no way you're getting off this ship unless you release the child." This voice was even more famil-iar, so familiar that Sunny found herself creeping closer to the airlock just in time to hear a booming *thwump* and watch Makenna and the stable hand fly through the air, the New Earther's blaster shooting in a wide arc that burned a hole into the ceiling straight through to the deck above them. They landed hard against the wall, suspended there in some sort of sticky, black webbing.

Shit, shit, shit. Makenna was one of Chahna's security officers.

<Sunny. They're going to take me.>

<Be brave, Sai. Be brave like Captain Zorba and Bartholomew from your books. Can you do that?>

"Everyone in the shuttle, now," commanded Tano while—in a supreme act of blind absurdity—Sunny raised her hands into the air, palms facing out, and skirted past the wall where Makenna and the stable hand struggled against their webbing.

"Sunny!" Makenna slurred against the webbing covering her mouth. "Don't!"

The airlock she stepped into was smaller than her pod, and she quickly found herself face-to-face with four heavily armed Kravaxians and one very scared ten-year-old.

"Sunny," Axel said, looking almost amused as he holstered the web-shooter he'd used to subdue Makenna and the stable hand. "What are you doing here?"

She lowered her hands and aimed for her most non-threatening smile. "I heard you were leaving, and I never let my guests leave my ship without a personal send-off."

Tano raised his web-shooter and aimed it directly at her chest.

Sunny kept her tone light, playful, while inwardly she resisted every life-preserving urge to run. "No need for that. I'm unarmed and harbor no secret military training whatsoever. I'm as threatening as a cleaning drone. Cross my heart."

"What do you want?" This was the first time she'd actually heard Marisia speak. Her words were clipped, but her voice was much softer than Sunny had expected, like a highly irritable ball of cotton.

Nervous laughter burst from Sunny's throat, chirped and brittle. "Oh, it gets boring on this ship. And why take only one hostage when you could have two?" She knew attempting to get them to take her instead would be pointless. They needed the senator's son for leverage. The best she could do was make sure Sai wasn't alone and hope against hope that the rumors of Kravaxian cannibalism were baseless.

"She's got a point," said Axel, his brow arched.

Sunny exhaled because she'd been banking on Axel agreeing to take her. Flirting had an impeccable track record of getting her what she wanted.

"Fine, take her. But we must leave now," ordered Tano, hauling Sai into the shuttle by his cuffed wrists.

Axel strode toward Sunny, reaching out to grab her arm.

Her voice was inexplicably calm considering the torrent of panic rushing through her. They could harm her. They could kill her. It didn't matter—she wouldn't leave Sai. "No need for manhandling," she said, smiling at Axel. "I'll come willingly."

Axel shook his head, laughing under his breath while he secured mag-cuffs around her wrists. "This is probably not your smartest move," he said into her ear, nudging her forward into the shuttle.

"Sunny, what are you doing here? Have you lost your mind?" whispered Sai.

"Yes. What of it?" she responded, trembling like a rain-soaked fungus rat as Axel deposited her into the jumpseat next to Sai, securing a second set of mag-cuffs around her ankles, then connecting both sets of cuffs with some sort of elastic cable that gave her arms just enough rein to scratch her nose.

"My moms?" Sai's eyes were huge, the whites nearly swallowed by deep brown pools.

"Alive," Sunny assured him, squinting hard at Axel as if begging him to disagree while he finished connecting her cuffs. "Your moms will be fine. And so will you."

Sai muttered, "Doesn't feel like it," as Axel joined Tano and Marisia in readying the shuttle for undocking.

Reya rose from her seat to place thin, metal bands around their heads. "This won't hurt, I promise." Her voice wavered, her eyes red and puffy.

"What are these?" Sai asked.

"Short-range EMPs. They'll frag your VC. That's all."

Her VC... <Freddie,> Sunny Vcommed while she still could, <I'm with the boy. We're unharmed. They're shorting our VCs.>

<Sunny, you're being followed—Captain Jones and Morgath in cloaked ships. Try not to let them jum—>

And with a flick of a switch, Freddie's voice vanished, and Sunny's mind was thrust into an abrupt, disorienting silence. The shuttle's faster-than-light drive whirred, spooling up for a jump, and Sunny realized she had no worldly notion how Freddie expected her to keep that from happening.

Reya moved in close to Sunny. "You shouldn't have come, but they won't harm you or the boy. They aren't like that."

Sunny scoffed. "Darling, they—*you*—are kidnapping us. Forgive me if I don't believe you."

"I know. I know this looks bad," Reya whispered, her voice breaking, hands shaking. "But we aren't bad people."

"Reya!" Tano barked a warning.

She stood, wiping her eyes. "Just stay quiet and do whatever Tano says."

Sunny watched Reya join the rest of the Kravaxians at the front of the shuttle, then she leaned over and whispered to Sai, "Any idea how to stall an FTL jump?"

"I'm ten years old," he whispered back, incredulous. "So, no."

Tano cursed in Kravaxian, something about *Orion's balls*, as two warning shots from one of the *Ignisar*'s exterior defensive mechs soared over the shuttle's nose. "How long until the drive is ready?" he snapped.

"Thirty seconds," Marisia responded. Despite the onslaught of super-heated metal, she appeared entirely unruffled. Sunny would have been impressed if she wasn't so busy nearly pissing herself with fear.

"That long?" asked Reya, nervously clenching her fists until her knuckles turned white.

"Worry not, young one," assured Tano. "They will not shoot us. Not with the boy here."

"Tano, stand down. We have you surrounded." Captain Jones's voice thundered through the shuttle comms. "Return Sunny and Sai, and we will be lenient. You have my word."

Tano did not respond. After a few tense moments and a gut churning instant of suspended gravity, Sunny placed her cuffed hands over Sai's and squeezed as the FTL drive engaged and they jumped away from the *Ignisar*, into the black void of open space.

"Welcome to Kravax," said Axel, stepping away from the window to give Sunny and Sai a view of the dark-green planet, rotating just off the starboard side of the shuttle.

"It's much smaller than I'd expected," Sunny japed, measuring the unimpressive size of the planet between her thumb and first finger. She was green to the gills. She hated jumping. It felt like being compressed to the width of a single strand of hair, then rebounded violently to normal size like a shot rubber band. There was a mountain of pressure followed by several minutes of off-putting wobbling.

Axel smirked at her. "I assure you, Sunny. It's quite large."

Tano cleared his throat at this, the sound almost a growl. It made Sunny and Sai lean into each other on instinct.

Marisia glared at Tano as she slammed an overhead storage bin closed, then strapped herself furiously into her seat to prepare for entry into Kravax's atmosphere.

Once they landed, Tano and Axel hauled Sunny and Sai from the shuttle and led them toward an actual cave. Sunny sighed at the cave mouth sitting at the edge of a thick forest, thinking some planets just couldn't help but live up to their stereotypes.

The gravity on Kravax was heavy, at least twice what they simulated on the *Ignisar*, making Sunny and Sai stumble during what was a short but grueling hike from the ship to the cave. The cave itself offered little relief—dark and musty, the ground hard and cold. Sai and Sunny huddled together against a wall in a pitch-black corner until Tano lit a fire.

"You'll be here for a while," Tano said, scowling in the firelight. "So get comfortable."

"If I may," Sunny interjected, angling her body in front of Sai's. "I'm assuming this is a hostage for ransom arrangement and not some 'we are hungry and you look appetizing' situation?"

Tano's eyes rolled. "Despite popular belief, we are not cannibals. As long as you behave, you might even make it back to your ship unharmed."

Sunny bristled because 1. she never behaved, and 2. she didn't trust a single one of them as far as she could throw them, which with this gravity wouldn't be very far.

Tano stood, wiped his hands on his tactical pants, and left them to warm themselves by the fire—Sai in his pajamas, Sunny still in her silk jumpsuit, both of them bound in mag-cuffs.

"Are you all right?" Sunny looked Sai over, head to toe.

"I think so. I mean, no, obviously," he clarified, holding up his cuffed wrists. "But you know what I mean. Are you all right?"

"I'm better than if I'd decided to wear a dress tonight, so there's that at least." She scanned the cave looking for anything she could use as a weapon, then abandoned the search when she remembered she wouldn't have the faintest notion what to do with a weapon even if she found one. She was not a fighter. She was only good at one thing, and if they stood any chance of getting off this planet in one piece, she would need to play to her strengths.

"What do you think they want with us?" Sai whispered.

Sunny pressed her shoulder against his. "I'm not sure. My best guess is it has something to do with your mother. I think they're using us to get something from her. And once they get whatever that is, they'll let us go." She hoped she sounded more convincing than she felt.

Outside, Sunny heard Reya and Marisia arguing in Kravaxian.

"Will whatever they want hurt my moms?" Sai's voice broke at the mention of his parents. Sunny thought the boy might've been more scared for his mothers than he was for himself.

"No. I don't believe it will," she said. In truth, she had no idea, but she didn't want Sai to be scared.

He sighed, pushing his toes through the dirt. "You're lying to me. I can tell. But thanks for trying to make me feel better."

The sound of boots crunching across the cave floor ended their conversation.

"Well, how does it feel now to be *our* special guests?" asked Axel, striding over to the fire and squatting to warm his hands over the flames. He wore a wry, smug expression. It was the expression of someone who'd been sitting impatiently on a very big secret he could finally tell.

"Your hospitality is unparalleled," Sunny said shakily. She was scared, but she knew she'd be orders of magnitude more terrified if she hadn't come, if she was on the ship wondering where Sai was and if he was okay. This, she was certain, was what his moms were wondering at this precise moment.

Axel shook his head, laughing darkly, his coarse black bangs settling over his broad forehead. "Did you know that one of the things we worked hardest to learn in order to convince you all that we were a kinder, gentler breed of Kravaxians was sarcasm? Sarcasm is not a valid form of communication on Kravax. We find it dishonest, abhorrent. But above all other types of expression, sarcasm sets off-worlders most at ease. Why do you think that is?"

"We bore easily?" Sunny proposed dryly.

Sai kept his head down, his eyes trained on the fire like it was the tether that would keep him from floating off into space. And he might not be far off the mark. They were both shivering. Even with the fire, it was far too cold in the cave for their climate-controlled sensitivities and Sunny's skimpy attire.

Outside, Tano shouted in several sharp reports. Axel stood, turning toward the cavemouth, frowning. "What now?" he grumbled, then he pivoted back, ordering them to, "Stay put."

"Darling," Sunny raised her cuffed hands as far as she could, "where would we possibly go?"

"Do you think they jumped with us?" Sai asked once Axel was out of earshot.

"Who?"

"Morgath, Rax. Captain Jones. I'm sure they were out there, probably in cloaked shuttles or something."

Again, Sunny was stunned by Sai's cleverness.

"Do you think they followed us?" he asked.

"I don't know. Isn't it next to impossible to follow a ship into a jump if you don't know exactly where they're going?"

His lips curled up at the corners, his eyes bright. "It used to be, but there's a new thing. Morgath told me."

"*Morgath* told you? Big twin Morgath? You've spent time with Morgath?"

Sai nodded enthusiastically. "Oh yeah, lots of time. Rax too," he continued. Sunny's jaw dropped. "Anyway, it's a tracker thing. Like a giant laser gun. Morgath said if you shot it at a ship, you could tag the ship and track it through an FTL jump."

"How in the stars did you end up talking about faster-than-light travel with the head of security on my ship?" This notion struck Sunny as somehow even more outrageous than the fact that they were freezing their asses off in a Kravaxian cave.

"He read my book with me one day. Captain Zorba was trying to catch a jewel thief before he jumped and got away, and Morgath said if he'd used the tracker gun, he could've followed the thief into the jump. It was the coolest."

"Morgath read to you? When? How?" Sunny was almost speechless.

"When he boosted the security around our suite. He took a break to have some lunch. I was reading. He joined me. It's not all that strange, is it?"

Sunny's wide eyes joined her gaping mouth in total agreement that the notion that giant, grumpy Morgath of all people had read a child's book to an actual child was indeed extremely strange. But if Sunny had learned anything in her tenure as a hospitality specialist, it was that every single being possessed untold hidden depths. "Sai," she said, "did Morgath tell you he had one of those trackers?"

"He did better than that," whispered Sai. "He showed it to me."

30

SUNNY HAD A FEELING

THAT EVENING, SITTING AROUND THE FIRE, SUNNY AND SAI WATCHED the Kravaxians tear into an animal Marisia had shot with this terrifying automatic crossbow while they drank steaming cups of tea made from berries and spruce. Reya offered them some meat, but Sai was a vegetarian and had adamantly refused. Sunny declined as well, in solidarity. But the tea was actually quite nice.

After dinner, when Sunny felt certain the boy had fallen asleep on her shoulder, she pretended to follow suit, closing her eyes and resting her head over his. She wasn't sleeping, she was listening. If she had any hope of figuring out why the FFKs wanted the boy and when—if ever—they might be released, eavesdropping was her only option.

They only spoke in Kravaxian, and after a lifetime spent having her VC translate every language into Common, words she didn't understand fascinated her. It became clear that Tano, Marisia, and Axel presented a united front which Reya continually pushed against. They weren't arguing, necessarily, but tension was mounting in the cave. Eventually, their conversation faded behind the crackling of the fire, and Sunny had nearly drifted off to sleep for real, her adrenaline fading as the fire finally warmed her through, when she heard a single, heart-stopping word.

Becks.

At first Sunny thought she'd imagined it, some half-dream insinuating itself into her subconscious. But then she heard the name again, "Becks," in Axel's clipped voice, followed by a hissing sound from Tano, as if scolding the younger man for saying this name out loud. And like one of Freddie's puzzle pieces locking firmly into place, Sunny realized why Tano had looked so familiar to her all along.

She'd never met the man in person, but his forehead, cheek-bones, jawline—those she'd seen plenty, everyone had, considering the vain bastard had them carved into the CAK's Central Park hedge maze. And while Tano's features weren't identical, there was no mistaking that he was related in some way to the unconventional, audacious, and evidently *Kravaxian* CEO of LunaCorp, Becks Karlovich!

Suddenly it all made sense, LunaCorp funding initiatives to benefit Kravax, the FFKs coming aboard the *Ignisar* at the same time as a senator who was about to propose legislation that would penalize corporate monopolies, and Sai being abducted to shut Chahna up so that her proposition would never see the light of day. Since nobody would ever think to question who was behind this act—kidnapping for ransom a common enough practice for Kravaxian pirates—LunaCorp and Becks Karlovich would get exactly what they wanted without garnering a single smudge of guilt. *Cunning, merciless, and resilient, indeed.*

This information also gave Sunny a fair indication of how long she and Sai would have to spend in this cave before the FFKs either released or killed them. The Senate meeting on Portis was in four days' time. Best case scenario, if Chahna killed the proposition, the FFKs would release them, and they would all go about their lives with a fun story to tell their friends. Worst case, and what Sunny now thought was much more likely since Karlovich was involved, she and Sai would die here in this cave.

Even on the off chance they did let Sunny and Sai go, no one would ever believe her when she revealed that a Kravaxian ran LunaCorp. She needed that proposition to pass, the entire KU did. There was no way around it—if they wanted to live, she and Sai needed to escape, and they needed to do it soon.

An ominous silence descended over the cave, and Sunny wondered if the FFKs had realized she was awake and listening. Was she tensing her muscles? Were her eyelids twitching? Had her breath caught? It wasn't until she heard the first rumbling snore that she exhaled. The FFKs weren't planning her untimely demise, they'd simply fallen asleep.

She waited as patiently as she could until she saw through her cracked lids that all four of their captors slept nestled along the cave walls, Tano and Marisia making the shape of spoons with his arm draped over her waist, Axel on his back with his arms crossed over his chest, and Reya huddled in a corner, curled inward upon herself like a snail, knees pulled up tight into her chest.

"What is that?" Sai, apparently just as awake as Sunny was, whispered, his face turned to look down the top of her jumpsuit.

Sunny was surprised by this turn of events and not entirely certain how to proceed. *Is this some teachable moment?* "Well, Sai, those are called breas—"

"Stop. No. Not what I meant. And I know what they're called," he said, only mildly flustered. "I mean, what is *that*? Your necklace?"

Reya stirred, pulling her knees in even tighter before settling again.

"Orion's Tooth," Sunny answered, having forgotten all about her pendant.

"I need that. I can *use* that," he said, making a very pointed gesture toward his magcuffs.

"You can?"

"Yeah. These are just another puzzle. Can I have it?"

Hooking a thumb under the chain of her necklace, she lifted the Tooth safely free of her cleavage, then gave a little tug on the chain, breaking the clasp. "It's yours. But don't do anything yet. We need a plan."

"They're going to kill us if we stay here, you know that right?" Sai whispered, staring into her eyes.

Sunny smiled grimly. "I hope not, but you may be right."

Before they fell asleep, because neither of them had any experience in planning daring escapes, they settled on a simple plan that hinged on something Sunny would have to risk trying. Something that could go very wrong, very quickly. But Sunny had a feeling, and her feelings about these things were rarely wrong.

"Is Tig okay?" Reya whispered, her voice trembling. "She didn't get hurt, did she?"

Sunny peered up from where she squatted in the dirt, surrounded by a copse of tall conifers with narrow trunks. She'd asked for one of the FFKs to take her to relieve herself, objecting when Axel offered his services and silently rejoicing when Reya stepped up to the task. Without Reya, she and Sai and their fledgling plan were sunk.

The hollow, dark circles carved under Reya's eyes made Sunny wonder if she'd actually slept at all last night. And if not, had she heard her conversation with Sai? Either way, Sunny had her alone. It was now or never.

"I have no idea, Reya. The last I heard before you fragged my VC was that Elanie found her crying on the floor of the control room."

Reya turned away, her shoulders pulled up toward her ears. "I didn't want this, Sunny. I never wanted any of this."

After pulling her jumpsuit back on, Sunny stood, taking a

moment to reconnoiter, trying to figure out where she and Sai would go after escaping from the cave in the middle of the night on a foreign and hostile planet. It was actually beautiful, wherever they were—a narrow valley surrounded by snow-covered cliffs on one side, rolling hills on the other, and behind them, a dense forest of pines. Since Sunny's shoes were hardly appropriate for climbing cliffs and the rolling hills were far too exposed, only one choice for escape remained: the forest.

"Reya, darling, what is 'this' anyway? I thought you were different. I thought you wanted change for your people."

Reya wheeled around, pointing a finger angrily at Sunny's chest. "You don't understand, you couldn't possibly. Kravax is not the rest of the KU. Beliefs here are not modern. We are not evolved. We do what our elders say—always. We don't have a choice. But," she paused, closing her eyes, "I really did hope that would change." When Reya's eyes opened again, Sunny could see how hard she was straining to hide the well of emotion behind them.

"Did you know all along?" Sunny asked softly. "Did you know the plan was always to take the boy?"

Hugging herself now, Reya's chin dropped to her chest, her black hair flowing forward to curtain her face. "I thought BLIX was real. I was actually excited about something for the first time in my life. And then, when I met all of you, when I met Tig, I thought maybe with her I could finally be," she shrugged, "myself. But no, I didn't know. Tano told me and Axel an hour before he made his move."

"And you felt compelled to go along because that's just how things are here." Sunny wasn't questioning or judging, she was only validating.

Reya nodded. "I shouldn't have. I should have pushed back, told Rax or Morgath or you. Maybe," she paused, and a single tear rolled down her cheek, "if I had, I could have stopped it. I should have been stronger, braver. I failed."

I should have been stronger. How many times had Sunny said this same thing to herself?

A bird twittered above their heads, pine needles crunching under Sunny's feet as she stepped toward Reya to place a hand over her crossed arms. "Tig will understand," she said softly.

Reya's head jerked up, the movement sending another tear down her cheek. "No she won't. She'll never forgive me."

This was Sunny's window. "She will because she will know that you are not your people. She will know that you are strong and brave. You are special to her, and she is special to you. That sort of thing doesn't happen all the time." Sunny's heart squeezed out its next few beats, Freddie's worried eyes flashing in her mind.

Reya looked around nervously, as if making sure they weren't being overheard. "That sort of thing *never* happens on Kravax. That kind of love is forbidden."

Sunny squeezed Reya's arm. Time to go all in. "Listen to me. The universe is vast and open, and your place in it is not defined by where you were born, what lies you've been told about what is right or wrong, or who you choose to love."

"But how?" she said miserably. "How can I find my place? I'm here. I'm stuck here."

"I'll tell you how. You are going to fight for what you want, for type of life you want to live, and you are going to start by helping me get that boy back to his mothers."

31

SNEAKY SCHEMER

TANO WAITED FOR SUNNY AND REYA AT THE CAVEMOUTH, HIS STANCE wide, his arms stiff at his sides. "Where have you been?" he asked, irritated, suspicious.

Reya's head ducked under his glare. Sunny was less affected. "Apologies, darling," she said. "It was a woman thing."

Those pale Becks Karlovich cheeks of his flushed pink. "Get back inside."

"Yes, sir," Sunny said obediently, then, steeling herself, she gave Tano a very obvious, very intentional thumbs-up before making her way back into the cave, her shoulder brushing against his as she stepped past him.

Tano's widening eyes, followed by his smug, self-satisfied grin told her well enough that Freddie's warning about this hand gesture being a Kravaxian come-on had been right on the money. As if on cue, Marisia grunted, scowling at Sunny, then glowering at Tano.

"What are you doing?" asked Sai when she returned to his side. His brows were knitted in confusion after he'd witnessed her little performance. "Doesn't thumbs-up mean sex stuff on Kravax?"

Her head whipped his way. "Sex stuff? How do you know these things?"

"Seriously, Sunny. What are you doing?"

Her mouth quirked. "I'm doing my job. If Tano is busy thinking about me, and Marisia is busy thinking about him—"

"They'll both be less busy thinking about us," he finished.

"Precisely."

Sai grinned. "I knew I could learn a great deal from you, Sunastara Jeka."

They passed the day by telling stories, picking at the tart yellow berries Axel had harvested for them, and, in the brief moments when they were alone in the cave, discussing their plan for escape. Sai was suspicious. He didn't think Reya would actually help them. But while Sai knew puzzles, Sunny knew people. Reya would come through, Sunny just hoped she wouldn't get hurt in the process.

After the sun set, Tano returned to the cave. He sat across from Sunny and Sai and lit another fire. Marisia, Axel, and Reya left the cave once Tano had returned, presumably to hunt for dinner. Poor Sai would be skin and bones by the time this ordeal ended. He couldn't live on berries alone.

"So, what's the plan here, Tano?" Sunny asked boldly, figuring he'd respond best to directness. "How long are you planning to keep us in this cave?"

His eyes narrowed. "And what makes you think I will tell you anything?"

"No harm in asking," Sunny said. "We can't really go anywhere or talk to anyone anyway." Her voice dropped to a whisper. "Your secrets are safe with us."

He only grunted. *Charming.* Overt flirting not hitting its mark, Sunny changed tactics. "Is Marisia your wife?"

He grunted again. "I have taken no wife."

"Really?" Sunny said. "Why not? She seems like she'd make a fine wife."

What Sunny could see—and Tano could not—was that Marisia had returned to the cave and stood in its entryway, a string of small, dead rodents dangling from her right hand.

"She would not make me a fine wife. She has no fire," Tano said as the flames picked up, golden light flickering in his eyes which stared fixedly into Sunny's. Regardless from which planet they hailed, men were so clueless sometimes it boggled Sunny's mind.

Marisia made a strangled, disgusted noise, dropped the rodents onto the cave floor, and stalked back out into the greying evening.

"You sure about that?" Sunny said, her eyebrow arched. "She seems pretty *fiery* to me."

Tano grunted for a third time, getting to his feet and walking to the cave mouth. Before he left, he stooped to pick up the rodents, flung them back so that they lay in a heap in front of the fire, and grumbled, "Mind your own business. I will go find the boy more berries."

Sai and Sunny sat in silence, watching Tano, Axel, and Reya chew on roasted rodents, and Marisia, declining to eat, on her resentment instead. While Marisia sent Tano searing glares and furrowed-brow scowls, Sunny passed him fleeting, furtive glances under her lashes, popping berries into her mouth and licking the tips of her fingers. Kravax might have cornered the market on violence and intimidation, but Sunny thought they had much to learn about interpersonal relationships and how easily those relationships could be manipulated to sow general dissent among the ranks by a sneaky schemer like her.

After dinner, Sai—who must have been both exhausted and starving yet had not once uttered a single complaint—fell asleep with his head in Sunny's lap. Leaning back against the rocky wall,

Sunny let her eyes fall shut on Tano and Marisia, sleeping on opposite sides of the cave, Axel snoring by the fire, and Reya sitting at the entrance, keeping watch.

Sunny waited another hour or so, until she was certain everyone but Reya was sleeping soundly. This part had been Reya's idea, since only she knew where to find the special berries that evidently induced sleep. Reya had gathered the berries earlier in the day, and then slipped them into the evening tea that Sunny, Sai, and Reya had only pretended to drink. When Sunny ran her fingers over Sai's soft hair, he opened his eyes and turned his head to look up at her. Her affirmative nod answered the question in his eyes.

Sai took a deep breath, then slipped his fingers into his sock and pulled out Orion's Tooth.

Sunny didn't know how he managed it, but with a press of the Tooth's tip, a tiny jiggle, and a firm twist, the cuffs on her wrists, then her ankles, unlinked. Sai couldn't reach his own cuffs, and Sunny was unable to unlock them with her fumbling fingers. So after he slipped the Tooth back into his sock, Sai put his bound hands into one of Sunny's and she led him silently past Axel, still snoring, then between Tano and Marisia, both with their backs turned stubbornly to each other, each conveniently facing opposites sides of the cave wall and also snoring. *That must have been some strong tea,* Sunny thought.

When they reached Reya, she placed a finger to her lips, then silently drew landmarks and arrows in the dirt as a reminder of the directions she'd told Sunny to run earlier in the day, directions that would hopefully lead them to a village where they might be able to find comms. Not Viewchips, but maybe the low-tech, surface-to-orbit radios Reya said were prevalent in the villages in this region of Kravax.

It was a risk, they knew, trusting Reya, running through an unfamiliar forest in the dark, hoping the twins or the captain had followed them through the jump and were now orbiting above them. But neither of them thought they'd ever get a better chance than this one. Before they left the cave, Sunny reached down, extending her hand to Reya. "Come with us," she mouthed.

Reya shook her head, then mouthed in return, "Tell Tig I'm sorry."

Sunny nodded, took a breath, then grabbed Sai's hand again. Once they'd tiptoed out of the cave, Sunny ditched her heels in the dirt, then she and Sai ran like the wind straight into the cold, dark forest.

32

DRAGONS

They'd not made it fifty meters into the trees when an explosion of sound and light had them sliding to a halt and spinning around. Sunny's chest heaved as Sai panted beside her and asked, "What was that?"

Sunny wondered if they were coming for them, if Reya had double-crossed them. She made to pull Sai into a run again when Tano's fearful shouting echoed through the trees and another flash lit up the sky like a lightning storm.

Sunny gasped and Sai whispered, "Whoa!" as a massive, flaming dragon burst into the night sky. For a fleeting moment, her adrenalin-fueled brain thought it was real, but then she realized out loud, "Magic! *Stars above*, Sai. They've found us."

A smile stretched across his face as he hopped up and down. "It's Makenna!"

Sunny took ahold of his shoulders. "Sai, did you know Makenna was one of your mom's SOs?"

He scoffed, ducking to hide behind a tree while they watched the fire dragon swoop over the cave. "Of course I knew. She's like my aunt." His grin grew impossibly wider. "The FFKs must be freaking out! I don't think they have magic on Kravax—or dragons." He started laughing. "This is just *so* Makenna. She's hysterical."

"Wait, what about Reya?" Sunny gasped. "If Makenna is here, Rax and Morgath must be here too. What if they try to hurt Reya? They won't know she helped us. I have to go back, but you need to stay here."

"Yeah, right. I'm not staying alone in the woods. I'll get eaten by something. I'm coming with you."

Sai led the way this time as they ran back toward the treeline, the sounds of magic effects and shouting growing with every step they took. Sunny couldn't make heads or tails of the chaos as magical oorthorses, dragons, and even fiery stampeding kurots assaulted the silence of the woods. Once she and Sai reached the clearing, she saw the FFKs huddled in their cave, one of them ducking a head out occasionally to cower in fear at the fire in the sky. But when Sunny looked around the clearing, she couldn't spot Makenna or her crew anywhere.

The magic dragon hovered outside the Kravaxian's cave, flapping its massive wings and slashing at the air with its glowing talons. "Let them go at once!" it roared. "Or perish!"

"That's rather dramatic," Sunny whispered.

"That's Makenna," Sai replied.

"They are not here!" bellowed Tano, white-faced, practically pleading with the dragon image towering over him. "They escaped. We do not have them anymore."

Finally, Sunny noticed Captain Declan Jones's head pop up from his hiding spot behind a boulder. He scanned the forest—for them, Sunny presumed.

She pointed out the captain to Sai, and they slid through the remaining trees until only a few tall pines separated them from the action. Kneeling down, Sunny grabbed a rock from the ground and threw it at the captain. The first rock fell well in front of him, unnoticed. The second rock, however, hit him squarely between his brows.

He jerked back. The poor man probably thought he'd been shot at. Sunny winced, cursing her horrible aim. But then he rubbed at his forehead and relief seemed to wash over him when he finally spotted Sunny and Sai in the woods. Sunny waved at him, and he held his hand out, palm facing the trees in a very clear *stay put* gesture. But Sunny rarely did as she was told. Instead she made her way, hunched and silent, to tell the captain not to hurt Reya. Sai, she noticed, hunched right alongside her.

They'd made it mere yards from the captain when strong fingers grasped at Sunny's hair and yanked her back off her feet. Before she stumbled, she pushed Sai as hard as she could toward the captain, who burst out from behind his boulder to grab the boy.

Marisia held her in a death grip, the woman's solid, well-muscled arm wrapped so tightly around Sunny's neck she could barely breathe.

"I do not fear your tricks," Marisia hissed.

Spots appeared in Sunny's vision as an otherworldly pressure built from the base of her throat to throb behind her temples.

"I do not fear your tricks!" Marisia repeated in a roar loud enough to echo through the valley, swinging Sunny's quickly flagging body from side to side. "Come out! Surrender, or I will kill her!"

"Marisia, no!" bellowed Tano from the cave. "You must not anger these spirits of fire!"

"Ha!" she cried, tightening her grip around Sunny's throat. "No, Tano. You must not anger *me*!"

"Put Sunny down!" barked Morgath, stepping out from his hiding place behind a tree.

He pointed a sonic cannon at Marisia and, by extension, Sunny. And while Sunny felt relief at the sight of the nonlethal weapon, a profound misery overcame her because she knew that one way or another, either from Marisia's chokehold or the sensory bombardment of the sonic cannon, she was about to be knocked out.

Deciding to have at least a tiny bit of say in her own survival,

Sunny raised her foot, smashed it down on Marisia's instep, and threw her head back as hard as she could. But it was too late.

The last thing she registered before Morgath's sonic boom robbed her of her hearing, then her consciousness was pain searing across the back of her head, Marisia screaming in her ear, and the satisfying crack of what she hoped was a broken Kravaxian nose.

33

SMOOCH

"WAKE UP." SAI'S VOICE WAS A SOFT ECHO, LIKE SHE WAS DREAMING it. "Wake up, Sunny."

"I'm up," she groaned, pushing herself up into a sitting position. "I'm up. I'm good." Without preamble, she doubled over and vomited onto the dirt.

"Ew, gross," hissed Sai, leaning away from her.

She wiped the back of her hand over her mouth. "Where is Morgath?"

"I'm not sure. Why?"

"Because I need to kill him."

Captain Jones covered Sai with a blanket, then draped another over her shoulders. "Morgath is a little busy detaining some Kravaxians at the moment, but I'll be sure to tell him you're looking for him," he said, dabbing at a wound on his forehead with the sleeve of his jacket.

Sunny grimaced. "That's not from... I didn't...did I?"

"Hell of an arm you've got there, Sunny," he said, wincing as he touched his sleeve once more to the place where her rock had bounced off his forehead.

"Reya!" Sunny blurted, coming to her senses. "She helped us. Don't hurt her. She—"

The captain cut in while offering her a canteen of cold water. "We know. Sai told us. We're detaining her with the others for now. But once we get them to Imperion for judgment, we will explain her situation to the courts."

"You're taking them to Imperion?"

"They kidnapped a senator's son, Sunny. This is a KU governmental matter now."

She hadn't fully considered the ramifications of their little adventure. There would be a trial. Sai and Sunny would be called to testify. She stood on unsteady legs. "Captain, there's so much more to this story than a kidnapping for ransom. We could all be in grave danger."

"The boy told us everything," said the captain. "Quite the story, but it does explain a lot."

"Sai already told you everything?" Sunny said, eyes wide. "How long have I been out?"

"Not long," said the captain. "Sai was very excited. He told us about Karlovich, then he said you'd devised the escape plan, played the Kravaxians against each other, and convinced Reya to help you."

"All in a day's work, Captain," Sunny deflected, a dull, abysmal headache hammering behind her eyes.

Captain Jones handed her a comm. "Someone would like to speak with you." Then he left to assist Morgath in securing the FFKs for transport to Imperion.

She clicked the Talk button on the captain's comm. "Hello?"

Freddie's voice ruined her. "Thank the stars you're all right," he whispered. "That was... I was worried."

"I know, darling. I'm so sorry." Tears stung her eyes.

"Don't be sorry, just be in my arms. Come home. Please come home."

"We're taking her to the ship now, Freddie," Rax shouted as he walked to Sunny's side, giving her a stern look that told her she would comply. "She'll be close enough to smooch in no time."

"Smooch?" Sai said, following this up with another, "Gross."

Sunny pocketed the comm and let Rax help her to her feet. On the way to the shuttle, Makenna stopped them, dropping to her knees to take Sai's face in her hands. "Are you all right? Did they hurt you?"

Sai shook his head bravely, but Sunny noticed his little chin quivering as Makenna crushed him to her chest. She had to look away when her own chin wobbled.

Makenna release Sai and got back to her feet. "Are you unharmed, Sunny?"

Sunny squinted, less in disapproval that Makenna had lied to the crew—including Chan—for weeks (well, maybe a bit in disapproval) but more to focus the three versions of her into one through her post-concussion vision. "You're a devious little one, aren't you?"

Makenna's lips pressed together tightly. "Only when I have to be. Thank you," her voice cracked, "for protecting Sai. Thank you."

Sunny waved her off, feeling like she might actually faint if she didn't lie down soon. "No problem, anytime."

Makenna grabbed her elbow. "Come on. You look like you're about to fall over. Let's get you to the shuttle."

Despite her aching head, blurred vision, and rubbery, adrenalin-wrecked muscles, she marched to the shuttle, walking past the FFKs, all on their knees, all cuffed in a similar fashion to how she had spent the last forty-eight hours. And for a brief moment, for all but Reya, she allowed herself to enjoy the symmetry.

"Sunny!" Sai shouted when they entered the shuttle. "There's food!" He ran back to his seat, digging into a plate of pita bread and hummus which looked and smelled divine.

Morgath stepped into the shuttle behind them, his head ducked, broad shoulders hunched in contrition. "Hi, Sunny."

Unable to stand a moment longer, Sunny sank onto her seat. "Morgath," she said, scowling. "A sonic cannon? Really?"

His head ducked so much now that his green chin rested on his chest. "Sorry. It seemed like a good idea at the time."

"It's all right. Thank you for saving our lives."

He came to kneel at her side, which still put his face above hers. "I'm sorry we weren't quicker. It took longer than we'd hoped to follow through the jump, we kept losing the signal."

"So the laser-tracker thing actually worked?" asked Sai with a mouth full of hummus.

Morgath nodded, ruffling Sai's hair. "Totally! I'll tell you all about it once we're in the air."

Sai slept with his head on Sunny's lap the entire journey back to the *Ignisar*, her fingers running slowly through his hair. When they finally docked with the *Ignisar*, she disembarked the shuttle to find Freddie standing in the airlock, waiting for her with a hand-written sign that read, *Welcome home, Sunastara. Please don't ever leave us again.*

The *Ignisar* had been her home for the last five years, but now, she realized as her eyes filled with tears, Freddie was her home. A lightness overcame her, put there by his smile, his sign, the tears he wiped from his cheeks. She stepped over the airlock threshold and into his arms, letting him hold her so tightly the pressure almost convinced her body that it was safe again. But then her heart froze in her chest as Lena and Chahna raced around the corner and fell to their knees in relief at the sight of their son.

"I can't," she whispered into Freddie's ear. "I can't see this. Get me out of here. Please."

It was too much. Seeing the relief she'd never been lucky enough to feel on Lena's and Chahna's faces, the absolute joy and fear and love and relief as they took Sai into their arms and held him. It was unbearable.

Freddie ushered her away toward the elevator, telling her, "I've got you, sweetheart. I've got you. You did it, Sunny. You saved him."

She spent the next hour sobbing in Freddie's arms, on his bed, his hand brushing over her hair, passing long strokes over her back until she finally cried herself to sleep. But when she woke, still held tightly in his arms, she felt safe and warm. And, most importantly, understood.

"I love you, Freddie," she whispered, placing her hand over his heart where its steady rhythm thumped under her fingers.

His hand floated up to cover hers. "I love you too, Sunny."

34

HOME

"Cheers." Sunny held her glass out to Chan. He clinked his glass to hers, but there, in the bar above the main deck atrium, in the orange light of sunset sim, he wore the same troubled expression he'd worn since she had returned to the ship two weeks ago. "Darling, what is it?" she asked, resting her hand over his.

His mouth pinched. "I don't know, Sunny. I thought... I let myself think that maybe this time it was real. It was really happening. And maybe I wouldn't be alone anymore."

He was speaking of Makenna, who'd left with the senator and her family last week, taking a piece of Sunny's heart with them in the shape of a ten-year-old boy. Perhaps their departure had taken a piece of Chan's as well.

"I'm sorry, Chan." Sunny didn't know what else to say.

His shoulders rose and fell, his hover chair humming softly. "I should have known it was all a trick. She seemed *way* too into me. She barely even flinched when I accidentally asked her if her eyelashes were real."

Sunny bit back the laugh rising up from her belly.

"I got carried away," he said, then he straightened. "It won't happen again."

This crushed Sunny's heart. Chan cared for Makenna, and he'd thought she'd cared for him. It was so similar to her conversations with Tig since she'd returned to the ship. Both Chan and Tig felt betrayed by someone they'd thought had cared for them. Every single one of them: Chan, Tig, Rax, Morgath, herself and Freddie, maybe even Elanie—they all spent far too much time on this ship, seeing the best and worst of love played out in real time in their every waking moment. When they finally risked holding out hope of having a love of their own, it was devastating when it all fell apart.

"I understand," she said to him out loud, but in her mind she told him, *I will make sure it happens again for you, if it's the last thing I do.*

After they shared another silent, pensive glass of Venusian whiskey, Chan turned to Sunny, his expression solemn. "Tell me what happened to you, Sunny. Not what happened on Kravax, but before. I know something happened, something awful, something you've kept hidden. You don't have to keep hiding it from me."

This request was so unexpected that she could only stare at him, blinking, speechless.

"I'm your friend, Sunny. You can tell me."

As the sun set over the treetops, casting long pink-and-purple shadows onto their table, Sunny realized he was right. She could tell him about Jonathan. And so she did.

Chan didn't say a word, no stranger to loss, but his hand squeezed Sunny's as tears lined his eyes. They sat together until the first twinkling of simulated starlight pierced the darkening dome suspended over the atrium.

"Chan," Sunny finally said after draining her third glass of whiskey, "will we be okay?"

"I suppose," he replied, somewhat slurred. "We carry on, don't we? What else is there to do?"

"If it's any consolation," Sunny's words grew thick as the

whiskey sank in, "even with the eyelash comment, I think your game is improving."

His head swiveled toward hers. "You do? I've really been working on it. I've been reading romance novels."

She smiled, proud and beaming. "Absolutely."

They'd been so busy over the last few weeks that Freddie and Sunny had barely had a moment alone. After the press interviews, the sentencing trials for the FFKs, and the fallout and restructuring of LunaCorp after Proposition 2126 passed the KU Senate by a wide margin, life aboard the ship, Sunny hoped, was finally returning to normal.

<What are you up to?> Freddie Vcommed while Sunny made her way back from the airlock to the staff pods.

<Just welcoming that adorable pop band from New Earth Korea aboard. I'm headed up to twelve now.>

<Adorable? How adorable?>

Sunny grinned. <I do love it when you get jealous. And very.>

<Did you chat with Sai today?>

Sunny's smile grew while she pushed the elevator button for deck twelve. <I did. He's starting school next week. He's nervous.> Sunny and Sai had a standing video chat every week, something she hoped would continue so she could watch Sai grow, with the ultimate end game of becoming his campaign manager when he ran for KU President.

<Aw. Poor kid. He'll be smashing.>

<That's *precisely* what I told him.>

<We received a digcard today,> Freddie said while she stepped out of the elevator. <An invitation to Garran and Kasa's hand-joining.>

"What!" Sunny accidentally screamed out loud. <Really? That's wonderful! The best news I've heard in an age!>

<Next year on Argos. We could take a vacation, combine the nuptials with a visit to Tranquis. If you wanted to, that is.>

Sunny's pace slowed. <You want to visit Tranquis?>

After a brief pause, Freddie replied, <I thought maybe I could —only if you agreed—meet your parents.>

<Freddie, you want to meet my parents?> Sunny's cheeks hurt now from all the smiling.

<I do,> he replied, making her chest swell. But then she spotted Elanie storming toward her, her eyes red and swollen.

<I do too. I think it's a wonderful idea, and I very much want to come and kiss you for coming up with it. But something is up with Elanie. It may take me a moment.>

"Out of my way, Sunny," Elanie barked when Sunny stepped into her path with her arms out wide like she was attempting to halt the progress of stampeding kurot.

"I'm not moving," Sunny said sternly. "Not until you tell me what's made you so upset."

Elanie slowed to a halt, buried her face in her hands, and began to weep.

Sunny grabbed her by the elbow and frog-marched her back to her pod.

"What in the worlds is going on?" Sunny asked after she plopped Elanie down on the edge of her bed. "Why are you crying?"

Through her tears, she said haltingly, "He...he told me... He said he thought I was beautiful."

Sunny frowned. "Who? Who told you that? And why are you crying over it?"

Elanie blew her nose on the tissue Sunny passed her. "His name is Blake. He was the bionic staring at me at New Year's. I said hello to him in the hallway one time, and now he won't leave me alone! He keeps smiling at me whenever I see him, asking me how my day is going. Why is he tormenting me like this?"

Elanie was distressed. She was *emotional*. Sunny stumbled back a step, running ass-first into her dresser. "Elanie, have you upgraded?"

"Whatever!" she cried, throwing her hands up. "Who even cares? It's all so ridiculous!"

Sunny shrieked. "You upgraded without even telling me?"

Elanie's shoulders slumped forward, her arms hanging limply from her sides over the edge of the bed. "I hate it. I can't think straight. Everything hurts. But you and Freddie seemed so happy, so I thought maybe I could be happy too. Well, guess what? Joke's on me! I am absolutely miserable!"

Sunny joined Elanie on the bed. "Darling, this requires a lengthy conversation—and a lot of food. Would you like to get some ice cream?"

With a shuddering breath, Elanie sniffled and said, "Ice cream? That sounds really good actually."

"I know it does, darling. I know it does," Sunny said, pulling Elanie in close.

After gorging on ice cream at the malt shop on deck twenty-two while Elanie spilled all the details about Blake the bionic, Sunny stepped into the elevator and very deliberately pressed the button for deck sixteen.

She knew Freddie was waiting for her, but she hadn't been to this pool a single time since the Delphinian Wizards had reversed the trick that had drained it dry. The pool was blue and empty, and the starlight shining through the flexglass roof shimmered over the water.

She stripped down to her underwear and dove headfirst into the deep end. After coming up for air, she opened her Squee app and sent a message. <Joshua, your services are required at the pool on deck sixteen, immediately.> Even though they were openly dating, every now and then they still liked to play.

In the space of two heartbeats, he responded sportingly, <Good evening, Phoebe. I am on my way.>

She was floating on her back when he finally stepped into the room and locked the door behind him. "*Stars*," he said, staring down at her. "You are the single most beautiful woman I have ever laid eyes upon. How in the worlds did I get so lucky?"

Rolling over onto her belly, she swam to where he stood at the edge of the pool, leaning forward to place a single wet kiss onto the top of his left shoe. "I'm the lucky one. Come swim with me."

She loved watching him undress, slowly shedding his suit coat, tie, pants—the professional, polite costume of Freddie the L&C falling to the ground to reveal the soft skin, long limbs, and devious, stormy eyes of Freddie the man, the one who schemed and laughed and lived, the man she loved.

He dove into the pool with predictable grace, and when his head emerged above the water, the heat in his gaze melted every strained muscle and resilient bone in Sunny's body.

Reaching behind her back, she unhooked her bra and tossed it onto the deck. "Come here."

Instead of walking the short distance between them, Freddie dove under the water. When he reached her, his fingers slipped into the waistband of her underwear, pulling down until they slid over her hips, down past her knees, off one foot and then the other. After coming back up to the surface, he pushed her back to the edge of the pool and set her underwear up onto the deck with a wet, smacking sound. He kissed her, his tongue sliding between her lips, his fingers wrapping around the back of her neck. His other hand cupped her ass, and he raised her out of the water, sitting her on the edge, kissing her belly, pulling her hips toward him. Moving down her body, he hooked her legs over his shoulders, sliding his fingers up her thighs, nestling in between them.

She buried her fingers into his wet hair.

"So beautiful," he said.

"To whom are you speaking, darling?" she asked, looking down at him.

He didn't take his eyes from between her legs. "Both of you."

She laughed, then sighed, then panted and writhed and cried out his name as he worked on her, his tongue sending her into her own orbit of pleasure, white heat flashing through her as bright as the stars above them.

He wasted no time pulling her back into the water with him, and she surrounded him with her body, sheathing him deeply inside her, her legs wrapped around his hips, her arms around his shoulders, her chest pressed against his so tightly that she felt his heart beating right next to hers.

"You have, you know?" she told him, kissing his shoulder.

"Have what?" he asked, squeezing her even tighter.

"From the poem you recited to me, that one about sleep. You've become like the air to me—that necessary. I never thought I'd let someone become necessary to me again, but you have, you are."

"I feel the same," was all he needed to say.

And as they floated in the water, holding each other, moving together, Sunny looked up through the flexglass into the infinity of time and space above them, where stars burned and expanded and collapsed, where planets spun and revolved around their suns, where it was the fate of all objects to push inexorably away from one another. Except for them.

Despite the odds, despite the gravity of their pasts conspiring to keep them apart, they had found each other, they'd held on, and they were both finally home.

***

Thank you for reading! Did you enjoy? Please add your review because nothing helps an author more and encourages readers to take a chance on a book than a review.

And don't miss more of the Ignisar series, by Jess K. Hardy, coming soon!

Until then, find more Mystic Owl books with <u>THE ASSASSIN AND THE LIBERTINE</u> by Lily Riley. Turn the page for a sneak peek!

You can also sign up for the City Owl Press newsletter to receive notice of all book releases!

SNEAK PEEK OF THE ASSASSIN AND THE LIBERTINE

BY LILY RILEY

January 17, 1765
Paris

I watched him, patiently, from behind my carved ivory fan. He appeared to be a capable servant—unobtrusive, almost preternaturally aware of the needs of the duke's guests, and just on the attractive side of plain in his dark gray livery. When he finally flicked his gaze to me, I lowered my lashes flirtatiously and drew my fan across my lips—an open invitation for a clandestine dalliance. The corner of his mouth twitched, and he nodded almost imperceptibly.

From the edge of the stifling ballroom, a gong sounded, announcing dinner. Gentlemen paired off with ladies, making their way into the dining room.

"Madame, shall we go in?"

The fat, thick-headed, wealthy lout at my elbow held out his arm. He'd been trying to monopolize my attentions all evening, despite my thinly concealed distaste. He reminded me of an overfed leech, pawing at me with his slimy, limp appendages and grinning with his yellow, toothy mouth. I covered my grimace with a wan smile.

"*Monsieur le Vicomte,*" I answered. "Please, do go in and find your seat. I need a moment to refresh myself. I'll be along shortly."

The leech eyed me up and down, offering a prurient wink. Unable to suppress my disgust much longer, I turned from him before he could see my expression.

The smell of food wafted in through the open doors. I hadn't eaten all day, but truthfully, I was not hungry—for *dinner*.

I left the gilt opulence of the ballroom and made my way down a candlelit corridor, discreetly checking the rooms for errant party-goers and trysting courtiers. I required absolute solitude, and fortune appeared to be on my side tonight. The duke's Parisian townhouse was impressive—if a little dated with all its *baroque* enthusiasm—and seldom in use. Like some members of court, he lived almost year-round at Versailles. Years before, King Louis XIV's paranoia had set that precedent for the aristocracy. *If you wish to feel the warmth of the Sun King, you must remain within his orbit.*

How suffocating. I was almost glad my husband had fled to Italy in disgrace, despite him leaving me to the absent mercy of the wolves of Versailles. At least I was free to maintain my own residence—and more importantly, I was free of him. The thought of my vile, abusive husband soured my stomach.

It seemed that King Louis XV, the Beloved, had a more relaxed view of things. *But for how long,* I wondered. France was changing at the speed of infection. The king could not continue to ignore *la peste du sang* that was starting to seep through the streets of Paris. The blood plague was upon us and I feared what was happening to the people of France.

Several doors down, I found what I was looking for—the duke's empty study. A few candles flickered inside, casting dancing shadows upon the gold brocade of the walls. Hopefully, young Giles had accepted my invitation and I wouldn't have to wait long.

I perched on the edge of the large desk, careful not to bend my panniers, and adjusted my navy skirts around me. The dark color was somewhat unfashionable this season, but I wasn't at Versailles and tonight I favored a gown that was a touch more utilitarian. The pastel palette of the court was hellacious for us more *active* members of the nobility. The stains could be murder.

Movement outside caught my eye, and I went to the window to observe. Snow had started to fall in soft, downy clumps. I watched the flakes drift gently onto the balcony terrace and smiled to myself. I flung the doors open, letting in a flurry of frigid air.

I almost didn't hear the soft click of the door closing behind me, but I'd been waiting.

Without turning, I spoke out to the snowy balcony.

"I'm so glad you came, darling Giles. I've been waiting all evening to get you alone."

Strong arms circled my waist, turning me to him and pulling me back inside the study. His eyes glittered fiercely, hungrily.

Without a word, he crushed his mouth to mine. His hands roamed my body, seeking the softness of skin beneath the silken layers of my gown.

"I don't have long," he grunted. He pushed me roughly against the wall, attempting to lift my heavy skirts.

"*Oui,* I know, *ma cher.* Neither do I." He'd found my legs beneath the copious underskirts and ran a cold hand up my thigh. I grabbed him by the shoulders and reversed our positions, pressing his body to the wall with my hips. He gasped in excitement and fumbled for the buttons of his breeches. I kissed him softly.

Dispassionately.

With him distracted, it was almost too easy for me to stab him through the heart.

He pushed me away—bewildered, pained—as smoke curled from the small wound in his chest. I slid the thin wooden stake out, wiped the blood on his livery, and tucked it back in my garter for my next assignment.

Only then did his fangs distend.

"*Putain de salope*," he hissed. His skin turned a mottled grey and he slumped to the floor.

I *tsked*. "Oh, Giles. How long did you think you could carry on like this—feeding your way through His Grace's housemaids? Six young girls are dead already, Giles. Six! Did you think we wouldn't notice a rotten little *sanguisuge* in our midst?"

He groaned in pain and glared at me.

"You're with them, then. *The Order*. Didn't think they allowed women in."

"Yes, well, what a lesson for you to learn today. *We are everywhere.* Too bad you won't be able to share that news with your filthy parasite friends, eh?"

The dying footman rasped a laugh, coughing up a trickle of black blood that steamed in the cold room.

"It won't matter if you're *everywhere*. It won't matter how many you are, how much money the aristocracy has or how good The Order's spies are. None of it will save you from what's coming."

A chill went up my spine that had nothing to do with the snow blowing in through the open terrace doors.

"What's coming?" I demanded, leaning in.

"*La mort.*"

His eyes dulled on a final exhale, and the young vampire Giles sagged against the wall. I dragged his body to the balcony and heaved it over, leaving it in the snow-dusted bushes for another agent to find and dispose of. I never asked anyone at The Order what they did with the bodies of all the vampires we dispatched. Truthfully, I couldn't bring myself to care.

After setting the room and my gown to rights, I exited the study and made my way to the dining room. I passed a note to a footman —a coded message for The Order that read *assignment complete, target retrieval requested*—and sat next to the Leech, who would no doubt boast about spending the entirety of the evening flirting with the *duchesse de Duras*, thus providing me with an unattractive, dim-witted, but unquestionable alibi.

The remainder of the evening passed as planned. Giles likely wouldn't be discovered missing until the morning, and even then, people would suspect he'd run off with one of the "missing" house-maids. Even though the job was done, a whisper of unease went through me at his dying words. I tried to dismiss it as a final attempt to frighten me, or swear some kind of undead vengeance, but I didn't really believe that. Giles knew something.

Death. Death was coming.

***

That Same Evening
Palace of Versailles

Just before her pleasure crested, my fangs lengthened and I nipped firmly at her thigh, drawing the blood I needed to survive. I'd waited too long to feed again, and the hunger clawed at my insides. I forced myself to take only what she could give without suffering. Fortunately, it was enough. *Barely.*

"*Très magnifique,*" she panted, reaching for me. "Now I under-stand what Yvette meant when she said you were a delightful beast."

The marquise giggled and sighed. I lifted my head from beneath her hideous orange skirts and grinned wolfishly at her, but the words had stung.

A delightful beast.

"What would the marquis say if he found you in bed with such a beast?"

The marquise snorted and stood from the chaise we'd been enjoying. She adjusted the bodice of her unfashionable gown and straightened the powdered mass of curls atop her head.

"He stupidly thinks I don't know about his penchant for the servant girls. If I were interested in catching his eye, I'd just have to don some depressing brown wool and bow gracelessly before bringing him dinner."

The marquise de Balay was a dangerous conquest—she was

fiercely intelligent, wealthy as sin, and—as a distant relation to the king—her witless husband enjoyed an impressive set of privileges at court. Her opinions formed his, and so if I needed help to sway the king's mind, I needed her manipulations at my disposal. The marquise de Balay, despite her unfortunate taste in clothing, was a powerful influence.

"He wouldn't be offended to find his wife *fraternizing* with a vampire?" I pressed.

She cut me a disdainful look and arched a supercilious brow.

"Possibly. But you're not like the rest of them, are you? Your father was the former vicomte de Noailles. Even if he was disgraced, you come from noble blood. The rest of those plague bloodsuckers are all peasants, aren't they? Farmers. The *poor*. You're the king's appointed emissary and advisor on how to deal with the *sanguisuge* menace. You aren't really one of them," she sniffed.

She left off, *you aren't really one of us, either,* but the words seemed to hang in the air, nonetheless.

Anger burned through me at her distaste toward my family and my kind. With a flare of disappointment, I realized she wouldn't be willing to join my cause. *Vampire rights* were a joke to the over-primped peacocks mincing through the halls of Versailles. She didn't see the tension stretching between the classes—the danger we were all in as the impoverished vampire populace grew. She, like the rest of the court, was blind to the true threats to France. Terror would not come from the battles fought on foreign soil. It would come from within.

And nobody would heed my warnings.

"Besides, The Order will certainly stop them," she offered casually. She was replacing her diamond chandelier earrings—fat, colorless stones that winked in the candlelight.

I stilled.

"What do you know of The Order? I always heard they were a myth." I laughed. I knew they were *not* a myth, but it surprised me to hear the marquise discuss them so openly.

She shrugged. "Only the gossip, I suppose. Surely you've heard?"

"I haven't." I *had*. They'd sent two assassins after me already—one disguised as a cut-purse, and the other masquerading as a drunken brawler in one of my favorite taverns. I'd smelled the lies on their clothes before they'd had the chance to stake me. At least their blood had sustained me for a while. The intervening years of poverty between my father's disgrace and my royal appointment had taught me that much—*waste not, want not.*

The marquise waved her hand dismissively. "You know, they've finally gotten sensible about the plague and excommunicated the members of The Order from the lower classes. I mean, if it's only the weakest peasants that suffer the infection, it's right that the stronger elites should decide what to do about it. We have the intelligence, the funds, the breeding. Don't expect me to listen to some dirt farmer about how to save my noble soul."

She giggled venomously. My stomach churned with her snobbish blood. I swallowed my disgust and nodded.

"We should return to the party," I said. "I believe I'm wanted for a card game."

The marquise smiled, but it didn't quite reach her eyes.

"Thank you for the distraction," she said as she turned for the door. "It was rather...*animal.*"

Instead of following her back to the party, I summoned my carriage and returned to my château. Only when I was safely ensconced in my familial home did I allow myself the pleasure of venting my rage by smashing my fist through the wall.

She didn't care. None of them did. Despite my attempts to stop it—to prevent it from happening, nobody else could see what was coming. And many of them would pay with their lives.

‡

Don't stop now. Keep reading f Mystic Owl books with your copy of <u>THE ASSASSIN AND THE LIBERTINE</u> by Lily Riley.

And find more from Jess K. Hardy at
<u>www.jesskhardy.com</u>

Don't miss more of the Ignisar series coming soon and find more from Jess K. Hardy at
www.jesskhardy.com

Until then, find more Mystic Owl books with THE ASSASSIN AND THE LIBERTINE by Lily Riley.

The fate of France itself is at stake if these sworn enemies cannot change their ways—and their hearts.

Daphne de Duras is a proper French duchess by day and fledgling assassin by night. Her latest mission is to dispatch justice and protect the French aristocracy by executing Étienne de Noailles, disgraced former noble, legendary rake, and vampire emissary to the court of King Louis XV.

But Étienne's alleged crime—the gruesome murder of Madame de Pompadour, the King's mistress and Daphne's friend—doesn't quite fit the dashing vampire's nature. With his immortal days suddenly numbered, Étienne needs to convince his would-be executioner not only of his innocence, but that they should hunt the real killer together—a challenge almost as difficult as convincing himself that he isn't falling for her.

Daphne reluctantly agrees to a temporary partnership when Étienne persuades her that something more sinister is afoot. He can, after all, help her find answers in places she's unable to go alone. And despite her deep loathing for any and all vampires, she can't help but start thinking of a few other places she'd like to go with him.

Please sign up for the City Owl Press newsletter for chances to win special subscriber-only contests and giveaways as well as receiving information on upcoming releases and special excerpts.

All reviews are **welcome** and **appreciated**. Please consider leaving one on your favorite social media and book buying sites.

Escape Your World. Get Lost in Ours! City Owl Press at www.cityowlpress.com.

ACKNOWLEDGMENTS

Sometimes book ideas come from personal experiences. Sometimes they come from dreams. The idea for *Love in the Time of Wormholes* came from another book, *Dark Age* by Pierce Brown, specifically chapter 66. If you've read the book, you might understand how I could have been so thoroughly devastated that the only possible way to process my feelings was to write my way through them. This is how Sunastara Jeka was born, a spitfire of a woman bulldozing her way through life five years after unspeakable loss rocked her world to its foundation. Processing the death of a child is no easy subject, but it is one I tried as hard as I could to be sensitive and careful portraying. The scene with Freddie and Sunny in the sensory room is the only scene I have ever written out of order. But I was stuck in Sunny's head, in her pain, in her insistence that her life was as good as it would ever get. Her life wasn't perfect, but maybe she didn't deserve perfect. Maybe she didn't deserve to move on. She didn't deserve to be happy. *She* didn't deserve these things and—while I was stuck in that place and time with her—neither did I. I had to write that scene, hammering out words through my tears. I had to get both of us to the point where she forgave herself before I could stay with her for one more second. This is a fun story, a delightful story, a sexy story, but it is also a painful story. I only hope I was able to tell it with the honesty and thoughtfulness it deserved. In light of this, and for countless other reasons, there are many wonderful people I need to thank for helping this story get told.

First, a massively huge thanks to my unbearably talented and unfairly brilliant critique partner, Paul Grealish. Thank you for every encouraging note, every suggestion, every late-night texting session when I was going to bed and you were getting up and we boosted each other up or tore the world down because there is little about writing books that is easy. You are as important to my writing as my laptop, as my hands. Thank you.

To Angela Crocker, my dear friend, my twin Eeyore, meme wizard, and mother of my son's favorite Minecraft partner, thank you. Thank you for being such a damn good writer, because it inspires me to be better. Thank you for your support and humor and for making me realize that we are never too old to find a new best friend. I love you.

To J Calamy, thank you for getting me, for making me cackle, for our epic plot development and character name brainstorming sessions (it's Levi, or maybe Hank. Definitely Hank). Thank you for cheering for this book and for your friendship.

Thank you to all of my early readers (and I will probably forget some, please forgive me). EG Deaile, Cate Pearce, Anita Kelly, Gabrielle Ash, Katie Golding, Nikki Payne, Kat Turner, Ruby Barrett. You are all, quite literally, the best. Thank you to my fabulous editor, Heather McCorkle. Thank you for taking a chance on this story and for loving Sunny and Freddie as much as I do. You are the best cheerleader! Thank you to everyone at City Owl for championing sci-fi and fantasy romance stories. To my husband

and son, sisters, brother, parents, thank you for your love and support and for being the most important people in my life. Lastly, thank you from the bottom of my heart to every single being who reads this book. I hope you will join me for more adventures aboard the *Ignisar*.

ABOUT THE AUTHOR

A Montana transplant who has her roots in deep, JESS K. HARDY is a lover of mountains and snow, long nights and fireplaces. She has been a sandwich artist, a student, a horse trainer, a physical therapist, a wife, a mother, and also a writer. She writes speculative and contemporary adult romance with plenty of heat and all the feels.

www.jesskhardy.com

ABOUT THE PUBLISHER

City Owl Press is a cutting edge indie publishing company, bringing the world of romance and speculative fiction to discerning readers.

Escape Your World. Get Lost in Ours!

www.cityowlpress.com

facebook.com/YourCityOwlPress
twitter.com/cityowlpress
instagram.com/cityowlbooks
pinterest.com/cityowlpress